Lia Britton and Lucas Dwyer in

HER HEART'S DESIRE

His eyebrows rose. He scooted back several feet, his back resting against the brick wall and his legs stretched out long. He laced his fingers together behind his head, and she wanted to believe the move was to keep himself from reaching for her. Clearly, he wrestled with some mental demon.

Then he patted the floor beside him.

"Really?" she groaned. Taking him up on the offer, she sat next to him, hip to hip, and waited. His kisses weren't chaste or brotherly. He had to see her as a woman. Waiting a minute more wouldn't hurt, but he wanted to talk *now*? The ache deep in her core said he better talk fast, otherwise her need for him would take control. For once, she wouldn't stop it.

When the silence grew, she folded and unfolded her hands, forcing herself not to touch. Her fingers itched to caress him. Another few seconds ticked by. She hummed and gently rocked. She folded her arms and held her elbows. Dread dropped like a brick in her gut. Maybe he didn't feel the same sizzle when he kissed her. Maybe he wanted a second chance to know his attraction to her didn't run deep. Or maybe he couldn't get past her being the *little sister*. If he regretted kissing her for one single second, it would leave a hole in her heart, one the size of the state of Kansas.

"Lucas?"

Lucas punched his fist into his open hand. The smack of skin against skin startled Lia. "This isn't what I had planned," he told her.

"You came with a plan?" There was nothing about any plan she wanted to hear. "Let's talk plans later."

"Amelia, let's take a moment here."

"How many moments?"

Lucas sighed and raised an eyebrow.

"Fine. We'll do this your way for now. How did you find me?" She rushed her words. She refused to hear regret come from his lips. He could have another thirty seconds. Only that long. Her lips refused to wait any longer. This could be her final chance to convince him of her feelings, and she intended to take it.

Also by Linda Joyce

Fleur de Lis series
Bayou Born, book one
Bayou Bound, book two
Bayou Beckons, book three

"Readers will root for Linda Joyce's inspiring characters as they reach for their Heart's Desire." ~ Melissa Klein, author of *Her Hometown Hero*

Her Heart's Desire offers an evocative and entertaining reminder that sometimes the things we need most have been right in front of us the whole time.
~ Leigh Jones, co-author of *Infinite Monster*

"Linda Joyce breathes life into her characters, with an ease that makes reading a joy and pleasure."
~ April Hollingworth author of *Double Magick in the Falls*

"Linda Joyce's characters walk off the pages into your heart."
~ Jackie Rod, *Finding Love's Magic*

Her Heart's Desire
Sunflower series, book one

Contact Information: info@wordworkspress.com

Cover Art by Kerry Klein
Image: Copyright istockphoto.com/000053217712

Published by:
Word Works Press, LLC
P.O. Box 625
Acworth, GA 30101
Visit Word Works Press at
http://www.wordworkspress.com

Publishing History
Print ISBN-13:978-0-9965811-0-3
Digital ISBN-13:978-0-9965811-1-0

Her Heart's Desire

By

Linda Joyce

Dedication

This book is dedicated to all my
Midwest friends.
I miss you more than you know.
And to my personal hero, Donald, thank you for
your unlimited love,
steadfast friendship, and unwavering support.

Acknowledgements

For a dozen years, I called Kansas home. Sunflowers. Corn. Cold winters. Blazing hot summers. Tornados. Endless cracks about the *Wizard of Oz*. And when I moved south again, I left behind wonderful Midwest friends. All of whom helped inspire this story. Especially, Karen LaRue, Amy Curtis, Mailan Le, Madelyn Genglebach, Diane Howard, Bobbie Martin, and Goldie Edwards. I cherish what you've given to me through your friendship.

Many thanks to Peggy O'Keefe and Amy Curtis for Beta Reading for me. I value your input and enjoy our connection through our love of books.

My gratitude goes to Terry Galloway Trahan of TnT Proofreading/Editing Services and to Cheryl Walz for their expertise in making this book shine. (Thanks for making me look good.)

I bow humbly to my critique group, Leah Sims, Leigh Jones, and Melissa Kline. Without you, this story wouldn't "show" the way it does. Thank you for always encouraging me to always stretch and grow.

I am so thankful to each member of Linda's Lovelies for the cheers and support. Thank you for sharing your love of books with me. A special thanks to Terry Galloway Trahan, Nancy Wolfe, Jo Ann Reinhold, Teresa Russ, Doreen Keele, Mary Woodruff, Latasha Clements, Linda Rimer-Como, Kay Gammone, Goldie Edwards, and Gina Hooten Popp.

A big hug for Tracey Gee and LovExtra for seeing me through the hair-pulling stress of bringing this book to completion.

To Maurice Baalman, a very kind man. He allowed me to pepper him with questions about farming in Kansas. I'm grateful he took the time to share with me his vast knowledge.

The writing groups in my life have provided me with valuable writing education: Romance Writers of America, Georgia Romance Writers, and Southeastern Writers Association.

And I am most grateful for readers. I enjoy meeting you at events, book signings, through emails and our connections on social media.

Chapter 1

Lia grimaced.

"*You will fail*." Her brother's words echoed in her mind as she marched to her truck. She needed to charge her brother rent for occupying space in her brain. But sometimes, she mused, strangling Craig might be easier. His words clanged in her head, causing a tug-of-war between remembering them and shutting them out.

Midstride, she tripped. The toe of her boot caught a stone at the edge of the driveway. Packages flew from her arms. She wobbled and managed to right herself, but boxes littered the concrete. Tormenting frustration scratched its way up to her throat. She swallowed hard, forcing back the choking sensation.

"Could today get any worse?" she shouted and looked up, expecting to find a dark cloud hovering over her head. Instead, September's clear blue sky stretched far and wide. Hummingbirds, thick like a herd of cows, flitted from one feeder to another along the fence line. Breezes carried a *neigh* from her neighbor's horse in the next pasture.

Out near the road, a cloud of dust rolled by. A battered blue pickup kicked up dirt. Once again, Lucas didn't bother to stop. She'd already failed with him.

The world continued around her, just another day

in paradise, except for almost a year she'd only been chasing serenity that paradise promised. It was almost in her grasp, yet one misstep would ruin everything. She'd go down fighting to prove her brother wrong. She just refused to fail.

Lia collected the packages and stacked them neatly on the back seat of her Ford pickup. When she turned the key in the ignition, the diesel engine rumbled to a start. Putting the truck in gear, she sailed toward town with a sliver of renewed hope the day would somehow get better. It took some fight, but she vowed to remain a *glass is half-full* kind of girl.

Behind her truck, the two-lane farm road disappeared in a cloud of brown dust. Wearing her best cowboy boots, she let up on the gas just before the truck hit a pothole the size of a wagon wheel. She bounced hard as though on the back of a bull, so hard it rattled her teeth. She'd suffered many bumps in the last year, and as bad as they were, they hadn't crushed her yet. Almost didn't count.

She glanced behind to the boxes now scattered as though someone had pitched them like a deck of cards into the air and let them fall. The stuff in the boxes, on their way to new homes, was money in the bank. Money that kept her in groceries and gas, but never prevented life's next bump from crashing into her world. With a little serendipity—she didn't dare wish for the full-blown luck of the Irish, just a tad to help cover looming debts—she would manage to keep her farm for another year. One year at a time.

Pushing away all thoughts of Craig and future tomorrows, she recited her list of errands. "Drop off the outgoing mail at the post office. Pick mine up.

Drive ten streets to the opposite side of town for Karl Turner."

Since she hadn't had more than a second date with any man in the last year, she set her sights on the new manager who'd moved down from Chicago and worked at his uncle's farm store. He thought she was coming in for a large order of tulip, daffodil, and crocus bulbs for fall planting.

"News flash! Lia Britton trolls for a date," she said aloud.

The information would shock every last person in Harvest, Kansas, given her family's position as upstanding pillars of the community, a family who dotted i's and crossed all t's. The Brittons were proper people, proper with a capital P.

For once, she wanted to get past the inquiry of first and second dates. "What's your favorite food? What's your favorite color?" Though several months ago, on a blind date, a man asked, "What brand of condom do you prefer?" Stunned, her sense of humor stalled, and she left before dessert.

Even a lowly artist and farm girl enjoyed a good meal and good conversation in the company of a good man. She was no exception. Would her dark denim skirt and off-the-shoulder, soft pink peasant blouse, something she'd discovered in one of the hundreds of unopened boxes in the barn, along with a bright smile prove country enough to catch Karl's eye? She'd worn the outfit hoping it would bring success to her mission.

She needed a date.

Besides, there was no reason he had to know why next Saturday night held such special significance. If she managed to land a rendezvous with him, it would give her something to look forward to...something to get her past the haunting pain of tomorrow.

Lia slowed, bumping the truck onto the fresh asphalt of Main Street and into the afternoon shadows cast by two-story buildings. She flicked a quick wave at Helen Carter standing in the window of the Sunflower Café, rolling by without slowing. Last week, the older woman had cornered her when she went in to order a birthday cake. Helen insisted on telling her fortune, which Lia hadn't wanted to know. Bad news was something she preferred to read in the paper rather than worry and wait for it to come true. Like sour milk, it could ruin a day...or a life. She'd had enough negative news to last a lifetime. But Helen, whose accuracy rate matched a master sharpshooter at a gun range, grabbed Lia's wrist when she offered her credit card to pay. Helen then proceeded to announce to coffee-klatch customers how Lia would soon have a man in her life. A man she already knew.

"Yeah, right," Lia mumbled, remembering the group's hearty applause and her own reddening embarrassment. An irritating flush heated her cheeks. There was only one man she wanted, but he'd rejected her, avoiding all entanglement except those resembling a brother-sister relationship. She had a brother. Didn't want another one.

She angled the pickup into an empty place in front of the post office. "A man in my life." She grunted. "As if men have been beating down my door."

Lia stepped onto the truck's running board, then

hopped down, hoping to make a graceful exit in a skirt. With the first of three stacks of boxes in her arms, she carried them in for mailing.

"Afternoon, Lia," Zoë Marshall, Lia's friend since grade school, called out from behind the counter. "How many this time? Single-handedly you've kept this station in business for the last year."

"Don't know. More in the truck." Lia plopped the boxes on the counter. A delivery service would pick up at the farm, but that's how hundreds of boxes ended up there in the first place. A service would've been easier than hauling boxes to town each week, but she'd never see a living soul if she didn't make the weekly trek to the post office and to church. At the farm, corn listened well; however, other than rustling with the wind, it never talked back. Hard to have a conversation even though there were acres of ears and only one of her.

After Lia stacked the final load of packages on the counter, Zoë weighed each one, punched numbers into a machine, totaled the cost, and handed a receipt to Lia. "We need a girls' weekend away. Before the cold blows in, let's go to the Renaissance Fair in Lawrence."

"Sorry, you know I don't like costumes."

"Well, then, how about that blues club over in KC?"

"I love their barbecue, but don't like smelling like it."

"Why do you keep putting me off?" Zoë pouted.

"How about horseback riding? A neighbor will loan us a couple horses for an afternoon."

"Lia, we have to do something to get you off the

farm." Zoë's tone chastised. "God knows it was awful what happened to your parents, but dang, girl, you didn't die with them."

Lia flinched. The painful rawness of her parents' death had healed, but a tender spot still remained. "I'm not the wild child I was when we were in high school. The old place is comforting. Makes me miss my parents less. Besides, you see me every week, sometimes twice with church."

"There's only so much to paint on the prairie. I thought surely you'd be ready to head back to the city after a few months." Zoë paused before whispering, "Of all of us, I thought you'd be the one to make it out for good."

She'd thought so, too. Except now, the rolling hills dotted with farms surrounding Harvest offered her endless inspiration. The same field, or stream, or copse looked different with each season. A simple tree dropped leaves in winter. Sprouted fresh green in spring. Bloomed rich deep green in summer, then turned red, gold, and orange in the fall. Every season offered a colorful palette. The fields had character, too. A blue sky transformed at dusk, glowing pink, gold, and even lavender. The scent of fresh-cut hay was like the warm embrace of an old friend.

Sometimes she missed the city, missed her students more, but here she could breathe deep with the wide-open sky. Here, she vibrated with life as though the country had tapped her with a tuning fork and together they pulsed with the same frequency. It had taken leaving and returning for her to figure it out.

Zoë leaned over the counter and waved

Lia closer.

"Are you mad at me because that cowboy at Rockets asked me out for Saturday night?" Zoë whispered.

Lia lowered her eyes and shook her head, trying hard not to laugh. Good-hearted Zoë, with her dark brown eyes expressing her every emotion, would be pleased to know she hoped to wrangle a date with the newest man in town, and the cowboy in question would never be her type.

"If you're interested, really interested, I'll let you have him."

"Oh, no, Zoë. I'm doing just fine. Are you mad at me because you don't have a place to crash in the city? Is that why you keep wanting me to leave?"

"No." Zoë drew back and placed a hand over her heart as though mortally wounded.

"But?" Lia whispered.

"The cowboy fits the description of the man Helen said would come into your life." Zoë furrowed her brow. "I can't mess with fate, nor should you."

"You go on and have a great time with him tomorrow night. You know, this could be the time when Helen is wrong. No one's perfect."

Zoë gasped and shook her head as if to negate Lia's uttered blasphemy.

Lia shrugged. People publicly shied away from conversations about Helen's abilities, but they sure lined up whenever she offered free palm readings or gave away free dessert. Just one of the anomalies of Harvest. Palm reading and pie.

Lia flashed a wide grin before walking around the corner to her post office box, the heels of her boots clicking against the worn linoleum floor. She paused before opening the small door. Her breath hitched. She hoped just once she'd find a greeting card or postcard, something personal from someone who cared, even if that someone turned out to be her brother.

She turned the key in the lock. The small door opened. She bent to peer inside, only a flyer for pool products and a gun catalog. A quick stab of sadness shot to her chest. Happiness had taken a holiday and forgotten to write. If she wanted snail mail, she'd have to send it to herself. Gee, what fun that would be...and oh, so pathetic.

At the door, she waved good-bye to Zoë and hoped her smile appeared convincing.

Driving at the exact speed limit along tree-lined Main Street guaranteed a green light when she reached Fifth Avenue, the only intersection in town with a stoplight. The sheriff and his deputy staked it out on weekends, especially in the fall, to catch speeders or red-light runners—usually tourists headed for the only antique and what-not store for miles. They made exceptions for bus drivers delivering potential customers on their trips from Kansas City to Denver.

Lia rolled through a green light, passed the other streets, and turned left on Tenth.

"Townspeople have all day to shop," she muttered when cars filled all the parking spaces in front of the store. Today was the final day of the fall bulb sale. Garden club matrons wanted the best show of spring color around public spaces, which made the annual flower sale a big hit. Every year they planted existing gardens with more bulbs, replacing the ones squirrels and rabbits had munched on over the winter.

Lia raked her fingers through her shoulder length auburn hair, then fluffed her loose curls, the result of struggling with a curling iron. Steering the truck to the rear parking lot, she spied a too-familiar, battered blue pickup. Dread dropped free-fall into her stomach. She had no parachute to cushion the landing.

The last person she wanted to see was Lucas Dwyer.

****

Nothing but the arrival of his younger sister or madness would make Lucas brave Mr. Turner's farm store on Friday afternoon during the last day of the annual bulb sale.

"Excuse me, ma'am." Lucas bumped his way through the long line that began at the cash register and snaked around bins filled with toy tractors, rolled fleece blankets, and assorted tools. At six feet, he stood at least a head taller than the horde of women, mostly blue hairs, all chirping at once like parakeets in a cage. It reminded him of one of the few vacations his family took when he was a kid—he'd been lost at Bird World. He shuddered at the memory.

Near the back of the store, the manager worked at the key-making machine.

"Hey, Karl," Lucas shouted over the roar of the grinding wheel. "Did you have time to fill my order?"

Karl looked up and nodded before bending again to focus on the key.

Lucas checked his watch. He had time to kill before Craig arrived from St. Louis. Time to finish errands and grab a shower. Later, they'd visit Rockets, eat some barbecue, and hoist a few brews. But Craig would want a full report about Amelia. Lucas's gut tightened, twisting like someone wringing an old-fashioned mop. He'd never kept information from Craig before.

Glancing at the crowd, he spotted the corporate farm manager chatting up the very elderly Mrs. Watts. He wanted to hate the man for managing what should've been his farm, but in the end, the man had no fault. That man hadn't left his family and joined the Air Force after college. Guilt stabbed Lucas, a knife to his heart. He turned his attention to the array of plumbing supplies, but the pain of losing the farm rubbed like salt in a fresh wound. While he'd been away on active duty, his dad made some bad decisions, which over time cost them their farmstead. Their thousand acres, minus ten, now belonged to a corporation. At least they still held the title to their family home and the plot of land—free and clear. He had to remember that.

Karl shut off the grinder. "I've got that bag of stuff in the breakroom in the back." Karl grinned and looked him over, old black work boots, faded jeans, and chambray shirt torn at the elbow. "I never took you for that type of gardener, Combine."

Lucas rolled his eyes and followed Karl. Lucas didn't care for the nickname the guy had pinned on him. He'd started a combining company to harvest commercially when he left the Air Force, but there was more to him than farming. However, it seemed as though giving people silly nicknames was the only way Karl could remember who was who in Harvest. It wasn't that Karl wasn't a good guy. He just tried too hard to be country. After a month, he still oozed with city slickness. Plus, he mistakenly assumed all his neighbors were hicks—never been anywhere, never seen anything. Karl liked to jaw about his travels. Lucas had seen lots during college and nearly thirteen years of military service. He had nothing to prove. Karl seemed smart enough. He'd figure out who was who and what was what...or he'd leave, like Mr. Turner's other nephew who'd tried to run the farm store and failed to ever fit in.

In the back storeroom, away from the chaos of little old ladies and their chirping noises, Lucas paused as Karl plopped a big burlap bag onto an old wooden table and pointed.

"Crocuses and daffodils. I threw in some hostas, too. My thank-you to you for sort of teaching me the ropes about Harvest."

"They're for my sister," Lucas said, wondering where the urge to explain his purchase came from.

"Sister?"

He'd promised himself to maintain the homestead like his folks had before they moved to a retirement community in Arizona. He wanted his younger sister to have all the comforts of home when she visited from college, including flowerbeds filled with blooms in spring. To accomplish that required some replenishing each fall.

"Her name is Megan."

"Oh, sure," Karl replied. His smirk suggested he didn't believe a word of it. "I haven't seen her around."

"Well, you wouldn't. This isn't Manhattan,

Kansas, or K-State. She's a student there. Only comes home once in a while." He wasn't about to explain the reason for her weekend homecoming—but come Sunday, the bulbs would work as a distraction. A time when they could plant side-by-side and talk about stuff. That worked best for them. They weren't ones to bare their souls to anyone, much less each other, but talking while working gave them a way to connect. And his way of keeping up with her without prying much.

Karl shifted his weight from one foot to the other. He looked down.

"What?" Lucas asked.

"Dude, is there more to do around here than Rockets on the weekend?"

"Sure, but most of it looks like farm work. Come to think of it, feels like farm work, too."

He hated being referred to as *Dude*. That offended him more than Combine.

"So what about…" Karl looked down again.

Lucas waited. If Karl had something more on his mind, he needed to spit it out. Guessing games were a waste of time, and he didn't have Helen Carter's mind-reading abilities.

Karl leaned in close. "What about the ladies?"

Lucas's brow wrinkled. "What about them?"

"Like, how do I get one? Seems there's all kinds of unwritten rules around here. Things you can say and do with one person that you can't say and do with another."

"Where'd you say you'd moved from?" Lucas asked.

"Chicago."

"Well, I don't know how things go in Chicago, but around here, you need to treat a female like a lady or you could have the whole town against you."

"But what about that Britton one? She's not really from around here, is she? Isn't she from Kansas City? Am I gonna step on anyone's toes if I ask her for a date?"

The punch to the gut surprised Lucas. His body stiffened. No had ever referred to Amelia as *that Britton one* before. No, the man could not have a date with Amelia, but Karl wasn't exactly asking permission. Should he clue in the hardware store manager or let him discover the situation for himself? After all, Craig would arrive in a few hours. Amelia's brother would have plenty to say, in no uncertain terms, about why Karl, or any man from Harvest, shouldn't date his sister.

Before Lucas could answer, *click-clack* of boot heels against the tired linoleum echoed down the dimly lit hall.

"Karl?"

"Yah? In here."

Lucas groaned inwardly as Amelia stood framed in the doorway. He gritted his teeth but couldn't stop from staring. She'd lost her farm-work clothes—baggy overalls and grungy t-shirt—replaced them with a curve-hugging denim skirt, a sexy top, and she glowed like her face was lit by a spotlight. Her hair hung in loose waves around her face. She had haunted his dreams, and now she haunted his personal space.

"Speak of the devil," Karl murmured and bumped his elbow against Lucas's side. Lucas grunted.

"Hey! How are you? What can I help you with?" Karl asked taking a step forward.

Lucas caught Amelia's frown, which she quickly lifted into a wide smile, aiming it at Karl. "I can come back another time. I didn't know you were busy. Mr. Turner said I would find you back here, but again, I didn't know you were with a customer."

"Amelia." Lucas nodded to her. He wouldn't allow her to ignore him, and if he hadn't been watching for it, her return nod could've been missed.

"Amelia? I thought your name was Lia Britton." Karl's expression turned puzzled as he looked at Lucas, then to Lia, and back to Lucas again.

She smiled sweetly. "My given name is Amelia, but no one calls me that anymore."

"Only family," Lucas bit out more harshly than intended.

"Huh?" Karl asked. "You two related?"

"No!" Lia snapped as if poked with a cattle prod. Her brown eyes glowered as though she wanted to stab him with one.

"Craig will be here by dinner." Lucas kept his voice low and even.

"Your boyfriend?" Karl asked, looking worried.

"Brother," Lucas said at the same time as Lia.

"Oh." Karl relaxed, flexing his shoulders. "In that case, I was wondering if you'd like to go out tomorrow night."

"No," Lucas said.

"I wasn't asking *you*," Karl snapped.

"Doesn't matter. She's got plans tomorrow."

Lia scowled so hard that if she'd had special, super-hero powers Lucas was certain his eyebrows

14

and lashes would be singed, probably burned off his face.

"Karl, I'm sorry, but I do have a longstanding engagement for tomorrow. However," she brightened, "I came to ask *you* if you would like to go out next Saturday night? There's a bistro on the river in Atchison. I thought we might go there."

"Yeah. I'd like that." Karl perked up like a strutting rooster in a yard full of hens. "What time shall I pick you up?"

Lucas frowned. "Amelia, Craig's not going to like this."

Chapter 2

Outside the farm store, Lia stomped her way to the truck, fuming and wishing she could snort fire. Squeezing her fist tightly, the keys in her hand bit into her skin, pinching the flesh of her palm. She punched the air before loosening her death grip. The intense pain subsided to a dull throb. "The nerve of that man!"

He had no right to look so good. Tall, lean, muscular and tan—her knees practically buckled. Her heart bounced as though it rode on the back of a bucking bull. But who was he to tell her anything? And better yet, who was he to discourage Karl from asking her out? Just because Lucas and her brother had been best friends since forever, he had no right butting in. None. And, he *dared* to invoke a threat using her big brother's name? As if Craig would want her to live like a maiden hermit all her life. He wanted what was best for her, though they couldn't agree on what that was. Thank goodness, Karl had a mind of his own and ignored Lucas, which earned him major points. The highlight of the day: Karl had asked her out first.

How about them apples, Lucas Dwyer?

Once inside the truck, Lia slammed the door. Lucas had broken her heart years ago. The pain of his rejection after she gathered her courage and thrown herself at him, back during her college days, still stung. Since then, he'd maintained an arm's length distance, except for the heart-stealing kiss after her parents' funeral. Somehow over the last year, he'd taken on the role of big brother while her older brother tried to force himself into the role of parent.

At least Karl was interested in spending time with her. That assuaged her pride and boosted her waning confidence a degree or two. The upside to the ridiculous scene—she'd go home and put the adrenalized anger to good use by painting, by slashing color on a canvas, darks fading into lights with textures of smooth and rough. When she finished emoting, maybe the painting would strike a chord with someone's imagination, or better yet, touch their heart. She didn't paint only to sell. She painted because it kept her grounded. Some people needed to listen to music or drink or some activity to help them block out the world. She, however, channeled her emotions into art.

Tapping her fingers on the steering wheel as though playing piano keys, she wrestled with anxiety while putting the truck in gear. Emotional overload. That could be why she'd been so darn prolific and produced some of her best work since grief had flooded her world, rising up the same way floodwaters covered fields and created murky spots with depths unknown. There were moments over the last year when she feared she might drown. She teetered between the joy of being back on the farm and the utter anguish of missing her parents. Either way, emotions pushed her to paint.

Funny how she hadn't recognized that fact

before. Tomorrow was the one-year anniversary of her parents' funeral. For weeks, she'd tried to keep her thoughts from drifting there, but like a broken farmhouse shutter banging in a storm, they refused to be silent, some days banging so hard they gave her a migraine. But here and now is what she had, along with a date with Karl. Balancing on the pinpoint of happiness, she had to share the news with someone else, otherwise, it would never feel real.

She pulled into the same parking spot in front of the post office she'd vacated an hour before. Squaring her shoulders, she took a breath before entering. The only person she trusted to keep her total confidence was Zoë.

Lia shoved open the outer door to the post office. The inside doors mechanically *whooshed* open. A line of customers waited.

"Hey! Lia. How's it going?" Butch called out. He was third in a line of six waiting for service. "Bring the truck over to the shop first thing Monday. I've got the new tailgate in. Will get it fixed for you then."

Lia smiled, nodded, and headed for the front of the line. On the way, she heard the farmer behind Butch say, "What happened to the tailgate?"

"She tried to unhook a trailer."

"Oh. Women farmers."

Lia locked her jaw and narrowed her eyes and continued to the counter. She was determined to remain silent and not launch into a word battle with the old-timer. Why men still contended a woman alone couldn't make a go of farming pushed her frustration button as quick as Lucas Dwyer had about going on a date with Karl. Leaning across the counter, she motioned to Zoë for paper and pen since she didn't trust herself to speak without shouting out in anger. Lia scribbled a note asking her to meet at Rockets the moment she got off work.

"Sure thing," Zoë said, motioning to the next person in line.

Lia scowled at the farmer as she passed him. Oblivious, the man continued to lament about the faults of women to Butch, who shot her an apologetic smile. Outside, Lia paused and took deep long breaths. Once. Twice. Three times. But it didn't quell her anger. Maybe sharing good news over food and a drink before heading home would balance out her mood. The unrestrained urge to paint was already there. She just needed to channel it in the right direction...although the last angry black and red painting she'd sold brought in a thousand dollars.

Scanning the skyline for Rockets, she spotted the rooftop ornament of the bar. Sighting the landmark filled her with a shot of comfort and steadied her nerves a bit. Much in her life had changed during the year since her parents had passed, but not so with the skyline of the town.

Rockets was an institution. The bar got its name from the first owner back in the 50s who had a replica V-2 American rocket mounted on the roof like a church steeple. The town welcomed the first bar within the city limits with a gusto that matched a bull rider's successful nine-second ride for big prize money. However, the owner fought city council for approval of the building's iconic rooftop decoration. The council balked with the determination of a mule refusing to plow, unwilling to issue a final permit as long as the signature icon stood higher than any church's steeple. Somehow, Rockets won.

Her only problem now? Walk or drive. Driving was five minutes, walking took ten, and Zoë had another half-hour of work. She'd never waited inside a bar alone. The Britton family reputation prohibited it, not that Rockets was a bad place, just not a kid-family-friendly kind of establishment.

Trepidation fluttered in Lia's chest as she reached the bar. Scanning either side of the street, she was alone, no one approaching on the sidewalk. She pulled hard on the heavy door. A year of grieving would end tomorrow. A turning point. If she truly wanted to prove her independence and make Craig take notice of how capable she'd grown—on the farm and handling her own life—then she could start by sitting alone at the bar while waiting for a friend. After all, on the rare occasion a fight broke out at Rockets, it usually happened after midnight. While the September sun had lowered in the sky, plenty of daylight still remained. Darkness was hours away.

"Lia?" The bartender approached.

"Hello. Um…lemonade please?" Lia asked, trying to sound cultured and offhanded. Bethany, the bartender and her high-school classmate voted Freshman Beauty, and by senior year, nominated for Most Likely to Succeed, had married the current owner of the bar.

"You want a lemonade? This isn't the Sunflower Café."

Lia shifted slightly and rested her hand on the bar top. "Beer."

"Which one?" Bethany played Vanna White and

pointed toward the beer pulls, and then with a flourish, showed off the collection of bottled beers arranged on the bottom glass shelf with the liquor displayed on the shelves above. "Draft or bottle?"

Since she rarely drank beer and only knew them from commercials, her knowledge left her without an answer. Playing on Bethany's vanity, Lia suggested, "You choose the best one for me." She hopped on a barstool parked at the end of the long polished wooden bar. It provided a perfect view of anyone entering or leaving by the front door.

"Boulevard Pale Ale on draft," Bethany said, placing a full mug on the bar in front of Lia.

"For a quart of Ale is a meal for a King."

"What?"

"Shakespeare."

Bethany chuckled. "You, of course, would know that. Always the artsy one. But I'd bet money you can't walk after a pint."

Lia ignored the jab. "I'll take some nachos with barbecue pulled pork."

"Coming right up," Bethany tapped the computer screen behind the bar.

Observing the place with a painter's eye, Lia marveled at the golden light filtering through the slatted brown blinds. The punched-copper ceiling, showing a rich patina, had to be original to the old building. Black tufted booths lined the walls, but the round tables and wooden chairs filling the open spaces resembled the style from old western movies. When Kip Moore belted out *Beer Money* through the sound system, Lia held up her frosted mug in salute. After a sip, she turned her attention to the closest big screen TV mounted on the wall where the pre-five o'clock news scrolled ticker-tape style on the bottom of the screen.

Rockets, she decided, had a very respectable atmosphere during the day despite its less than distinguished late-night reputation.

A few minutes later, the door to the bar opened.

"Hey, Bethany, I'll take a draft of whatever's on special today," Zoë called as she entered and headed in Lia's direction.

"How was work?" Lia asked when her friend hoisted herself on the next barstool.

"I can tell from that frown you really don't want to talk about that, although I could give you stories that would keep you in stitches all day. What's up?"

"Lucas Dwyer."

"What's he done now?" Zoë shook her head.

Lia paused as Bethany lingered while dropping off Zoë's beer and Lia's plate of nachos.

"Ah, we'll run a tab," Lia said and waited for the bartender to slide her way back to the far end of the bar.

"Forget about Lucas for a moment. I have good news. Great news! I have a date for next Saturday night." Lia beamed.

"Ducks do fly south for the winter. Who's the dude?"

"Karl Turner."

"*The* Karl Turner? The new nephew at the farm store? Nice."

Lia smiled. "He asked me out for tomorrow night…but," she paused when her heart slammed in her chest knowing what tomorrow represented. "We have a date for next Saturday night."

"*Next* Saturday night?" Zoë's brow furrowed.

"Lucas had the gall to tell him I couldn't go out with him tomorrow night."

"Lucas said that? Well, you *could* go."

Lia sighed. "Yes, but I wouldn't be good company. I hate it when Lucas is right."

"But, think about it. Maybe going out is exactly what you need."

"I will, but *next* Saturday night."

"I've met Karl once. He seems...more mature than the last nephew Mr. Turner imported to help out. It's not like Lucas to butt in."

"He's been an ache in my backside for the last year"—Lia lowered her voice—"I think…and oh, is Craig going to catch it…I think my brother appointed Lucas as my watchdog."

Zoë's eyes grew round.

Lia nodded. "That would explain why Lucas, not Craig, fought with me about who would put in the crop last spring, who would help me with the mowing, even who should harvest the corn. All along, I just thought he wanted the business. When I complained to Craig about Lucas Dwyer, my brother dearest encouraged me to let Lucas handle things if I wanted the farm to succeed. I think Craig feels guilty because he couldn't pull strings to help the Dwyers keep their farm."

"Wouldn't you?'

Lia frowned. "Yeah, probably. If I were Craig. But I don't know about finances like he does, and I can't depend on Lucas. He's gone in the fall combining. Craig said Lucas travels as much as a thousand miles to a farm for work during the season."

"And that's got what to do with giving the man a contract? Give Lucas some credit. He's helping pay for Megan's education."

Lia narrowed her eyes. A ripple of unease rode a rollercoaster from her brain to her heart. "Do you still have a crush on him?" she asked quietly. "I thought you were long over Lucas."

"Hey, sister!" a voice shouted, interrupting her study of Zoë. Lia turned to see Zoë's younger brother racing toward them.

Zoë hopped down from the barstool and let out a squeal. "Whee!" She raced toward her brother. "Seth! How come you never told anyone you were coming home?"

The uniformed solider stopped, saluted, and then grabbed Zoë around the waist and twirled her round and round. The few customers in the bar clapped. Bethany reappeared from the kitchen and joined in the applause.

"Welcome home, Seth," Lia called out, but she couldn't help but wonder if Zoë had purposefully avoided the question about Lucas—their unrequited love during their high school years.

Chapter 3

Lia waved her hand. "Hello? Bethany. Another of whatever beer Zoë's drinking and the same for her brother," Lia said to the mesmerized bartender as Seth and Zoë walked toward her spot at the bar.

"I just love a man in a uniform," Bethany gushed. Lia worried the woman might fall into an old-fashioned swoon, something like Scarlett O'Hara might pull. Lia's mother had endowed their Midwest family values with a smattering of southern culture from her side of the family. An iconic swooning couch had held court in the living room all of her life.

Seth saluted Bethany, who blushed deep pink.

"Drinks coming right up. *His* is on the house." Bethany hurried away.

Seth leaned over and hugged Lia. "The famous artist comes to town. Good to see you."

"You aren't the little runt who followed your sister and me around. I'd salute you, but would probably make a mess of it, and I don't want to insult. How about a toast instead?"

Bethany placed a beer directly in front of Seth and Zoë's second one within reach.

Lia stood and lifted her mug. "Here's to all brave men who serve with honor. And to you, Seth Marshall, for making your family proud and coming home alive." She clinked the glass together with her friends and took a sip.

"To Seth," the other dozen patrons in the bar shouted.

Seth turned and waved to the well-wishers. "Thanks. It's good to be home."

"I'm going to leave. You two have some catching up to do," Lia said, picking up her keys from the bar.

"But you haven't finished half your drink," Seth pointed out. "Don't go on my account."

"I feel even more inspired to paint now. It's all taking shape in my brain." She hugged Seth, then Zoë. "I'll see you tomorrow," Lia whispered. "About two. Rain or shine." A touch of sadness tweaked her heart. Celebrating Seth's return, a brave man home from war, and seeing the joy in Zoë's eyes over his homecoming made the ache of missing her parents and the family life they'd shared greater in the moment. Not that she expected things to be a hundred percent different tomorrow, but maybe getting past the first anniversary of the funeral would be like finishing a book about an epic journey. Starting a new story might lighten the remaining sadness stuck in her heart.

Walking out of the dark bar, Lia shaded her eyes, allowing them to adjust to the sunlight. She crossed the street in the shadow of the bar's rocket steeple before turning the corner and making her way back to her truck. She mused about the differences between her and Zoë. She was taller, curvier, auburn haired, with not much family compared to Zoë with her petite build, model thin, blonde bobbed hair, blue eyes, and a large boisterous family. Their goals in life were different, too. While she loved to paint and enjoyed teaching, Zoë preferred the spotlight. Harvest didn't have a theater, but maybe it could use one where her oldest friend from grade school could perform and charm any audience. If Zoë had pursued a career in sales, her friend would be rich. Her smile endeared her to everyone.

"But then, if she wasn't here, I wouldn't have her to lean on right now," Lia said, climbing into her truck. Their differences didn't interfere with their friendship. However, she envied Zoë one thing—as an older sister to siblings, her friend received family respect—unlike Lia's brother, who looked at her more and more like a child since their parents had died, which made the challenge of proving her farming capabilities that much more difficult. If Craig would only see reason, he'd be proud of her, instead of doubting her.

Two years in age difference was a lot when they were in high school, she a sophomore to his senior status, or when they were in college, but not now. Just because he majored in business and she in art didn't mean she couldn't manage the farm like a business. In the face of Mister Doubter, as long as the weather held and the crop came in—fingers crossed—she'd break even on her first, fulltime farming effort. He'd given her a year to fail.

Just the same, even with mixed feelings, she'd be happy to see him. Family history and grief knitted them together, a special kind of bond. She sighed. Craig was headed home for the weekend to spend time with her and to pay respects to their parents. She couldn't pull off the small graveside memorial service tomorrow afternoon without him. Lucas and Megan would be there and Zoë, too. A few other close friends and neighbors had been included. If she were a betting woman, she'd put money on the fact that Craig had other items on his agenda, like trying to talk her into selling the farm again. He had better be ready for a shocker...did he even understand the two-letter word, no? If he decided to sell his half, she'd find a way to deal with it, but her inheritance wasn't for sale. End of story.

Lia pulled into a quick-stop station shaded by tall grain silos, filled up the truck with diesel, then ran through the car wash before heading back to the farm, traveling the two-lane blacktop highway rather than farm roads to keep the truck clean. As she drove, she noticed hints of changing color. The sun appeared more golden, rather than summer lemon. Leaves showed the first fall tinge of orange and gold. Fields of sunflowers turned their heads to the light. Tassels on corn glinted like golden silk thread in fields spreading out for miles, signs of summer slipping into fall. Any day now, a first soft frost could arrive and make the world look different. A Kansas fall was like a rose bud—it opened fast and faded too soon.

But she could capture it all in a painting to preserve the feeling year round.

Arriving at the farm, she nosed the truck into the garage. Gentleman Jack greeted her with loud barks from the mudroom where she'd left him. For a Brittany Spaniel, he obeyed well, yet true to his bloodline, whenever able, he'd cast for quail and pheasant—no matter the season.

"Were you a good boy?" She let the dog loose. He bounced past her in a spurt of energy before sprinting back. Together they walked around the old two-story farmhouse. Spring a year ago, her father had replaced all of the windows with efficient double-paned ones. It lowered the heating and cooling costs, which made a difference in her budget between eating well or not. The butter-yellow paint on the house had faded along with the black on the shutters. With the right ladders, she could save money by tackling the job herself. Well, with the right ladders and a few male friends with strong forearms. She had a few candidates in mind, men she could bribe with good food and beer. Maybe she could ask Lucas to organize a painting party. After all, if he was going to keep inserting himself into her life, he might as well be useful.

The house was more than just a structure built on some land. It represented her past and her future. Safety. Comfort. She loved it, but loved Lucas as much. That was a secret she shared only with the house. How would he react if he knew her honest feelings? Would he brush her off this time, like the times in the past, all because she was Craig's sister?

For some reason she hadn't figured out yet, she feared Lucas knowing the true depths of her feelings. Telling him was a risk she wasn't willing to take at this point. Her heart still ached over the loss of her parents, and she couldn't handle rejection from him again.

If she let him know how much she cared, and he didn't share the same feelings, it could very well be her final heartbreak. Only then, would she consider moving off the farm. Torture would be seeing him with another woman. If he married...then Craig just might get his wish. She'd be the one to plant the For Sale sign by the road. But she held on to a thin thread of hope about Lucas. As much as the man infuriated her, fighting with him was better than not having him in her life at all.

Walking with Gentleman Jack through the yard and around the house, she surveyed what she owned. The house rested on the crest of a rolling hill. A hundred yards away, oak and hedge apple trees lined a stream slicing through the thousand-acre property. Passing the line of birdfeeders, she made a mental note to refill them. She selected different feed for each one to attract different species of birds. Cardinals, blue jays, and a few bluebirds came, along with brown wrens and gray doves. Just beyond the yard surrounding the house, as far as she could see, corn whispered in the wind and one field of sunflowers lifted their faces to the sun. Here the wind always blew. She missed it whenever she traveled.

Satisfaction settled over her like a warm blanket on a cool night. She'd show Craig. The crop had been planted with a lot of hard work, and she'd already contracted to have it harvested within the month. No way would she miss the mortgage payments. The sale of the corn, yellow like gold, would provide enough money for her to make it through the winter, plus pay for planting in spring…as long as internet sales of the boxed stuff her mother had left hidden in the barn remained steady for the next few months. However, to ensure her success, it was time for plan B, a visit to the gallery in Kansas City requesting to show her work. If her collection of paintings sold, she'd be in *high cotton*, as her mother used to say.

A trail of dust caught her attention. A truck traveled up the hill on the mostly hard-packed clay road. She glanced at her watch. The delivery driver was right on time, but as usual, he passed the house, continuing on his route to one of the neighbors down the road. Had her mother kept watch through the sunroom window and anxiously waited for the arrival of new packages?

"Here, Jack!" Lia called. The dog ran to her with his ears peaked and his tongue hanging out. She bent to pet him, rubbing behind his ears. "I guess it's a good thing after all that you never bit the FedEx man who delivered all that stuff to Mother."

The news of her parents' death had been difficult enough to take, but when she and Craig got to the hard part of disposing of some of their parents' belongings, in the barn along with equipment and tools, they'd discovered a room built into the back corner with a lock on the door. When they busted in, to their surprise, they uncovered a ten-by-ten space stacked from the wooden floor to the fourteen-foot ceiling with unopened boxes. The mystery of the packages revealed itself after they searched a file cabinet and found receipts providing information identifying the contents of the multitude of packages. But the reason for the merchandise was only a guess. By all appearances, their mother, a meticulous bookkeeper, became an internet shopaholic after Lia went off to college more than ten years ago.

Lia crossed her arms, hugging her shoulders, and wished she could hug her mother to make the tightness in her chest lessen. She blinked back tears. Mother had lived for their family. Left her home and relatives in Louisiana to marry a farmer and take on a completely different life than the one she'd known. She brought a taste of Cajun culture to the Midwest, but the folks didn't understand Twelfth Night and thought Mardi Gras was an excuse for debauchery, which their local minister preached against. Had her mother been so lonely she tried to fill her cloistered farm life with stuff? Had the highlight of her day been a delivery from the FedEx man? What had her father thought about all of it? Her parents, as far as she knew, had the perfect marriage. Lia shook her head. She'd probably never uncover the secret to her mother's behavior.

Lia had shared her secret fears about her mom only with Zoë. It would kill her if people gossiped about Mother now that she wasn't around anymore.

The wind whipped up. Pushing her hair behind her ears, she grabbed its length to keep it from her eyes, closed them, and lifted her face into the gust. The breeze carried some of her sadness away. When she opened her eyes, pride thudded a steady beat in her chest as she gazed at the fields of corn. Her mother wouldn't want her to wallow. That wasn't allowed. She had three reasons to celebrate. A trip to KC with her artwork. Dinner with Karl on her birthday. And Gus harvesting the corn.

A sound on the wind distracted her.

"Amelia."

The wind muffled her brother's voice. She ran as fast as the back slit in her skit would allow, happy Craig had arrived safely.

"Go get him, Jack!" Lia shouted. "Go see Craig."

The dog took off on her command flying across

the yard and around the corner of the house. When she finally spotted Craig, her heart warmed. He playfully petted Jack. But the warming turned cool. Behind her brother, she spotted a black car. He'd traded up to a new BMW, another marker of his intention to prove city life was better than life in the country. It shouted, "I'm doing well." He would never buy a car on credit. Cash only. She shook her head. That car wouldn't last on farm roads.

Drawing nearer to Craig, she couldn't hold back a smile when he bent at the waist, swaying from side to side. Jack grabbed for Craig's dangling tie as though it were part of a game.

"Good boy, Jackers." Craig laughed, yanking off the tie and tossing it through the open driver's window.

"Sit, Jack," Lia said. The dog obeyed. She eyed her brother. "Did you rush from a meeting? Drove for hours with a tie? You've become the definition of stuffy."

"So nice of you to worry about me. Hello, to you, too. I was on the phone for business most of the way here. It's always the same. Semis hogging the road. There's nothing new to see on I-70 when you've driven it a thousand times."

Craig opened his arms. She hugged him tight, enjoying the security he offered since their parents had died. A moment later, she pushed back and punched her finger against his chest. "We need to have a serious chat."

Craig's eyebrows shot up. He shook his head and waved his finger back and forth like a metronome as if to say she wasn't the boss of him. The stern expression and gesture were all too familiar, probably how he had reacted when she was born.

In the distance, another cloud of dust moved up the hill. Wind never swirled the dirt into a wall unless it was a twister. That kind of cloud only came from an approaching vehicle. A moment later, she recognized the battered work truck turning down the lane toward the house. "I should've known," she grumbled.

"I'm going out with Lucas." Craig smiled. "Want to join us?"

"Nope." Lia stormed to the back door, turning only to order Gentleman Jack inside. She visualized a painting in need of a canvas. Her earlier checked anger had returned with the approaching truck. If Craig were lucky, tomorrow morning for breakfast, she'd cook eggs instead of throwing raw ones at him. He might be a Wall Street-type with his fancy investment banking job in St. Louis, but she hadn't appointed him guardian of her life. They were going to come to a meaningful understanding about his interference. And, all interference from Lucas Dwyer on Craig's behalf had to stop.

"Amelia! Wait. It's only Lucas."

She opened the door and walked through without bothering to acknowledge him.

"Only Lucas," she muttered as she closed the door behind her. "The root of my problem today."

Chapter 4

Lucas gripped the door handle and braced his other hand against the car's console. When Craig punched the accelerator to ninety miles an hour, Lucas sucked in a breath. For a mile, the BMW sped along faster than a tornado.

Suddenly, Craig hit the brakes hard. Made a sharp turn. The rear fishtailed. Wind whirled through the open windows. Lucas blinked and imagined his brain bouncing side to side inside his skull like a batted ping-pong ball. Thankfully, the seatbelt locked him in place. He exhaled a ragged breath.

"Stop it." He grabbed Craig's arm.

The tires kicked up a cloud of dirt. The car jerked, rocked from side to side, fighting centrifugal force.

"You can't blow away the pain. Isn't it bad enough that tomorrow is the anniversary of your parents' funeral?" Lucas hollered. "Do you want your sister to have to plan another memorial service?"

Once completely through the turn, Craig let off the gas. The car slowed. Lucas's heart raced ahead as though in accelerated motion. His body yanked against the seatbelt again. "Ow!"

The car came to a final rest on the rise of a hill. Lucas swallowed the lump lodged in his throat. "Shit! Craig"—Lucas punched Craig's arm—"you want thrills? Sign up for a tour of duty in Afghanistan. Two tours of duty were enough for me. I want to live." Adrenaline coursed through him like a speeding train.

"Look." Craig pointed.

Before them, a smoldering orange sun hovered above a wide, flat green horizon. Red. Yellow. Pink. The sky blazed as though on fire. Something he missed when he visited Craig in St. Louis. Too much ambient light prevented a night-light show like this one.

"I understand why Amelia wants to stay on the farm," Craig said quietly. "Every star in the night sky is a reason."

Lucas nodded.

"I love it here, too. But there isn't opportunity for me. For now, St. Louis is my gateway."

"Don't get poetic on me. You haven't even had a drink yet," Lucas said dryly and folded his arms over his chest, still irritated by the kamikaze driving. His jackhammering heart slowed from overdrive to fast. He wanted to punch Craig for his fool stunt, but restraint was the better part of valor. Given his friend's mood, the night looked bleak. He doubted his friend would take the news he had to share with ease, but now was the time to move the line in the sand.

"I loved growing up here," Craig said. He gripped and released his hold on the steering wheel. "But I'm not a farmer, and farming is too hard for a woman alone."

"If I have my way, she won't be alone," Lucas muttered under his breath.

College days were far behind him. He'd been to war and survived. His family lost the farm. Accepting reality came when he started his own business. But after relocating his parents and moving his sister back to college, he finally admitted to himself Amelia was the reason he stayed. In Harvest, he'd never lingered long in any relationship. Thoughts of the woman he loved had kept him alive during his tours of duty. His plan to admit his attraction to her went to the bottom of his to-do pile when her parents suddenly died last year. If timing required luck, then his sucked.

He'd waited an entire year out of respect for the Britton's sense of propriety. The year of grieving ended tomorrow. In high school, he'd denied his attraction to her out of loyalty to Craig. In college, he kept Amelia at arm's length because a relationship proved improbable when he roomed with her brother. Later, she moved to the city. He couldn't make up for being a fool in the past. His reality had a new face, one that didn't sacrifice love for loyalty. The two could coexist. And if Craig had a notion to kill him in his fancy new car, he'd better tell Amelia his feelings fast or he'd take them to the grave.

Lucas coughed, breaking the silence in the car.

As though a switch had been flipped, Craig smiled. "Lucas, I hear a beer calling your name. I'll set my coordinates for the eatery." He made a U-turn, heading toward town.

White knuckled, Lucas held on.

Craig chuckled. "You're a brave man."

"More like a fool. You're one for driving like one. Me, a bigger one for tolerating it."

Craig slapped his shoulder. "You're the best friend. No one could ask for better. You've always been a brother to Amelia and me."

Lucas grunted rather than responding. Soon enough, Amelia's brother would know the truth.

Under a floodlight, across the street from the bar, Craig pulled into a parking space of a mostly full lot. As they entered Rockets, aromas of tangy and sweet and barbecue smoke wafted to Lucas's nose. His mouth watered. The smell of 'que always reminded him of Harvest. The farm. Family.

A hostess greeted them, led them to a booth at the far end away from the door, and placed menus on the table.

"Enjoy your meal, boys."

The din of voices and sports shows playing on the TVs scattered around the room almost drowned her out.

"So what's new?" Craig asked as he perused the food selection.

"Nothing."

"I don't mean on the menu. I mean with my sister. Why is she boiling mad at you?"

Lucas closed his menu and slapped the table. "This is wrong. I know it's wrong. I can't help you anymore."

Craig frowned, clasping his hands together and resting them on the table. "We agreed with my plan. What's caused the change of heart?"

"This really isn't the place, but in case you decide to kill us both on the ride home, I have to tell you the truth," Lucas said, hoping no one could overhear their conversation. Amelia hated gossip. If what he had to say leaked out, it could ruin everything. "She's a grown woman."

"That's not exactly news."

"You do remember that her birthday is a week away. In another year, she'll be thirty. She can make up her own mind. Make her own mistakes. I have a sneaking suspicion she'll come out just fine."

"I want her back in Kansas City."

"Have you ever thought about what she wants?" Lucas sat back in the booth and scrutinized his friend. Craig's folded fingers tightened, then relaxed, a telling sign of his desire to punch something.

"In case you've forgotten, she's a teacher *and* a painter. She's sold a number of paintings over the last couple of years. I had an expert check out the one she gave me. Without knowing the artist was my sister, he appraised the painting at forty-five hundred dollars. Can you imagine that?"

"She's got talent."

"Lucas, I know she's not painting by numbers or painting a house. This is fine art. She has a studio going to waste."

"Maybe, if you dropped the lease, that would save you money. Or better yet, take the money and rehab the barn into a bigger studio for her."

Craig leaned in, squinted one eye, and cocked his head. "What's going on here?"

Lucas paused. Now wasn't the time for a full confession. "I'm tired of running interference for you to keep things she wants from her…like, dating. I managed to persuade the guys who've asked her out that a couple of dates is all they get. No more. I gave up covert operations when I got out of the military. You need to be straight with her. Now she's got a date with Karl. *She* asked *him* out. I just happened to be there."

"My *little* sister asked a *man* for a date? I can only imagine my mother turning in her grave."

"In case you haven't noticed, your little sister is a fine-looking woman. I'd say *hot*, but it's you I'm talking to."

Lucas gave the waitress his attention when she appeared beside their table. "Ready to order?"

Craig leaned back and graced the woman with a warm smile. "Of course, but first, what did you say your name is?"

"I didn't. I thought you'd remember me."

Craig looked the woman up and down. His quizzical expression confirmed his faulty memory, but Lucas wasn't about to help his friend out of the jam.

"Your senior year of high school. Tractor pull. Kansas City. You almost took my tonsils out. No anesthesia required. Then you never called me again." The waitress's voice dripped with sarcasm.

As though mental gears had kicked into place, Craig beamed. "Crystal! Best night I ever had at a tractor pull. I left for college after that. Sorry. I figured you were nectar to bees and had guys all lined up. Just killing time with sorry me. You're as cute as you were then. Maybe we'll go out sometime."

The waitress blushed and lowered her chin. "So what's it going to be tonight?"

Lucas caught the waitress's double entendre. He cut Craig off before he could reply.

"Two Pale Ales. Full slab of beef ribs and the sides on the menu that go with it." Lucas clipped off the order. The waitress scribbled fast, and then grabbed the menus before sauntering away.

Chuckling, Craig shook his head. "Next time we eat first, talk later. Hunger makes you mean."

"Well, I'm here to eat cow. Doesn't get any meaner than that."

Bethany delivered their beers. "Saw Lia today," she said setting the mugs on coasters on the table.

"Amelia? In here?" Craig asked with surprise.

"What's wrong with *here*?" Bethany challenged. Her fists went to her hips.

"Nothing. Does she come in often?"

"No," she answered slowly. "Never alone. Ironic that you'd both be here on the same day. Don't see you around much anymore. Guess you've crossed over to the dark side...big city guy now."

"Aww, Bethany," Craig drawled. "You can take the boy out of the country, but you can't take the country out of the boy."

Bethany laughed, massaging Craig's shoulder. "You got that right," she said before walking away.

Lucas shook his head. "Where do you come up with this stuff? If you spent more time here, they'd have an auction and raffle you off to the highest bidder. Your kind of charm makes even a whorehouse Madame blush.

"Know about them, do you?"

"No, but remember, I did spend more than a few years in the Army. I saw life though a different lens, enough to know I like it here the best."

"So, my sister is picking up men? I can't imagine."

"Drink your beer," Lucas said, purposefully changing the subject. The idea of Amelia in the bar rattled his brain, too. She had been a wild child until high school, but the tomboy-type, running a four-wheeler all over the farm. Boys were the least of her interests, unless she could get them to sit for her while she painted. Her mother, the transplanted southern belle, tightened the stays and corseted Amelia's life once high school came around. Mrs. Britton taught deportment in etiquette classes after school and made Amelia sit in the front row.

"Do you remember the time your sister painted a mural on the side of the hay barn, the one that backs to the west cornfield? After the crop was harvested, only then did anyone notice the mural of a bayou, complete with cypress trees, a heron, and a gator."

"I'd forgotten about it. A reporter came all the way from Wichita to interview her about her *masterpiece* and snap some photos. Amelia was twelve. Painted from memory after a visit to our Louisiana grandparents. Dad finally painted over it when the mural had mostly blistered and peeled."

"She's got great talent," Lucas said.

"Who's Karl?"

Lucas drew back. A simple question, but the answer was complicated. "Mr. Turner's nephew. This is his younger sister's son. From Chicago. He's trying hard to fit in. Levi's. Tony Lamas. Charlie One Horse straw hat. If he's been on a horse, it had to be at Turner's place and long ago. He was asking me about asking Amelia out before she walked in the storeroom and asked him out herself."

"Hmm."

"Hmm, what? I let it slip that you might not be happy about the idea. I'm not interfering with your sister's life anymore. The two of you have to work it out."

"Okay."

"I'm going to punch you. Okay, what?"

"I'll let her ruin her life. Marry some guy who doesn't understand her art, wants her for the land and will give her lots of kids. That'll make her real happy, don't you think?"

Lucas narrowed his eyes. "You think a local guy can't give your sister a good life and love her for who she is?"

"Well, maybe. But it would be just too weird."

Crystal arrived with the food on a tray so large she struggled setting it down. Lucas rose to assist. The tray made it to the table without food sliding from the plates. Crystal placed the full slab of ribs, side items, and extra plates in front of them, along with a roll of paper towels.

"Always the Boy Scout, Lucas," Craig said.

"Always the gentleman," Crystal replied smugly. She picked up the empty tray and winked at Lucas before leaving.

"Have you gone out with her?" Craig asked.

"Long ago. After her tonsillectomy from you, but before we graduated college."

"Back to Amelia. I guess for her to ask a man for a date, either she's grown up more than I thought, or gotten pure lonely at the farm by herself. I hadn't considered that eventuality."

"I'm glad to finally hear your 'Amelia light bulb' is turned on," Lucas muttered. Maybe grief had clouded Craig's judgment, and now it was returning.

"Well, look." Craig pointed to a spot over Lucas's shoulder.

"Hey!" Zoë called out. "Look who it is. CB. How ya doin'?" She dropped down in the booth next to Lucas causing him to make room for her. Zoë reached for a piece of garlic bread, all the while grinning at Craig.

"I'd kiss you, girl, but I've got barbecue lips." Craig puckered and kissed the air. "How's your family? Seth doing okay?"

"Arrived home on leave today. I'm sure you'll see him. So...Houston, we have a problem. Lia's got a date next Saturday night. Plus, Helen told me Lia's already been by the café and ordered her own birthday cake. I'm going to have to let Karl in on the surprise if we hope to get her to the party," Zoë said between chews of bread.

"Karl seems to get around." Craig said.

Zoë elbowed Lucas. "Yeah, I hear you tried to put the kibosh on their date. What's up with that? Karl's a *good* lookin' guy. Been around, traveled a lot. Knows more than how to grow corn or fix a tractor. He's the white-collar type. Like our friend here who only wears suits now. Karl could be good for her."

"I was following orders," Lucas grumbled.

"Huh? Craig, that was your fault? I don't want to believe it, but Lucas never lies."

"So, can Karl be trusted or do we stage a kidnapping?" Craig asked.

The suggestion must have been to Zoë's liking. She smiled and drummed her fingers, playing a drum roll on the table. "A staged kidnapping sounds exciting."

Lucas groaned. "No. Too undignified. Amelia

would hate it, which would ruin the party for her. Remember, the whole reason we're doing this is for her."

"Well," Craig interrupted. "If you think we can trust a newbie like Karl, then we'll let him in on the secret, but you'd better be real sure he can keep a confidence. Amelia refused to celebrate her birthday last year. Too close after the funeral. We're making up for last year and celebrating this one, too. You know how my mother was big on birthdays."

"Let *me* talk to him, Lucas," Zoë purred. "I think I can persuade the man that talking isn't in his best interest. And, their date is the perfect cover for the surprise party. Lia will be so many shades of embarrassed when she gets there we'll need a fire hose to cool her cheeks."

"No, Zoë. I should be the one to take her to dinner before the party. I'm a better decoy," Lucas insisted.

Zoë turned and looked him up and down. "That may have been true once, but I think she's over you. You had your chance, dude...and blew it. Several times. If you asked Lia out now, she'd know for certain something is up. Besides, you're the world's worst liar. That's one of the things we all love about you."

"If I thought Lia would agree to dinner with you and believe everything was normal, I'd say ask her," Craig said. "But, we all know, you asking her out now would be the same as writing *Warning, Amelia* on the billboard at the entrance to town. She sees through you like cellophane."

"If she could see through me, then she wouldn't

be asking Karl out," Lucas muttered through a clenched jaw. His frustration shot up like mercury rising in a thermometer facing the Midwest sun.

"I don't like it. Craig, why don't *you* take your sister out for a family dinner?" Amelia together with Karl, under any circumstances, would push his blood pressure into the danger zone.

"She's barely speaking to me."

"Talk her into it. Charm her. That way, we all know our secret is safe." He couldn't tell Craig about his attraction to Amelia before he'd had a chance to show the woman he loved how much she meant to him. In his plan, they'd break the news to her brother together. But first, he had to get past the guards holding Amelia's heart in lockdown. Zoë was right. He'd had chances in the past and blew them, but he was resourceful. Now he'd create a new one.

"Karl is our decoy." Zoë rose. "Got to get back to the horde. See you both tomorrow."

"Glad that's settled," Craig said, digging into his food.

Lucas frowned as Zoë rejoined her family. Karl a decoy? That idea churned his irritation like a carnival round-up ride, the twirling centrifuge. Somehow, he had to move Karl out of the picture.

"Hey, where are you?" Craig waved his hand. "Look, I know you said you were through with my plan to get Amelia back to the city, but I need your help, man, one last time. Have a chat with Karl. Tell him no more than two dates. I'm going to protect Amelia's interest and will do so until I die. She's moving back to the city. That's the end of that."

Lucas grunted. "Okay. This *one* last time."

He'd help, but only because it served his interests, too, and an idea began taking shape, and soon he'd allow his feelings for Amelia to unfurl.

But was Zoë right? Was he too late?

Chapter 5

Lia sat alone on the wide back deck with her legs stretched long in a chaise lounge. Gentle breezes ruffled her hair and whispered through the corn. A few birds warbled, calling to each other in the nearby trees. A butterfly danced from flower to flower in the garden surrounding the deck. She flipped her robe closed to cover her legs. Her mood matched the overcast sky. Low hanging clouds brought hope for a chance of rain to water the crops. Yet the same gray clouds dragged in dreariness, hid sunlight, and swept cheerfulness away. Compared to this time last year, her heart lifted buoyantly, but would it ever totally heal?

She sipped Earl Grey tea strongly dosed with cream and sugar and tried to distract her mind from the movie playing repeatedly in her head, the one from a year ago when the whole town and half the county had turned out for her parents' funeral. With Craig by her side, they'd greeted everyone and thanked them for coming. The funeral at the Methodist church seemed more like a bad dream. She'd pinched herself through the entire service. To her ears, each breath she took produced a roar like that of water rushing over a dam. The noise drowned out most of the service. When the funeral home attendants simultaneously closed the caskets on her mother and father, she had drowned in tears.

The painful memory remained emblazed in her mind. With the sleeve of her robe, she dotted the tears now trickling down her cheeks. If Lucas hadn't been there that day, she might have died of heartbreak. He was solid. Salt of the earth. A man deserving of praise and respect, and in her case, adoration. Her lips gravitated to his. Just thinking of him warmed her. He personified the best of every ancient hero she'd ever read about, but when it came understanding her feelings for him, Lucas hadn't connected the dots any better than Lois Lane had between Clark Kent and Superman. How could Lucas *not* see her feelings for him?

Last year during the funeral service at church, she and Craig had sat alone in the first pew. Just the two of them, like orphans. No family came from Louisiana. No long-lost Midwest cousins arrived. Lucas and his sister, Megan, sat in the middle of the pew behind them. Zoë and her big family flanked them. Craig maintained his composure—actually, the ordeal left him numb, shocked, emotionless, so much so it frightened her. She, on the other hand, had emoted enough grief for the two of them.

Later, about a month after the funeral, the first time Lia had ventured to town, she waited in line at the Sunflower Café and overheard a conversation. An elderly woman whispered, not so quietly, that she'd never seen a more gallant gesture than Lucas's at the funeral.

"My heart ached when the Brittons' caskets were closed. Amelia began wailing to wake...well, the dead. Lucas climbed over the pew—never minding anyone—and cradled Lia while she sobbed. That man held her like she was the most precious thing in the world."

Lia pretended she hadn't heard a word, but on her way out of the shop, the elderly woman grasped Lia's arm, squeezed, nodding, she said, "Lucas is a keeper."

Lucas had offered comfort that day. He folded her into his arms while she trembled and cried until she had finally caught her breath.

She still couldn't recall the rest of the service.

But she remembered Lucas's strength, the safety of his embrace. When she'd buried her face next to his warm chest, his heart beat with life when everything else around her reeked of coldness and death.

And, she remembered with great clarity, much later that night, his kiss. Warm. Loving. Tender.

"Good morning!" Craig slid the glass door to the porch open. "Thanks for making coffee for me."

Startled, she shook her head to clear the clouds hanging around. Had she fallen asleep? She lifted a finger to her lips, expecting to feel the lingering heat of Lucas's lips. When she didn't, the measure of disappointment surprised her.

"You're welcome. Are you ready for today?" she asked, her voice throaty, as though she'd just woken.

Craig squeezed her shoulder before sliding into the chair next to hers. "It's been a hard year." The graveness of his voice let her know he, too, experienced the gravity of the day. "A year of firsts."

"No Halloween party in the barn, no Thanksgiving dinner. Christmas without them.

Ringing in the New Year without seed catalogs and dates for farm equipment auctions," she whispered.

"Amelia, you can't hide this holiday season. We only get out of life what we put in it. Our world didn't completely die because we buried them. They'll haunt us if we don't set aside our grief and get on with living."

Lia reached for his hand. "You've managed that quite nicely. Promotion at work. New sports car. I know you're trying to do the big brother thing for me. Believe it or not, I'm stepping into new shoes today."

"Something you found in one of those boxes in the barn?"

Lia chuckled. "Well, I meant it figuratively, but now that you brought it up. Yes, I found a box with new shoes. I'll wear them this afternoon. They're scandalous for a memorial service. Purple suede with gold platform bottoms. Totally like Mother."

"Speaking of firsts, you asked the newbie out on a date?"

"News travels fast. You haven't been home for twenty-four hours and you know all the latest gossip. Yes, I have a date with Karl next Saturday. I don't want to talk about it, at least not until tomorrow. I just need to feel today… I know this service will be different from last year's, which had me quaking in my boots. I'd never before lost control like that."

"Yeah, you worried me," Craig said so quietly, she almost didn't hear him.

Gentleman Jack ran up on the deck with a stuffed toy pheasant in his mouth. He dropped it at Craig's feet, then plopped, and rested his head on the toy, as if he, too, understood the sadness of the cloudy day, and also why neither of them had come out with him to play.

"You have to help me clean." Lia rose and swatted at Craig's shoulder trying to lighten the mood. "Do you remember how to do that?"

"Hey! My cleaning lady only comes once a month. I do it the rest of the time."

"Well, then, Mr. Janitor Junior, you clean the guest bathroom. I did the rest yesterday morning. I've got biscuits to make and a ham to put in the oven. You can help by setting the dining room table for the buffet."

She turned on the CD player. Faith Hill kept them company while they worked at their chores before going to their rooms to change for the memorial service.

From her dresser, Lia picked up a framed photograph of her parents taken on their last vacation. There were days when the frame lay face down. She couldn't bear to look at it. Other days, she carried it from room to room, needing the comfort of their smiling faces. She would've never made it through the year had she not come back to the farm. Craig would have to get used to the fact that she intended to stay. She had accepted his move a half-day's drive away. Now she wanted his moral support about her decisions. She would get back to the business of living.

But only at the farm.

As if she, too, had been planted in the spring with the crops, she'd put down new roots in familiar ground, and then grown, just like the crops, from seeds to stalks. Her grief had followed the seasons, gray in winter, lightened in the spring, and brightened during the summer. Her paintings reflected the changes in her, too. The family memories were gifts of joy now.

"Amelia, you ready?"

"Almost. Meet you in the car."

The breeze blew the clouds away while she dressed. Climbing into Craig's car, she breathed in the smell of new leather. Craig was doing well for himself, for that she was thankful.

She rode in silence next to her brother and focused on the bright sky. Its cheeriness irritated her sadness like an annoying loose tooth—even if you didn't mess with it, you still knew it was there.

She tried putting aside dreary thoughts to experience the beautiful rays of white light illuminating the countryside, images she'd love to capture with oils, but the joyfulness of the scene was wasted, overshadowed by her dark mood.

"I wonder if everyone will be there?" she said, thankful Craig had chosen silence over the noise of the radio.

"I've never known anyone to RSVP to a memorial service, but everyone we invited responded to the invite for the potluck afterward," Craig said quietly.

Lia fidgeted with the cuff of her blouse. The purple suede heels she had discovered in her mother's locked room in the barn added New Orleans pizzazz to the conservative black skirt and white silk blouse. The purple in the flowered scarf draping her neck matched the purple in the shoes. While her mother lived, Lia would've never considered wearing them, too loud and too attention-grabbing. Her mother would be thrilled to know she'd moved past some of her too conservative ways, and while she would never fill her mother's figurative shoes, she appreciated her mother's colorful flamboyance more now than ever.

"After the first month or so, I stopped going multiple times each week to visit them," she said, breaking the silence. "It got too cold. After that, I went only once a week."

"Wait. You'd said you visited their graves only a couple of times all summer."

Pressure built in her chest. Anxiety pinged like quick-firing pistons. She licked her lips, stalling before uttering the truth. In their younger years, Craig would've swatted her for lying. "We went together for Mother's Day and Father's Day, and that was the last time I stood graveside..."

"Spit it out, Amelia. We discussed your obsessive need to haunt the cemetery."

"Craig, you don't understand," she said quietly. "I feel so guilty about shutting mother out when I left for college. I was terrified I relied on her so much that I would fail at school...or life, if I didn't stand on my own. As a result of my rejection of her, she left me a legacy of boxes. Each and every one reminds me of her."

"You're wrong. She left you a legacy of memories and an example of how to live an honest life, be a good wife, and raise a happy family. Can't you see that?"

Lia snorted. "I do hold the memories dear. But I'm an artist, and I want to farm. My decision to stay doesn't diminish mother's dream for me." She raised her voice, "It's part of why I love it here. But you're unable to see that about me!" Clearing her throat, she composed herself. "I'm as capable of running the farm as I am painting, well, almost. As for the wife business, at this rate, I'll be an old maid forever. I can't manage anything beyond a second date."

"There are suitable men in the city," Craig grumbled.

"That doesn't do me any good here, now does it?"

"We're almost there. Let's not fight." Craig reached over and squeezed her forearm.

For a few minutes, her heightened anxiety subsided to a slow churn. Her brother had taken her mind off the purpose for his visit—to give grief a final rest.

Lia crossed her legs, bouncing her foot while she twisted her mother's engagement ring on the middle finger of her right hand. Mother had never declared her wishes. Did she want the ring to go to Craig for his someday-bride? Craig had decided she should keep the one-carat ring their father had given their mother. If he ever married, his bride would wear a modern new setting. Something to go with his new image, she suspected.

Having a family, a husband and children, without her mother to share in the joy colored the future with a shadow of gray. Today's memorial service was an important event. A marker of the passing of time. A year of grieving had come to an end. The rawness of her loss had healed, but a small scab remained. She fully expected it to scar. She picked at it mentally. Emotionally, it needed more healing time. Why had she taken her parents for granted?

Rumblings from a truck behind them drew her attention. A horn beeped.

"Who could be so rude?" she demanded. Craig shrugged, but his mouth moved into a lopsided grin. She flipped down the visor and adjusted the mirror.

Lia's hand went to her throat. Her chest tightened. Her eyes darted to the mirror again and locked on Lucas's smile. He waved. Heat rose in her cheeks while tingles traveled to her toes. Thinking of Lucas was like straddling barbwire. Either way she moved, it hurt.

A year ago, he'd kissed her. In the moment of that kiss, life wrapped her in a cocoon. She kissed him back. She'd waited for so long for that kiss. Her heart sang with joy, ecstatic as if she'd found a pot of gold in a cornfield after a tornado.

Only then to have Lucas snatch it away.

For the entire the last year, she'd waited for a repeat performance. It never came. The boy she'd fallen in love with had grown into a man, and neither boy nor man wanted her. The strain between them made them barely friends. "Of course, it's Lucas Dwyer."

Unrequited love was not the glorious thing poets made it out to be. Over-romanticized drivel. Lucas would never know how often she painted and watched for his truck to pass on the road. The sunroom with its walls of windows provided an exceptional view of the few vehicles coming and going.

Each week, then each month, since Lucas last kissed her, her hope dwindled. Just once, she wished he'd stop by the farm to see about her. Really see her, not check up on the crop, or do something for her brother.

Where had the passion and tenderness he'd given in her most desperate hour disappeared to? His reputation didn't include irresponsible behavior. In fact, his actions were usually the complete opposite. He considered every decision he made before he acted. But in her case, had he just overreacted to her tears? Pondering, she refused to accept any conclusion, at least not a satisfying one. The only good thing after that kiss—she'd poured her heart into her painting.

She sighed. Wouldn't Lucas be surprised if he knew she'd dreamed of him?

"I hope he doesn't pass us. Your new car will be covered with dust," Lia said.

Craig glanced in her direction. She smiled saccharine-sweet. "After all, this isn't St. Louis. You'll have to drive all the way to town for a carwash."

"I'm not worried about the car. I am wondering about you, though. Amelia, what's up with you and Lucas? You've been down on him from the moment I got home. He's family. The only way we, meaning you and I, could be closer to him is if..."

"If what?" she demanded.

"Nothing." Craig shook his head. "Let's not fight. I'm sure the anxiety of the service is weighing on both of us."

Rising apprehension bit at her nerves. Her shoulder muscles tightened. If a distraction didn't happen fast, she'd lose what remaining composure she possessed. This time, Lucas wouldn't be there to comfort her in the middle of a breakdown.

"Why, I don't know what you mean, big brother." Lia winked an eye repeatedly while bobbling her head and shrugging one shoulder.

"Great! Comic relief. Keep that up," Craig chuckled. "Dress up like a Zombie. You'll be a hit at Halloween."

Lia went still. "You know we don't get trick-or-treaters out here."

"Just several more reasons to be in the city. Trick-or-treat in your neighborhood. Halloween parties at school and in the West Bottoms."

"Drop it, Craig. You gave me a full calendar year. I won't fail. There's a good crop waiting for harvest. I've got enough boxes to help pay the bills. And, I've got some income from my art work. I'm not going back."

Craig heaved out a deep sigh. "You're stubborn, just like Dad. Everything might work out this year, but what about next year, and the year after? Amelia, I'm begging you, go back to the city and paint. Become a famous artist. Become the toast of the town. Become teacher of the year, but don't ruin your life waiting on corn."

"When we get to the cemetery, don't you dare let on that we've been fighting," she snapped. "Not in front of everyone. Mom and Dad would be so embarrassed. It would break Mom's heart."

"Amelia, you're breaking mine."

Chapter 6

Craig scanned the crowd. More than a dozen people had gathered for the very private graveside memorial. Their support provided an anchor in his life. Appreciation radiated through him, reaching into the black Kansas dirt and nurturing the connection to his family roots. Each person took turns sharing a lighthearted memory of his parents. To his surprise, Amelia hadn't cried, though when she lifted the sunglasses from her face, her expression of sad resignation ripped his heart like an axe slamming into a tree. She used to smile freely, radiate with a joy contagious to all around her. When would a full smile replace her weak one?

When it was Lucas's turn to speak, he looked around at the people gathered in the circle. "They were second parents to me. Treated me like a son. Mrs. Britton sent me packages when I was in Afghanistan. Their passing has left empty spaces in my life. However, they would expect all of us to soldier on with chins up and shoulders back."

Everyone nodded.

"Mrs. Britton taught me to dance," Megan said. "You know, the tango and the box-step." She demonstrated the dance steps, swaying her hips. "Through her, I found confidence to be myself."

"She brought her New Orleans *joie de vivre* to

the plains," Helen said. "It took us a while to understand the southern in her. She was sweet like bread pudding and spicy like gumbo. Craig and Amelia"—Helen pointed across the circle at them—"your mother loved your father so much she moved up here to live her life. Your parents were role models for our community."

"Thank you, Helen, for your kind words." Craig replied. He understood better what his mother had given up to love and marry his father. She devoted her life to all of them, but she always remained a bit of a fish out of water in Kansas...same for him. As much as he loved his childhood memories, his sister, and his friends, St. Louis was more exciting than Harvest, Kansas had ever been. Farming would be last on the list of jobs he ever wanted. His father never understood that about him, but his mother had.

After all the guests had spoken, his sister took a half step forward into the circle. "Thank you for coming today. It means a lot to me to keep the memory of my parents alive. For as long as I'm able to stay on the farm"—Amelia glanced over her shoulder at him—"I will host a Twelfth Night celebration every year. Mother had her quirky ways, but I wouldn't trade her for another. Dad understood me best, though I'm not sure why. He always encouraged my painting. I hope to make my parents proud and put Harvest on the map someday. Thank you again for sharing this circle with Craig and me today."

Murmurs of agreement drifted around the ring as Amelia stepped back.

Craig walked into the middle of the circle and

stood between the headstones of his parents. "I'm grateful you came," he told the group. "It's nice to see familiar faces. I appreciate your support, be it from respect for our parents or support of us. Thanks for looking after my sister—even if she's stubborn like a mule's backside." Everyone but Amelia chuckled in response. "You know how much my father loved barbecue. His trophies remain on the shelves in the sunroom. Mother refused to display them on the mantle. So, let's go celebrate life. As Dad always said, 'The secret to good barbecue is sauce—it covers up all mistakes.' We're serving 'cue—pig and cow—and we'll wash it down with brew."

A little while later at the house, a convoy of vehicles parked on the lawn and along the lane leading from the dirt road to the driveway. Craig tapped the beer keg on the back deck with Lucas's help while Megan and Amelia placed bowls of potato salad and baked beans on the table.

"Amelia!" Craig hollered. "I'm ready for the burgers." Craig adjusted his father's black pitmaster apron with *Boss of the Sauce* in large red print on the front. His father had won it as a trophy at the American Royal BBQ five years earlier. Craig's mouth watered from the aromas drifting from the smoker. Beef and pork ribs. Long and slow.

The late afternoon breezes blew in a few lofty clouds. The sun played peek-a-boo, and streaks of light shone like spotlights on the surrounding sunflower fields. The back deck and yard buzzed with chatter, everyone sharing humorous stories and loving memories. His parents would be pleased by the fondness their friends and neighbors had shown.

Craig's heart swelled with pride.

Amelia stepped onto the wide back deck and started to hand him a platter at the same time as Zoë rounded the corner of the house with a man in tow Craig didn't recognize. Amelia's hand moved. Craig grabbed for the platter, catching it before it hit the deck. "Hey! Watch it." But Amelia appeared to be in a transfixed state, showing no signs of hearing him. Her gaze remained locked on the newcomer. And Zoë.

"Welcome, Karl."

The softness in Amelia's voice and the too bright smile reinforced the knot in his gut. Amelia had a genuine interest in this man? This guy had to be the newbie in town. Had Zoë invited him? Who crashed a cookout like this? His parents, had they been there, would've insisted the newcomer be welcomed.

"I hope you don't mind, I asked Karl to meet us here," Zoë said. She led Karl by the hand onto the deck. "I thought this would be a good way for him to get acquainted with some folks he hasn't met."

"And some he'll never meet," Craig grumbled. To the untrained ear, Zoë words were innocent enough, but he was certain she had purposefully arranged the encounter. Maybe it was her way for him to give Karl the once-over. Since his sister seemed bent on dating the guy, and since their surprise party next Saturday depended on Karl's discretion, he should be thankful for Zoë's fast thinking. But something about it pecked in his gut the way a woodpecker hammered away at tree. However, the best defense was a good offense, so he'd be polite, but with both ears and eyes on the guy.

"Karl, welcome. I'd shake your hand, but…" Craig lifted up the platter in one hand and the spatula in the other.

Karl grinned as Zoë and Amelia flanked him.

"Hey, Karl," Lucas said, coming through the back door from the house with a platter of cooked ribs. He set it on the table. "I didn't know you were coming. Grab a rib." Lucas cupped Amelia's elbow. "Amelia, we need a bottle opener in here, and if you want me to carve the ham, I need the carving knife."

Amelia appeared flustered, but when Lucas guided her into the house, she went.

"Karl, this is Craig, Lia's brother." Zoë made introductions.

Craig caught a quick flash of worry in the man's eyes. He leaned in for a private word. "So Zoë has recruited you for our plan?"

Karl nodded. "I won't let you down."

"Good to hear. Grab a drink from the cooler over there or the keg. Make yourself at home." He hoped to put Karl at ease, making it easier to study the guy.

"Should we offer to help Lia?" Karl asked.

"She'll be back in a few minutes," Zoë said reassuringly as she reached for Karl's hand, guiding him down the deck. They crossed the yard with Gentleman Jack running, and then scurrying back, as if to urge them to hurry along. Zoë headed in the direction of the creek.

She was taking the guy there? She giggled at something Karl said and gave him a little flirty shove. A knot formed in Craig's gut, twisting like water wrung from a towel.

Friendship and family loyalty played tug-of-war.

Did Amelia have a true interest in this guy? How hurt would she be when she discovered Zoë's interest? He'd read all of Zoë's signs. Big eyes, coy grins, a slight tilt of her head, and that friendly shove. He was well aware of them. She'd been his first serious crush back in high school, but no one knew. He hadn't even shared that information with Lucas. It would've been too weird, him dating his sister's best friend. That would be as ridiculous as Lucas dating Amelia.

Craig set the platter on a table. One by one, he tossed hamburger patties onto a grill and turned the country-style ribs on the second one. Sizzling from the heat, the barbecue with its tangy aroma made him miss his dad. He could never replace their father in Amelia's life, but he'd be the best big brother she would ever need, which meant doing everything in his power to make sure she never got hurt. A parent's duty, his father had reminded him when he was young and interested in calf roping, included finding the gift in a child and nurturing it. His dad had supported his efforts in rodeoing, but Craig soon learned it wasn't his forte. However, Amelia's gift was painting, and he hoped he'd made his father proud doing all he could to help further his sister's career.

Later that evening as the cookout came to a close and guests departed one by one, Craig finished wiping off the grills. The silence of the fields surrounded him. He tossed a dirty cloth into a bucket. Looking through the screen door, he peered inside the house. His line of sight to the kitchen was blocked by the couch and the corner. Where had his sister disappeared to?

"Hey, Amelia. Bring a couple of bottles and let's

sit out here."

No sound came from within the house. Gentleman Jack wandered from the yard where he'd been scouting for rabbits and lay down at Craig's feet. He petted the dog and called out, "Amelia?"

Still no answer.

Craig opened the door and waited for Jack to enter before following him in. "Jack, where's Amelia? I haven't seen her for at least an hour."

Jack looked up at him as if to say, "You really don't know where she is?" The dog bolted toward the kitchen. He sat at the door to Amelia's studio and pawed like a person might knock, but Amelia never answered. Strains of Samuel Barber's *Adagio for Strings* hummed in the air. Craig opened the door. Jack made a beeline for his bed, curled up, sighed, and closed his eyes.

Craig stood transfixed. He gazed at the tabletop. A purposefully arranged setting of an antique lace doily topped with a collection of different sizes and colors of bottles, including a tall blue one of German Riesling he remembered purchasing, matched the image on the large canvas before his sister. Amelia's detailed still life rivaled any of the masters. Pride swelled in his chest. If he could sing, he'd launch into a *Halleluiah* everyone in the county could hear. *Caterwauling* is what his grandmother had called his singing when he was young. Instead, he could do the he-man thing and beat his chest, but that would embarrass his sister.

After accusing him of lacking culture and substance beyond the business world, Amelia had taught him about art. He hoped by providing a studio for her in town, one day her work would hang in several galleries and collectors would seek her out.

She educated him about her favorites, and he particularly loved Jan Frans Van Dael's *Still Life with Roses* and Paul Cezanne's *Still Life with Cherries and Peaches*. Amelia's still-life work radiated with intensity and vibrant colors of those artists. She had said the old way of making and mixing colors was a lost art, but oils were the only thing she'd ever use to paint a still life. Her name graced only a handful in all her years as a painter. These type of paintings popped realistically on the canvas only when sadness overpowered her, which meant something troubled her deeply now.

And whatever troubled her, worried him.

When the music ended, Craig started to call out, but the music started from the beginning again, obviously on continuous play. Amelia, lost in an art world, sat on a rolling stool with a paintbrush in hand and swayed to the achingly, haunting music. She daubed paint from the palette resting on an old, wooden TV stand with wheels, which allowed her to roll around while she painted, or to roll it out of the way, so Jack wouldn't hit it and knock it over whenever he bolted for the door.

His sister never appreciated interruptions when she worked, however he needed to speak with her. Had she taken a deep melancholy plunge over seeing Karl and Zoë? When the two of them returned from the creek, Zoë and Amelia acted in their usual way, teasing and telling stories about their pigtail days. If Amelia had been bothered by Karl's presence, or her friend's interest in the man, she never let on.

Rather than startle his sister by calling out, Craig walked to the opposite side of the room and stood next to the table holding the sculptures. He waved. Amelia blinked several times. She paused with a paintbrush in midair as though returning from a faraway world.

"Have you been there long?" Amelia asked.

Craig shook his head. "I know you don't like to be bothered when you're painting, but I need to talk. Since I'm only home for the weekend, and I'd rather not have this conversation over the phone, will you take a break soon?"

"No." Her mouth formed a thin line. Her nostrils flared.

"You have to go to bed at some point. After all, you twisted my arm about going to church tomorrow morning."

"Yes."

Craig reached over and paused the CD player.

"No. Yes. Are we having a conversation? Or answering questions for a gameshow somewhere in your head?"

"No, I don't want to talk to you. Yes, I'm going to bed soon."

"Amelia, what did I do this time?"

His sister rose from the stool and kicked it aside. "I think I'm done for the night after all." The stool bumped the couch, changed trajectory, and came to rest beside Craig's legs. If she were shooting pool, it would've been a good trick shot.

"Here, Jack," she called. From his bed, the dog lifted his head, looked at each of them, before resting his head, ignoring them both.

"No. Yes," Craig said.

"What?" Amelia snapped.

"No, you're not going to ignore me. Yes, we're going to talk."

"Fine! Let's talk." Amelia stormed out of the room. "I won't let you invade my space and leave a negative imprint there."

He found her in the dining room pulling the top off a bottle of Basil Hayden. Their father's favorite George Jones song, *The King Is Gone and So Are You*, popped into his head. It was a song they shared as an inside joke, but given her anger, he didn't dare laugh. Before their parents died, just mentioning the song would have had Amelia in stitches. She loved to sing along with George Jones to entertain their father.

Amelia poured whiskey into a crystal glass, about three-fingers full. She handed it to him. Pulling another glass from the china cabinet, she splashed a small amount of liquid into that glass. When she tipped the bottom up, that surprised him.

"Whoa."

"Ahhh," she said, pouring another three-fingers width of liquid into the glass. "Let's talk." Before he could get a word out, she stomped across the living room and out to the back deck. He followed her, but just before he reached the open door, Jack scampered past him, clipping him at the knees. He grabbed for the door to keep from falling. Whiskey sloshed onto the deck. "No, Jack. That's not for you," he told the dog when Jack came to inspect the spilled liquid.

"Here," he shoved his glass at Amelia, who sat in a chaise lounge. Walking to the far end of the deck, he grabbed the bucket with dirty soapy water and poured it over the whiskey spot.

"And don't drink that either," he told the dog. In response, Jack jumped on the chaise and stretched out beside Amelia, resting his head in her lap.

"Please don't yell at Jack. It isn't his fault you're clumsy."

Craig pulled up a chair, straddled it, and faced his sister. Darkness mostly shrouded her face. He raked his fingers through his hair and let go of an exasperated sigh. "I'll take my drink, now," he said. She handed it over.

Leaning over with his elbows resting on his thighs, he cradled the glass. "Amelia—"

"How. Dare. You." Her voice came out low and deadly calm.

"There are several things I want to talk about, but you're going to have to clue me in. None of what I want to discuss could produce that level of intensity."

"I swear if you don't admit the truth, I'm going to start picking corn and chucking it at you until you're bloody. There'll be nowhere you can hide— until you put your butt back in that sports car you bought and leave. And you of all people know how dear my corn crop is to me."

"What?" he demanded. Trying to talk with her when her emotions whirled like a top was worse than a sailor trying to find dry land in the fog without a lighthouse to illuminate the way. He took a gulp of whiskey, ruining the pleasure of a fine sipping bourbon.

"You! You're blackmailing Lucas!"

Craig drew back.

"Are you crazy? I know today has been difficult,

which is why I wanted to check in with you, but to accuse me of...of doing that, to Lucas of all people! I going to call 9-1-1 and tell them a crazy person has carried off my sister." He peered closely at her. "Or are you some sort of clone?"

She leaned forward and swatted at him. He dropped the crystal glass. One of their mother's favorites. Amelia rose from the chaise so fast, she dumped Jack on the deck. He yelped, but scrambled, scratching the wood with his nails, and scampered away.

"Did it break?" she asked, her voice warbling as she searched the deck in the dark on her hands and knees.

He shook his head. "No." He scooped up the crystal glass. "All in one piece." Setting the glass on the deck beside the foot of his chair, he asked, "But are you?"

"I know you and Lucas have concocted some plot concerning me," she snapped, standing against the deck railing.

"There's no plot." Had she figured out about Karl and the surprise birthday party? Could Karl be worthless with a secret?

"It was clear today with Lucas. The minute Karl walked up, Lucas said he needed me to find a carving knife. He knows darn good and well where that knife is kept. And it all makes sense"—she pointed her finger at his nose—"you're the reason why a man only asks me out for one or two dates. Lucas would never stoop so low to interfere in my love life without prompting from you."

"Is Lucas trying to pin something on me?" Craig

asked.

"Of course not, he's too loyal for that. He'd fall on his sword for you."

"Interesting," Craig muttered. Did Lucas's feelings for Amelia run deeper than he let on? His interest in Amelia couldn't have turned...romantic? He groaned.

"Aha!" Amelia snapped her fingers.

"What?"

"That groan is as good as a confession. When I asked Karl out, Lucas happened to be there. His exact words were, 'Craig isn't going to like this.' You're purposely dissuading men from dating me. Lucas is doing your dirty work. You're a...a," she sputtered. "I can't even say what I think you are. Mother would turn in her grave. Dad would find a way to wash my mouth out. But know this, Craig Britton. I'm staying on the farm, and I'm going to date whomever I like."

Craig held up his hands in surrender. "Okay. I get it. At least about the dating part. However, like it or not, if the crop and your painting don't put you in the black, you'll be off the farm before Christmas. Sorry, Amelia, but it's a business decision. Nothing personal. I won't let you take me down over your silly sentiment." Let her stew on that. If it took tough love to make her see reason, then he'd dish it out.

"You're worse than the bank that stole the Dwyer's farm."

"A bank didn't *steal* it..." Craig stood. The conversation turned in a direction he hadn't wanted to go. Given the cost of Amelia's studio in the city—he paid the rent monthly—plus contributions to farm expenses, the business decisions had to be made rationally.

"Don't get all technical with me. The end result is the same." She sneered. His younger sister, the woman who had adored and looked up to him, acted as though he were the same as a bug on a pile of cow dung.

"Let's face facts. You've made it this year only because of the sales from the stuff Mother stashed in the barn. Once that's gone, that revenue stream is dry. Your only recourse is to paint more. And you can do that rent-free in the city."

"I'm not a robot," Amelia whispered. "I don't paint by numbers or paint on demand. It never occurred to me I'd ever see the day when you'd truly use the farm against me. Pull my home out from under me. I guess I need to talk to Lucas...ask for his advice...since you weren't able to help Mr. Dwyer save his farm. I now know I can't count on you to help me out. When the noose is around my neck, you'll be the one to tighten it."

Amelia knocked back the rest of the whiskey in her glass. "I'm going to finish off the bottle. I'd ask you to join me while I drown my sorrows, but I'm afraid you might really do it."

"Do what?" Craig asked.

"Drown me." Amelia opened the door, and Jack followed her inside. She slammed the door so hard the glass rattled. For a moment, he wondered if it might crack. That would be yet another expense to pay for.

He looked out over the property bathed by moonlight. He'd run the numbers again and again. He couldn't afford to indulge his sister in her fantasy of farming. Why was he the bad guy for being the voice of reason?

Had he been wrong to interfere in Amelia's life? Maybe. Probably not. All the numbers said he was correct. She needed to move back to the city.

How could he ever convince Amelia of that?

Chapter 7

Lucas stabbed the ground again with a shovel turning over the scooped earth. Garden cleanup. One of the necessary evils of life. Digging up all the existing bulbs, dividing the multiples, and replanting the flowerbed lining the back of the house, ate up more time than he had to spare, but he did it for Megan. A short break might soothe his boredom. With the sun continuing to rise in the sky along with the heat of the day, he preferred lemonade to quench his thirst rather than a beer. He wanted to set a good example for Megan.

"Quit grunting. I know you hate this. You want lunch in a few minutes?" Megan asked as she divided a clump of irises. "We've been at this for three hours now. I'll make sandwiches since you cooked breakfast. You've gotten good at ham and cheese omelets."

Lucas glanced at his sister. Streaks of light blond framed her face in the warm, fall sunlight. Jeans and a purple college jersey replaced her old farmer coveralls, the kind she'd worn as a kid when she followed their father around doing chores, feeding chickens, exercising horses, and tinkering with tractors. Watching her now, he still saw an innocent young girl who idolized their father. He wanted to believe she lived by the values their parents instilled in them. Honesty. Compassion. Integrity. He'd gone to war to fight, not only for freedom, but for their way of life—liberty and the pursuit of happiness—where a person had a chance to make something of his life regardless of his humble beginnings. He believed deeply in the American experiment and accepted setbacks came with forging new paths.

Sweet Megan. His brotherly protectiveness tugged hard at his heart, so hard it wouldn't surprise him if he sweated blood. She deserved a good life and he wanted that for her, just as he understood all the reasons Craig tried to protect Amelia. But the difference between Megan and Amelia was the difference between sunflowers and deep red roses. Sunflowers in their simplicity turned their faces to the sun and tracked its path across the sky, whereas the hardy winter roses used their heady fragrance to captivate and their velvety petals to seduce. Amelia was his red rose. She stood a much greater chance of succeeding on the farm alone than Megan ever would.

"Earth to Lucas." Megan waved at him.

"What?"

"Lunch?"

"Sure."

He surveyed their progress. Completion of the project would require another hour.

"Why women in this family insist on bulbs, especially tulips, I'll never know. Between icy cold winters and scorching hot summers, the darn things rot. If the weather doesn't destroy them, the squirrels and rabbits munch them," he grumbled. Tulips never stood much of a chance in a prairie garden. Only half the bulbs they'd planted last year came up this spring, though the daffodils, hyacinths, and irises had survived. Splotches of brown soil, visible between the plants, reminded him that his mother's garden had always looked colorful and charming.

"What are you so angry about?" Megan asked. She moved to sit in the grass next to the stone-edged garden and finished sifting through the surviving bulbs.

"Nothing. I got new bulbs for you, didn't I?"

Megan snorted. "Yeah, right about the bulbs, but since when did you start lying? If I guess what's wrong, will you tell me?"

Lucas continued to work the soil. When had his sister become such a chatterbox?

"You're mad about the land. But, you still own ten acres and the house." Megan stood and dusted off her jeans.

"No sense in being mad about losing the farm. We. Megan. We have ten acres."

"Nope. I've decided," Megan said with a determined jut of her chin. "Since you're helping me with all the expenses of school, my graduation present to you is my half of what we own."

Lucas stopped shoveling. "That's generous of you. I appreciate what you want to do, but ten acres doesn't keep a man employed to feed and clothe and educate an entire family."

"Not as a fulltime farmer, but it's enough land to produce food to eat, including some chickens. A house with four bedrooms, though not a sprawling two-story like the Britton's place, has enough space to raise a family. Besides, you have the combine contracts. You're the best around. I heard you even turned down business this year because you're in such high demand."

"Megan, really, I appreciate your offer. However, don't listen to gossip. And, combining is not farming."

Lucas glanced at his sister as he stabbed the shovel into the dirt point first, into earth so hard the farming tool stood upright on its own. Megan shook her head and sighed.

"I know you mean well," Lucas said. "Half of what we have is yours. I like the idea of us sharing this place together for holidays and summers. Here our kids will have a connection to each other. And to the land, especially since Dad was an only child, we never had cousins locally...we didn't see much of the ones out west."

"You sound like you're leaving." Megan's brow furrowed.

"I'll be on the road for the harvest season with my crew. I'm thinking about staying with Mom and Dad in Arizona after Christmas. Getting out of the Kansas cold for a while this winter."

"But…" Megan sputtered. "What about me?"

"What about you? You go back to school after the holiday. Your entire freshman year, you only came home to visit once each semester. Cell phones do connect in Arizona."

"But what if I want to come home more on weekends?"

"You've got a key."

Megan's eyes watered. She jumped up and bolted for the back door.

"Wait!" Lucas kicked the shovel and started after

her, but before he reached the door, a car horn blasted. He turned, surprised to see Amelia with Craig. They must have come straight from church.

Slam!

From inside the house, a door slammed. Megan and her anger. Maybe it was his punishment for not taking her to church, like his mother had insisted when they talked last night on the phone. Thank goodness Amelia had arrived. His sister would respond better to female intervention than a two-male invasion.

"Glad you could come by before you left," Lucas said to Craig. He turned to Amelia, "Could you talk Megan down? She's upset. She ran inside. If I'm not mistaken, she's crying. I think it was something I said, but...for the life of me, I don't know what's wrong."

"Brothers," Amelia grunted. "Can't live with them, can't kill 'em." She headed toward the back door. He watched her go. Her hips swayed as she picked her way across the yard in high heels. For months, whenever she was near, his gut clenched as though he'd been sucker punched. A deep ache made him want to take her in his arms and hold her. Feel her softness and her warmth. It had become near impossible to hide his feelings about her.

He jerked his attention to Craig to clamp down on his growing desire and to avoid alerting Craig to his true feelings. It would be uncomfortable if his friend caught him gawking at Amelia.

"You couldn't have planned that better," Craig said.

"How do you mean?"

"I can't believe I'm going to say this, but we need to talk."

Lucas pointed. "How about in there? It'll give us some privacy." They walked the worn path away from the house to the large metal building that served as a workshop and storage for farm equipment. Once inside, Lucas led Craig to the far corner where several easy chairs faced a flat screen TV. When he had time, he let his inner football fan cut loose. It wasn't a man cave, but a place of his own requiring cleaning only when he got around to it. Tiny dust particles danced in the light when Lucas flipped the switch and the fluorescents flickered on.

"What's your call?" Lucas asked, reaching for the fridge door.

"Root beer."

"Take your choice of seats." Lucas pointed to the grouping of easy chairs that had seen better days, then to the three-legged wooden stools by the workbench. Craig grabbed a dingy rag and wiped the top of a stool before parking on it. Lucas rolled his eyes. The city boy didn't want to get his suit pants smudged with a little dust. His friend had surely changed.

"Talk." He handed a bottle of root beer to Craig before settling on the next stool. A small motor on the workbench caught his eye. He needed to pick up parts to finish the repairs. Tasks awaited him everywhere he looked. And the garden wouldn't have a harvest if Megan didn't pull her weight and complete the task.

"I'm asking for your help."

"Go on." Lucas took a long draw on his root beer.

"Someone made me an offer on the farm. I'm

going to sell."

Lucas coughed, spurting a trickle of brown liquid. He wiped his mouth with his sleeve. The shock of Craig's confession had his brain turning round like a whirligig. Amelia would be crushed. "Say, what?"

"I want your help. Talk Amelia into leaving the farm." Craig set his drink on the workbench, rose from the stool, and began pacing. "I have an offer. Have had an offer, but the buyer wants the whole thing, not just my half. I never wanted to push her off the farm. I always wanted leaving to be her own decision. But...it's been a year. Now, she says she's resolved to stay. You and I know everything hinges on the harvest. I don't want her to fail. It will crush her if she loses the farm." Craig stopped in front of the large flat screen TV. "I want her to see *the truth* of the situation and decide to go on her own."

Lucas frowned. "Truth is a tricky thing sometimes. Your truth isn't necessarily hers."

Craig crossed the room and stood in front of Lucas. "You *have* to talk to her. Convince her."

"What makes you think Amelia will listen to me?" Shaking his head, Lucas stared at his friend. Had he truly heard Craig correctly? "You're going to sell? Who's the buyer?" he asked suspiciously.

"I'm not going to say just yet."

Lucas locked his jaw and glared. "It's not a *who*, but a *what*. That soulless corporation offered you big money." He never imagined his best friend would be a sell-out. Plenty of local farmers would want the Britton's land. He barely had enough for a down payment, but even he had an interest in the land.

However, he never wanted Amelia to think his interest in her was connected to the farm. He wanted her, not for her farm. Why would Craig turn traitor and destroy the tradition of family farming?

"It's practical. It makes sense, Lucas, and not just on paper. Afterward, I'll invest the money. Amelia can paint. Do what she wants without the headaches and the worry of the farm. She won't be at nature's mercy for income."

"You want an easy way out. You just don't get it." Lucas rose and kicked a stool, sending it toppling onto its side. It *clunked* against the cement floor. He sucked in a quick breath to check his frustration, which was rising like a flooding river. He lowered his tone and studied Craig. "She paints like a fiend here—*not* in the city. She's making ends meet. The crop this year is good. It'll put her in the black. You should have a little faith in your sister."

"But what about next year? Or the year after that?" Craig shouted. "Soon, all the boxes of stuff my mother bought and hoarded in the barn will be gone. Then what?" Craig slammed his bottle of root beer on the workbench. Liquid spewed from the top and trickled down the side. Craig shook his hand, shaking off the brown beverage. He grabbed for the rag and wiped up the mess. "Farming is gambling. Only worse. You put your heart and soul into it and just like that"—Craig snapped his fingers—"it's gone."

"If farming is gambling, then you should understand. You gamble with people's money every day. Isn't that what you do, Mr. Big Investor? Just wait until after the harvest." Lucas mopped his face with his hand. "Give her that much time. If the corporate operation is willing to buy now, they'll pay more after the harvest. It will give you leverage to up the price."

"You of all people should know," Craig sounded as though on the edge of defeat, "farming is always a huge risk. I won't remind you about what happened to your father. Look what it did to you! I don't want that for Amelia. I have to protect her."

He couldn't deny the truth of Craig's words. The loss of the farm still jabbed his gut, sometimes as a mild punch, other times like a fiery hot stab. He understood what it meant to have life ripped away. A life he'd fought for, risked his life for. Would it be worse if Amelia tried and failed? Maybe. Maybe not. He wasn't in the psychic business. That was Helen's bailiwick. But he wouldn't help *anyone*, not even Craig, yank dreams from another person, especially if that person was Amelia.

"I can't help you, man. I told you before." Luke bent to pick up the fallen stool. "I'm done running interference. I'm not sticking my nose into Amelia's business unless she asks me directly. You're on your own."

"What if," Craig's words came slow and even, "I made it worth your while?" Craig's eyebrows raised.

Lucas frowned. "A bribe?"

"Think of this as a business deal. The parcel of land between your house and ours. It could be yours. It will give you greater access to the creek. Your holding will go up from ten to ninety acres. They don't want the land where our house sits. It's a sweet deal."

"I think if you weren't my best friend, I'd punch

you out right now." Lucas locked his jaw. "If I wanted your land, I'd offer a deal to Amelia. Not you."

"Craig? Lucas?" Amelia's voice came from near the doorway. "Can you hear me? Are you in there? Want some lunch?"

"Consider the offer," Craig growled. "For the sake of our friendship. Amelia's always been like a sister to you. Help me do the right thing by her."

Lucas narrowed his eyes. He kept his voice low. "Well, consider this. Maybe I'll just marry her. That would solve her biggest problem—you."

Craig drew back. The shock on his face made the entire conversation worth it. "Let him *consider* it all the way back to St. Louis," Lucas muttered as he turned his back on Craig and walked toward the voice of the woman he loved.

****

"Megan, honey, you have to look at the good in the situation." Lia sat on the foot of Megan's bed with apprehension railing in her gut like Jerry Lee Lewis pounding piano keys. It broke her heart to see Megan cry. The transition from kid to grownup rarely went smoothly for anyone, but could she really offer adult advice to the almost twenty-year old sobbing into a pillow? Her brother, and for that matter, Megan's brother, often treated her with kid gloves, like she were still a child, which she resented. Would Megan reject her offer of support? Though Lia had been a teacher and dealt with children's emotions, Megan's pain cut so close to home. Lia started to reach out and pat the young woman on the back, but thought better of it. Megan didn't need to be patronized.

"If Lucas is out on a job or visiting your parents in Arizona"—Lia clutched her hands in her lap— "you can stay with me...if you don't want to be here all alone. You can even invite some of your friends from college for a weekend sleepover. Do college girls do that still? Just know this, I know what it's like to miss home."

The young woman flopped over and wiped her tear-stained face with the corner of a pillowcase. "You make me feel guilty. At least my parents are alive, but I always pictured myself coming home from college for holidays and having my parents here." Megan sniffed.

"I never understood how complicated parenting must be until mine died. I have many regrets now. I took my mom and dad for granted. My mom was upbeat and like a brilliant star. I always felt like I lived in her shadow," Lia confided. Tears welled in her eyes. She had to get a grip on her own sadness or she stood no chance of helping Megan.

"But...but," Megan sputtered. "It's like my dad gave up on life and our family. Lucas is now a parent to all of us. Something he didn't ask for. He's always had broad shoulders to carry the weight of our woes, but now, I'm worried about him...yet also feeling sorry for myself."

Lia reached for Megan's hand. She squeezed, offering support. "I know it's not the same with your parents moving out west. I know how life can feel unsafe because of all the changes. Craig takes his big brother responsibilities very seriously. I know he wants to protect me, just like Lucas wants to protect you."

"How is it that my dad, a fourth-generation farmer—I mean, our family survived the Dust Bowl!—leaves the farm?" Megan sat up and scooted on the bed, resting her back against the headboard. She pulled a pillow into her arms and hugged it. "My dad now spends his days swimming and playing shuffleboard at a retirement village. Every trailer looks the same. Okay, maybe the front doors are different colors. My mom knits and goes to book clubs. Who are those people?" she wailed. "What's become of my mom and dad? Why did they desert me?"

"Lucas works hard so they can have some comfort in their life," Lia said quietly. "He also does that for you. Do you really think he'd leave for more than a couple of weeks? Arizona might be nice in the winter, but Lucas is tied to this land. I've never talked with him about it, but as a former military officer, I'm guessing many large companies would be happy to have him. Yet, he chose to come home."

"Yeah." Megan sighed. "You're right."

"Remember what my mother always said?"

"*C'est la vie*," Megan whispered.

"That's life," Lia repeated. "Say it louder."

"C'est la vie!"

"Much better," Lia said. "We have to take life as it comes. You're counting on doom before it arrives. Not a good philosophy for living." She paused and tried to step away from the war of emotions battling in her heart. Guilt about her mother raged against practical reason, but so far, the war had no victor, and her heart remained battered and bruised. She might very well be on the way to a bleeding ulcer if she didn't heed her own advice. Megan had spent more time at the Britton's farm over the last five years before her parents died than she had. Maybe Megan had insights? "I've only told one other person this..."

"Yes?" Megan leaned forward.

"I loved my mother, but she made me uncomfortable sometimes. She was always the brightest star in the room. She made people feel welcomed. Growing up, I often felt awkward in her presence. She had a sense of grace and southern style, and she forgot to pass those genes to me."

"When I was in high school, I got off the bus at your house on Fridays," Megan said, a small smile appearing. She pulled a tissue from the side table and dabbed the corners of her eyes. "Your mom always had something wonderful cooking on the stove. The house smelled *heavenly* with spices. I didn't mind the long walk home, even in the winter wind or snow, although she always offered to drive me. I think it made my mother mad that I spent so much time with your mom."

Lia paused. "But you can't think it had anything to do with your parents moving to Arizona."

Megan shrugged.

"No," Lia insisted. "I think it has more to do with the embarrassment they must feel over what happened. Losing the farm, one that's been in the family for several generations, is hard. It's complicated. Emotions are messy. I understand embarrassment. Felt that way about my own mother sometimes. She would talk to anyone about anything."

"Wrong," Megan corrected. "She *listened* to

everyone, even those in line at the grocery store. She drew people out. She gave them a reason to smile. She made everyone she came in contact with feel special."

"Because she was so outgoing, and you know how small town gossip is, my parents strictly enforced propriety. Dotting all i's and crossing all t's was required. The fact is...my mother embarrassed me and, at the same time, she insisted I follow strict rules of conduct."

"I guess"—Megan shrugged—"we always want what's on the other side of the fence."

Lia laughed. "In this case, we've crossed the line into literal. May I ask you a personal question?" She chewed her bottom lip. Never would she want to sully her mother's sterling reputation, but there was so much she wanted to know, and she had no one to ask but Megan. "Did she ever talk with you about buying all that stuff? I don't know if my dad ever knew about the cache in the barn. Mom paid the bills and did the bookwork for the farm."

Megan grew pensive. "I don't want to speak out of turn. Your mom never said anything directly to me. It wouldn't be right for me to say. I don't want to speculate."

"Did she ever mention me?"

"Oh course! All the time! She beamed with pride about your art. About the recognition you've had. And, I hate to say this, but here goes—I'm on Craig's side. I think you should go back to the city and paint."

"So, you, Craig, and Lucas are ganging up on me. Nice to know I've got the support of my family and friends."

"As Lucas reminds me, sometimes we're unable to determine the direction of the wind, but we feel the effects. Anyway, now you know my vote, for whatever good that is. Um... How about lunch?" Megan swung her legs over the side of the bed. "Before you and Craig arrived, I told Lucas I'd make lunch."

"Now who's uncomfortable? It's three against one." Lia folded her arms over her chest and eyed Megan. "What else do you know?"

Megan's nose wrinkled. "All I'm going to say is you've got an ally, and you haven't figured that out yet."

"What do you mean?" Lia demanded.

"I think I hear Lucas calling me. I know he wants lunch. He's all hyped up on caffeine." Megan slid off the bed. "Let's go."

Megan left the room almost at a run. Lia stared at the empty space where the young woman had just been and frowned. The only person who might agree she should stay, at least until next Saturday night, was Karl, but he couldn't be counted as an ally. Even Zoë encouraged her to return to the city. Megan had some explaining to do.

Lia's hands rested over her heart. Who in Harvest could she trust?

Chapter 8

Lia set plates on the table. "Chicken salad sandwiches. Potato chips. Lucas likes the salt and vinegar kind." She opened the bag and poured a small pile of chips on each plate. It comforted her to know small details about Lucas's life.

Megan turned up her nose. "Those make my mouth pucker just thinking about the taste." She carried napkins to the table and placed one beside each plate. "He can have my share. I've got some fruit salad in the fridge. Shall I get it out?"

Before she could answer Megan, she caught sight of Lucas. He stalked into the house, his expression unreadable. The screen door bounced closed behind him. He went straight to the hall. She followed, but stopped short, peeking round the corner. The sound of water running came from the bathroom. When she turned around, she stood face to face with her brother, who did an about-face and went to the kitchen sink.

"Is something...wrong?" Lia asked Craig as he soaped up his hands.

"Wrong?" He shook his head. "No. Why?"

"If I didn't know better, I'd say Lucas was mad."

"He's wearing his military poker face," Megan said. "Not good." She opened the fridge and pulled out a bowl. "He's deadly serious about something."

"I can hear you," Lucas called out.

"We had a difference of opinion," Craig said. He dried his hands before making his way to the table. "Thanks for lunch, Megan."

When they were finally seated, Lia poured lemonade in glasses and passed them around. "The silence is deafening. What's the disagreement about?"

She pinned a stare on her brother, who then looked outside as though interested in the hummingbirds diving and darting around the feeders. Megan cast a glance at each of them, planted her elbow on the edge of the table, and rested her chin on her palm. A grin full of excited anticipation lit her face, like she'd just won a ticket to a ringside seat at a fashion runway show.

"Good lunch," Lucas said between bites of his sandwich.

"Awkward," Megan replied in a sing-song tone.

Lia frowned. Something was going on between Craig and Lucas. They had no right to be mad at each other. This was her time. She planned to seize the moment, hoist a conquering flag, confronting both men about their plot to ruin her social life in front of a witness. But as much as she wanted to battle with them, their silence brought uneasiness prickling up her spine, one she couldn't ignore. Adding fuel to an existing fire could result in a blaze they could all regret. In the many years of their friendship, the two men had few falling-outs. They had a way of balancing each other. Funny and serious. Loud and quiet. She had come to count on them as a team. That realization surprised her. No matter what the problem eating at them, she wouldn't kick them when they were down.

Megan, obviously bored with the silence, turned the conversation lively with stories of dorm life. Craig and Lucas chimed in, but neither spoke directly to the other. Lia rolled her eyes. Did they really think they were fooling anyone?

"Thanks for the hospitality. I've got to get back." Craig rose from the table and put his plate in the sink.

"I'm going to catch a ride home with Craig," Lia told Megan and Lucas. "Zoë's coming by in a bit."

Megan walked them to the door. Lucas remained at the table.

"Remember, I'm here to help," Lia said, hugging Megan tightly. "I love your wonderful memories of my mother."

Lia rode in silence with Craig to the farm. When they arrived, she hugged him before getting out of the car. "I wish you'd tell me what's going on. It's weird and unsettling, you and Lucas not speaking. I can't remember the last time you two had a problem...wait, I do. It was over a girl when you were in college." Lia paused. "Is it a girl now? Did you and Lucas meet someone new at Rockets?" She really didn't want to know the answer. It would break her heart if Lucas had a serious interest in someone else.

"Yes, it's about a woman."

Lia flinched.

"But not in that way. I've got to go. We'll talk about it later."

They're fighting over a woman? Who?

Worry began a slow shred of her self-confidence. Prickling sensation returned, moving up and down her spine like someone playing scales on a piano. She shuddered at the eerie vibrations. "Okay. Text me when you've made it to St. Louis. Even a younger sister can worry."

Lia entered the house. In need of a distraction from niggling apprehension, she donned bib overalls, the perfect stereotypical garb for a Kansas farmer, and went outside. Jack ran circles around her as she walked to the barn. "Dog, you make me dizzy."

A late afternoon breeze fluffed her hair. An orange sun in a cloudless sky hovered above the treetops. The days were growing shorter. She gazed over the green horizon—miles of corn and soybeans, a postcard of almost anywhere in the state of Kansas. The thought of leaving the beauty surrounding her produced an ache in her heart. Zoë didn't understand that even she would miss the land if she moved to the city. But some lessons were best learned from personal experience.

Inside the barn, Lia turned on the bright shop lights and surveyed the scene. An old croquet set she and her friends had used back in their junior high days, sawhorses, a long worn workbench lined the wall, rusted dog crates, and other junk too rusted or broken to discern the purpose they'd served when new. From the horse tack hanging from posts to the scattered hay on the floor, this place would make the perfect setting for a country music video.

She made her way to the very back of the barn and pulled open the door to the storage room. A light popped on. The room resembled a small warehouse, walls lined with shelves and racks in the center of the room. Her task until Zoë arrived would take her through each remaining box to create a complete inventory of what remained from her mother's secret shopping stash.

Awhile later, Lia pushed her hair behind her ears and surveyed her progress. Now only one wall displayed boxes. Cool air rippled along her back like a ghost running its hand from her neck to her butt. She shivered and scanned the room, half-expecting to find her mother sitting on the crate near the door.

"Momma, I miss you," she whispered, folding her arms over her chest. "Missing you so much. What do I do about Lucas? What will happen to me if I lose the farm?"

The rumble of a vehicle coming up the road drew Lia's attention. She stepped out of the room and peered through a window of the barn. A cloud of dust confirmed her suspicion. Someone traveled on the road to her house. Zoë?

A moment later, outside the barn, an engine died.

"Lia!"

"Back here."

Jingling keys allowed her to track Zoë's progress to the rear of the barn.

"How's it going?" Zoë asked. She shielded her eyes and squinted. "Wow! Not a whole lot left."

Lia nodded. She moved a package from the center rack to the last open space on the shelf against the wall. When all the shelves were empty and the packages shipped off to new destinations, would she be forced to go, too? Uncertainty rubbed her nerves the way a new boot rubbed a blister on the back of her heel.

"It's pretty bare compared to when I started. I made an inventory of the remaining items for sale and those pieces I'm going to keep. The problem is the

Lenox china. There's a place setting for eight. I have Mother's set of Lenox Autumn in the house, so I'm not sure what her plans were for the Lowell Dinnerware. Maybe she intended it as a wedding present. I guess, I should check with Craig to see if he's interested in it...for that someday event. But I imagine his bride will prefer to pick out her own china."

"I would," Zoë agreed.

"Over there"—Lia pointed—"are enough packages of seeds to plant a kitchen garden for everyone in the county. Mr. Turner said he'd take those off my hands."

"I can't fathom what made your mom, the mother-of-no-clutter, transform into a secret shopaholic."

"I've continued my search for clues. A diary. A journal. Notes stuffed in a drawer. All I found was a pocket folder with receipts. It makes me sad. I feel so guilty, as if somehow this is my fault." Her chest tightened. Guilt hit her hard.

"You've got to let it go. We've talked about this. Your mom wanted you to be a success. She was proud of your teaching and artwork. She chose your dad and life on the farm."

"Still...I believe she began this secret obsession after I left for college. The sales receipts indicate that."

"I'm a parrot. I'll say it again. You have to let it go. As your mom always said, C'est la vie. It's advice that's served us all very well. Consider it the best gift she ever gave you."

"Maybe." Lia shrugged. "Help me move these

94

boxes to the cleared workbench. I've sold this stack."

Zoë picked up the biggest box, square and awkward, her arms barely able to hold the sides. When she tried to adjust it in her grasp, it toppled and hit the floor sending up a cloud of dust. She coughed and swatted to clear the air of dancing particles.

"You okay?" Lia chuckled at Zoë's sheepish grin.

"Sorry. I hope whatever's in here didn't break."

Lia flipped open her steno pad and ran her finger down the page. "Nope. No worries. That's box 53. A blue and white sundress, matching blue sandals, and a big floppy white hat. The box is mostly filled with those air-filled packing pockets to protect the hat."

"The box isn't damaged, so that's good." Zoë resumed her trek toward the door and managed to get the box there without dropping it again.

Lia placed two small boxes in the Jeep. "I'll admit I'm worried. What if there's not enough money, even if I sell *all* the boxes, to keep me completely in the black all the way through spring? I've been working on Plan B. Emailing with a gallery in KC that sold a couple of my paintings last year. They've looked at my entire portfolio. They want to give me a showing. I'm taking a dozen paintings to them tomorrow."

"How many paintings do you have completed?"

"Between what I have here and in my studio in KC, a catalog of forty. That's every last unsold piece. A few of the paintings are almost fifteen years old."

"You kept the work you did in high school?"

"Absolutely. Someday when I'm famous, I think people will be most interested in my earliest work."

She grinned, wishing she really had that much faith about her painting future.

"I like you're confidence. It helps to stare uncertainty in the face. Unflinching tenacity is what it will take, especially if you truly mean to stay on the farm. So you want me to play Pony Express and mail these packages for you?" Zoë teased.

"You found me out. Now to keep with the western theme, you and I are having leftovers from the potluck while you explain to me what happened yesterday."

Lia did a double take at Zoë's bashful smile.

She wondered when Zoë would get around to talking about Karl. Did she know about the private conversation he had with Lucas that had Karl shaking his head like a bobblehead doll? Afterward, Karl had politely, but determinedly, insisted on leaving.

Gentleman Jack bounded to the barn door. He loped in the grass alongside Lia and Zoë as gravel crunched under their feet on the fifty-yard walk to the house. Inside, no evidence remained of the houseful of guests from the cookout.

"Does Craig help you clean when he comes home?" Zoë asked, running a finger along the edge of a bookshelf. She raised a spotless finger.

"What are you? The white-glove brigade?" Like her mother, who always had a clean house, Lia had stayed up late to tidy the place after the party. "Don't tell anyone. He'll only deny it, but he cleaned the downstairs hall bathroom, scrubbed the floor and all. He also cleaned his room. I don't go in there. I keep the door closed when he's gone. He's responsible for it."

"Mister Suit remembers his roots. Maybe the big city hasn't changed him as much as I'd thought."

"Maybe. Set the table. I'll reheat some food."

Zoë pulled blue and white Currier and Ives plates from the cabinet, utensils from the drawer, and two napkins from the holder. "So about yesterday. How interested are you in Karl?" she asked, placing the table settings on the breakfast counter.

"Will you pull the potato salad from the fridge?"

Closing the short distance, Zoë did as she requested. "Now, tell me. What about Karl?"

"I don't know." Lia stood by the stove and placed slices of ham into a frying pan. "I'll tell you more after my date next Saturday."

"Why'd you do that?"

"Ask Karl out?"

"We always celebrate birthdays together. I'm feeling like a third wheel."

"That would mean you'd be on the date with me and him, and that's *not* going to happen. I apologize. I should have talked to you about changing things up. However, if I'd told you what I had planned before I did it, I might have lost my nerve." It took all the bravado she could muster to ask a man out.

"I have to admit, that's pretty audacious for you. So, how would you feel if someone else was interested in him? Like really, truly interested."

Lia didn't need to ponder the question, but she wasn't yet ready to share the full truth. "Well, since I haven't kissed him yet, I don't have anything to compare him to."

Zoë grinned. "And whom might you be comparing him to?"

Lia turned away from her friend as heat flooded her cheeks.

"Lia Britton, you're holding out on me.'

"No. I'm. Not."

Zoë moved in close. Lia tried to turn away, but Zoë was nose-to-nose with her, staring her straight in the eye.

"You, like Lucas, never tell a lie. What gives?"

Lia turned back to the stove. "I can't stop thinking about kissing Lucas," she whispered. When she turned back to Zoë's widening grin, she wasn't sure which bothered her more, the smugness spread across Zoë's face or the unraveling of the façade she'd guarded for so many years. Her pulse raced.

Would Lucas reject her again?

Chapter 9

The next day, Lia backed the truck and U-Haul trailer from the barn to the driveway at the house. After opening the rear doors of the enclosed trailer, she rolled up the garage door. Donning leather work gloves, she dragged out a wooden rack designed to hold paintings upright while being transported. She broke a sweat wrestling the rack into place in the back of the trailer. Clearly, she needed a part-time job stacking hay. Working out regularly would make the loading process easier. Wouldn't Craig love to know a well-appointed gym and a personal trainer were things she missed about her life in the city? She'd never hear the end of it.

Sliding the contraption into position, she cinched it down with retractable straps. She stepped back to inspect her work. If a strap broke loose, it could mean disaster, unrepairable damage to one or more of her paintings. She'd only used the wood rack twice before, and then, had only carried four paintings on those trips to town, although, thank goodness, she had the foresight to design the holder for a dozen pieces of artwork—the exact number she needed to present to the gallery in Kansas City. The gallery owner hinted during their last phone call she may have already sold two or three based solely on the photographs Lia had sent.

Testing the straps one last time, Lia paused and wiped perspiration from her brow. What had her mother always said? Men sweat. Ladies mist. At this rate, she'd need another shower. Excessive misting had ruined her makeup. The September sun beat down as though it confused arid Arizona with the green plains of the Midwest. Deodorant hadn't been designed to work miracles.

"I might as well finish the job before showering again," she muttered, scanning the yard. If the corn in the field or the hummingbirds flitting around the feeders heard her talking to herself, none seemed to mind.

Opening the door to the sun porch, she stepped aside when Gentleman Jack bolted past her, his ears flopping and feet flying so quickly only two touched the ground at any one time. Zipping along, he galloped his way around the corner of the house and out of sight.

"You'll be back," Lia shouted after him.

Taking care, she wrapped each delicate painting to prevent damage. One by one, she loaded them onto the rack inside the trailer. The larger ones at one end, the rest in descending size order. When she finished laboring over the project, Jack reappeared. Panting hard, he dropped to the ground at her feet. He looked up at her as if to confirm he'd run the perimeter of the premises and all was in order. He was ready and waiting on her.

"Good fella." She bent and scratched behind his ear. "Want a cookie before I shower?"

Jack followed her inside where she treated him, then treated herself to a quick, cool rinse. She selected an outfit of black slacks and a pink and orange flowered top that said summer. While dressing, she replayed in her mind the conversation she'd shared yesterday with Zoë. Her friend's expressed shock over the confession about Lucas's innocent kiss surprised her. She still hadn't shaken off the uncomfortable feeling. Vulnerability made her want to hide.

"Lucas. Lucas Dwyer," Zoë had said. "No wonder you and he have acted so strange, especially lately. He's like a big brother to you. If we were back in grade school, I would've guessed you liked each other. Classic behavior. Now, whenever he's around, you zip it and either frown or just ignore him."

"You've got a vivid imagination."

"I'm not the one who paints pictures."

"Wait now. My paintings are my interpretation of what I see around me. Not some embellishment of the truth."

"Well, I've been blind all this time. I couldn't see what was in front of me. You like Lucas."

"Of course, I like him. As you said, he's like a brother to me."

"I'm thinking your feelings fail to fit into the *la familia* category."

Lia hadn't wanted to lie, so instead, she'd zipped it. Zoë was right. She did have feelings for Lucas. Deep ones. And some seesawed back and forth. She wanted him to fold her into his arms and kiss her again, not to offer a grieving woman comfort, but to offer love and happiness. A future together. At the same time, she wanted to swat him hard for interfering with her life, behind her back no less, at her brother's request. Could Lucas ever truly see her as more than Craig's sister? Was that hope a pipe dream? Lucas was right. Craig wouldn't like it.

Lia brushed her hair. Her mind continued its focus on Lucas Dwyer. Funny that her very first kiss has come from him back when she was a junior in high school and her prom date dumped her at the last minute for the hottest cheerleader on the Varsity squad. Lucas kissed her out of pity then. Somehow Craig learned of it and butted in, teasing Lucas so bad he hadn't spoken to her all summer, in fact, hadn't talked to her like she was anything more than a good buddy, never with any hint of recognition that she was female. It wasn't until he came home from college at Christmas during his freshman year that her heart, bursting with unrequited love, broke a second time.

When she caught him under the fake mistletoe hanging from the chandelier in the foyer, she kissed him. Mere contact of her lips to his, warm and gentle, sent shivers to her toes, and not because of the howling north wind descending from the Arctic on Kansas. Lucas's reaction embarrassed her. He pushed her away. His wide-eyed shock and surprise pained her like a knife to the heart. It hurt even more when he refused to talk about it. Not at the party or any time while he had visited over the holiday.

Was he shocked because she was a bad kisser? Or because he didn't feel the same chemistry racing through her veins?

The kiss from a year ago burned into her mind and forever sealed her heart. Lucas asked her to take a break from the funeral crowd gathered at the house and walk to the creek. They made their way in silence through the ankle-high grass while breezes brushed the hem of her black dress. Grief created a tension. Her entire body ached. It began the moment she heard the news of her parents' death and climbed each day. That afternoon, Lucas offered a safety net. The vibrating anxiety quieted a bit. With him, she could be herself and drop the too-brave veneer worn for everyone else's benefit.

When they were over the hill and beyond the prying eyes of the crowd, Lucas reached for her hand, a gentle gesture providing human contact she needed so badly. Still, he remained silent. Not wanting to break the peace of the moment, she made no comment. In the shadows of the tree line, they sat side by side on a large oak branch growing horizontally over the creek's slow trickling water, just as they had done as very young kids.

Cocooned from reality, submerged in temporary tranquility, Lucas quietly asked about her feelings. Her loss. Her grief. He urged her to talk even when she resisted. After a few false starts, she poured her heart out to him, sobbing over the pain of losing her parents. The boulders of her life had been forever removed. Her father represented stability. He plodded along, always on the straight and narrow, enjoying the benefits of a dutiful life. Her mother, the heartbeat of their family, the star casting a bright light over everyone, had ceased to shine, leaving drab emptiness.

With an arm draped around her shoulder, Lucas wiped away her tears just as he had at the funeral. Her skin warmed wherever he touched her. He cradled her face in his hands. Gently, he put his lips to hers. His touch seared. Her insides quivered and melted. He deepened the kiss. Her bones turned to Jello. Her heart pulsed as fast as hummingbird wings fluttering in flight. The gripping tension nearly strangling her since her parents' death let go. In those few moments with Lucas, the entire world slipped away—the ache of grief, the maddening pain, the fear of a bleak future—and melted into a bliss she'd never known.

They didn't speak, but continued to kiss. He seemed to savor the taste of her lips. He stroked her cheeks with his thumbs as though marveling at the smoothness of her skin. She deepened the kisses, brazenly caressing his lips with her tongue and sucking on his bottom lip. He moved, shifting his body. He pulled her closer.

All thoughts dissolved. Only need of Lucas remained. When she reached for the first button on his shirt, the need to feel his skin daringly urged her on. Passion flared like a bonfire. It demanded satisfaction. How she craved what could come next. Her heart pounded, a resounding thud to a deep thundering. Desire fueled her actions, blinding her to only that moment.

But Lucas captured her hands with his and kissed her palms. With extreme gentleness, he pressed her head to his shoulder.

It wasn't outright rejection.

She understood his actions. If anyone wandered down to the creek and discovered them, gossip would shoot rocket high. He meant to protect her from embarrassment. That elevated him to hero in her book. A seed of hope lodged itself in her heart.

Maybe Lucas did see her as a woman, someone with whom he could have a relationship. At the very least, he'd enjoyed kissing her.

A quiet closeness settled between them on their return walk to the house. However, halfway there, Craig again ruined everything. From the back deck, he'd hollered for help and Lucas had dropped her hand and went running at her brother's beck and call. The big emergency? A flame up on the grill.

Lia grabbed her keys and sighed. After that day, Lucas had maintained a respectable distance. And the only three kisses she'd shared with other men since his soul-melting ones were chaste goodnight kisses only after a second date. Never on the first. And no guy had asked her out beyond a second time.

Now she understood why.

Lucas had followed her brother's orders and made her a local dating pariah.

Picking up her purse and a portfolio of photos showing her paintings, she searched for Jack. "Males," she huffed. As for meddling male big brothers, Craig had skipped out yesterday before she could lay down the law to him about not poking around in her life. The weekend memorial service had her on emotional overload, which hadn't left her in the right mind to do battle with him. Soon, she'd confront him, just like David standing up to Goliath, and everyone knows who won that battle. Craig had better beware.

"Here, Gentleman Jack!" Lia called, wondering if the dog had snuck out the dog door and run off to the creek. She shaded her eyes and squinted in the noonish light, scanning the yard and nearest field.

Unable to spot the four-legged ball of energy, she walked around the side of the house. A hint of an early fall breeze caressed her face. She soaked in the change of season, hoping the last of scorching summer had slid away. Scanning the landscape, she called for Jack. Finally, she spied him at the edge of the back deck guarding a pile of toys. He'd harvested them from hiding places in the yard.

"Pick one, and let's go if you want to ride. Otherwise, I'll drop you off at Zoë's for the night."

Gentleman Jack barked, picked up a stuffed toy pheasant, then dropped it, picking up a blue rubber ball. He dropped that, too. He looked at her as if to say he was unable to choose only one of his prize possessions, and why didn't she help him by bringing them all along.

Lia bent down and grabbed a thick rope knotted at both ends. She held one end and dangled the other. After she took a few steps, her traveling partner grabbed the loose end. They walked rope-in-hand and rope-in-mouth to the truck.

"Load," Lia ordered. Jack dropped his end, backed up, and with a running start, hopped onto the backseat of the cab. Lia tossed in the rope and closed the truck door behind him.

She returned to the house. Checking the door to the sun porch, she didn't bother locking it. No one ever came nosing around. If a criminal wanted to rob the place, it would take work to find the house and for not much gain. After climbing into the cab, she started the truck and crept along the long gravel drive to the packed hard road, careful to avoid ruts. Her future rested inside the trailer. The precious cargo equaled money. Money to pay the bills all winter, painting supplies, plus pay for seed *and* the spring planting. In a couple of weeks, Gus, an old family friend, would begin harvesting. A small portion of the corn crop sale would pay his fees. The rest would pay the mortgage for six to eight months and provide a reasonable cushion to reinvest in the farm.

Lia shook her head. The whole delicate cycle reminded her of her students' working mothers trying to make ends meet. They worked to pay bills, but paying high costs for after-school childcare left them with barely enough to meet household expense. Still, they chose to work. It gave them a sense of pride and demonstrated perseverance to their children. She understood their struggles better now.

When she reached the blacktop road, a plume of dust rose around her. Someone bumped along the same road. Yet due to the hill and the breeze, she couldn't determine if they traveled in the same direction or were coming at her head-to-head. She slowed the truck to a crawl. As she topped a small rise, she met the other vehicle.

Lucas.

He beeped the horn and skidded to a stop, kicking up even more dust. She moved inches at a time until they were side by side, waiting for the wind to carry away the haze of dust before rolling down the window.

"You on your way to KC by yourself?" Lucas asked. It sounded like an accusation and she bristled.

"Yes, taking Gentleman Jack with me. Good guard protection...and just in case there's a pheasant or quail to point."

"I don't know why you have to be so stubborn. I told I'd come over to help load your paintings and drive you over. It isn't easy navigating a trailer through the city, especially on that narrow bridge."

"Semis do it all the time. I've had a lot of trailer practice in the last year. The tailgate on the truck is proof enough. When I return, I'll take it in for repairs. That will erase the obvious reminder. Besides, I'm staying overnight with a girlfriend." If things were different, she would've welcomed his company. But now it wouldn't be a good idea for her to be in such close quarters with him for a whole twenty-four hours. No way to remove temptation. The risk of her embarrassing herself by doing something stupid, like kissing him again, was very high. Who was she kidding? She'd love nothing more than an opportunity to seduce him. She would make the first move. This man of integrity and impeccable reputation would never put a move on his best friend's sister, even if she stood naked in front of him. Darn man with his high morals. It had to be a sin to be that good.

If she did seduce him, where would things go from there? A one-night stand wasn't in character for either of them. If they ever did make love, then what?

"How about humoring me?" Lucas said dryly. "Call me when you get there. I like knowing you're safe."

Lia shook her head. "I'm a big girl now. I appreciate your concern, but even Craig doesn't insist I check in with him when I travel." She paused, a daring urge hitting her. "Or do you want to come spend the night with me?"

Lucas glared. Had he growled? Was it a frustrated groan? She couldn't be sure, but what did that mean regarding the *big brother* responsibilities Craig had foisted on him?

"Call me, or"—Lucas pointed a finger—"I'll. Call. You." He rolled up the window and pulled away.

Had he actually given her an order?

Lia drove through Harvest. She waved at Helen who stood in the window at the café. She beeped the horn at Zoë as she passed the post office, and Gentleman Jack barked his greeting. Without hitting a single red light in Harvest, she made it all the way through Atchison, and then she left Kansas behind via the tall metal bridge spanning the Missouri River and linking two states together. When she finally hit the interstate, her confidence about the future anchored solidly in her heart as strong as steel-tough chert found in the Flint Hills.

Interstate traffic moved steadily. Ahead, a flashing sign advising drivers to prepare to stop due to construction caught Lia's attention. She pulled off I-29 and into a truck stop. They'd been on the road for only two hours, but there was no reason to die of thirst. Sitting in traffic would make her antsy. Jack, too. A pit stop would do them good.

White lines marked parking spaces with fronts of the cars pointing toward a building. She parked in the section for tractor-trailers, pulling between two, and grabbed her wallet before leashing Gentleman Jack, taking him to a grassy pet walk area directly on the far side of the parking lot.

Forty-five minutes later, after paying for a bottle

of water and a bag of chips, Lia pulled back on the highway.

"Jack," Lia said when the dog bumped her shoulder. "I gave you water and a cookie. This is my drink and the chips are my treat. Lie back down."

Unless traffic on the bridge crossing into Kansas City had been reduced to one lane, she'd make it to her one-thirty appointment.

At the construction zone, traffic narrowed to one lane on the approach to the bridge crossing the Missouri River, moving slowly, but steadily. She checked her watch. Shifting in her seat a moment later, she checked her watch again. Her fingers gripped the steering wheel. Even at the turtle's pace, she'd make it on time, but only if there were no other delays.

When she rounded a long sweeping curve, Kansas City rose on the hill before them.

"Gentleman Jack, look! I'm sure this was Oz in the movie with Dorothy and Toto."

Jack braced his paws on the armrest and barked excitedly. Lia lowered the windows to capture breezes as she navigated city traffic. When she finally reached the tree-lined streets of Brookside, she pulled into the art gallery's parking lot at the rear of the building. Excitement vibrated, tingling all the way to her toes. She hopped out of the truck and ran the few steps to the gallery's back door. The buzzer sounded. A moment later, a heavy steel door opened.

Janice Keller, one of the gallery owners, appeared. "Lia! Welcome! I can't wait to see the pieces." She rubbed her hands together in apparent anticipation.

"Ms. Keller, I am very honored that you've decided to give me a show."

"Call me Jan. It's only two weeks away. We sent out postcards made from the images you sent us. They looked professional and the work so refined. Let's get these paintings unloaded. Paul will be in after lunch to start hanging the art in our new wing. It's so exciting to share new talent."

Lia walked beside Jan toward the back of the trailer. Gentleman Jack barked excitedly as they passed the truck cab.

"I see you brought your own fan club." Jan chuckled, reaching through the open window to pet Jack. "I'm thrilled, too. Talent like yours doesn't come along every day."

"I think the paintings you've selected are some of my best work," Lia said, rounding the corner of the trailer, her feet wanting to tap dance. If she were any more excited, she'd bob above the ground, floating like a helium-filled balloon. She stopped. Staring at the lever holding the double doors closed, she blinked and looked again.

Hair on the back of her neck stood up. Slowly she shook her head and blinked again. "No!"

Jan jumped. "What?"

"It can't be. It just can't be." Grabbing the lever, Lia jerked it, throwing open the trailer doors.

Her greatest fear stared back, taunting her. The words of her brother whispered in her ear, "*You will fail.*"

Dread bloomed in her gut. She doubled over in pain.

"Oh no," Jan whispered.

All that remained inside was an empty wooden rack.

Chapter 10

Lia pushed her fingers impatiently into her hair, wanting to yank it out by the roots. Her anxiety was riding a rollercoaster. She fought back rising nausea and forced her feet to anchor to one spot inside the art gallery. Every nerve in her body urged her to hop in the pickup and return to the truck stop in search of the paintings.

There had to be a clue. Someone had to have seen something. Her mind recreated the events of the pit stop step-by-step. What had she overlooked? No one loitered about the trailer. Not that she saw, but then, she really hadn't paid much attention. How naive of her to believe all was safe because of a padlock.

"Trailer was locked?" a policeman asked as he handed back her driver's license and insurance card.

She stuffed the items in her purse. "Yes, Officer," she said calmly, holding back an impulse to shout, I already told you, *I had a padlock on it*. This was the third policeman she'd spoken to, each time before she'd been passed off to another police department. They each said the correct jurisdiction needed to investigate.

"Tumbler or key?"

"Key." She bit back a snarky retort—It was the kind of lock thieves used bolt cutters on. Key?

Tumbler? Who cares?

"And you think this happened at the truck stop?"

"It was the only place I stopped on the trip between home and here. The truck stop across the river. Before the construction work begins. I was there for"—she glanced at her watch—"maybe forty-five minutes. Long enough to walk Jack, my dog, go the restroom, and buy a soda."

"Twelve pieces of artwork." The officer scribbled notes.

"I have photos of the paintings," Jan interjected. "I can print them out for you now." She left them in the gallery in a hurry and headed for the office.

"That would be great, along with a list, the titles of each artwork, and the approximate amount of the loss. Then email me the photos, please," the officer called after her. Turning back to Lia, he asked, "You're positive you didn't have insurance on your work?"

"I think I would know."

The officer raised an eyebrow at her.

"What? You think I made up this story to collect insurance money?" Shocked, she took a step back. "I am not that kind of person!"

"I'm not saying you are or you aren't. I'm trying to get appropriate information to make my report. So, once again, you're sure there's no insurance on the paintings."

Wasn't that rich? The police considered her a suspect rather than a victim. Planned a heist to collect insurance money. The notion had never crossed her mind.

"Is there anyone else who might have insured the

paintings?"

"Not that I know of. In fact, my knowledge of how to insure art could be placed on a nail head."

The officer leaned in closer. "The gallery doesn't insure art for you, do they?"

"I'm sure they have insurance for their property and maybe the artwork before it's sold, but my work never made it through the door. I guess if my TV education is worth anything, you could ask Jan if they have surveillance cameras to corroborate my story."

"Anyone who might benefit from your loss?"

The name that settled in her mind made her swallow hard. Craig. Only her bother would stand to gain from her loss—he and some unnamed thief would reap the benefits loss of her misfortune. The loss of her artwork created the perfect storm, one where no money rained down in her direction. One where she couldn't pay the bills. One where the farm would be ripped from her just like Dorothy's house had been ripped off its foundation in the *Wizard of Oz*. "No. Can't think of anyone."

"Well, then," the officer snorted, "I wish I could give you more hope." He handed over his business card. "Here's the case number." He showed her the handwritten number at the bottom. "But when items are so portable..."

"Portable? One of the paintings is four feet by five feet! Most people couldn't pack that away inside their trunk, let alone get it into the backseat of their car." She clasped her hands together and sucked on her bottom lip to keep from making a further scene.

"I'll be in touch if I find anything."

"So, you're saying if with a capitol I and F," Lia

muttered as the officer left.

"Lia," Jan said, returning after walking the policeman out. "I'll get us some lemonade, and let's talk about this in the conference room." Jan pointed to a door across the gallery.

Lia set her purse on the table. When she dropped down into a high-back padded chair, rioting panic surged through her. Leaning over, shoulders hunched, elbows on the table, she closed her eyes tight and hid her face in her hands. Her paintings weren't Van Gogh or Monet, but her golden eggs, a reward at the end of the rainbow. In one swift blow, a stranger had ruined her life. Why?

She would lose the farm. Lose. The. Farm. Pain ripped a ragged tear in her heart. She curled her toes tight in her shoes. When she began to shake, she held her breath hoping to stop the tremors. It wasn't that she'd failed, just as Craig had predicted, but her connection to family land would be forever severed, an amputation of something so dear it was rooted in her DNA. Anguish burned in her chest. She fought back welling tears. Losing the farm was as painful as losing her parents all over again.

Clenching her hands, she banged them on the table until her fists hurt. What she wanted was a brick wall to bang her head. Sniffling, she swallowed hard. She would not cry in front of Jan. Being labeled a temperamental artist was one thing, but unprofessional was a word she wouldn't have attached to her name. She swallowed again and straightened in the chair. All of this heartache because of a stupid padlock. Would Lucas have recommended something different? Could the theft have been avoided if he'd been along?

Her thoughts continued to drift to him. How had he survived when he returned from the war to find his family farm sold out from under him? He never said much, just took over organizing his parents' relocation to Arizona and got Megan back in school. Whenever someone in town offered condolences over the loss, Lucas shook them off, said he was glad he'd made it back alive and that's what mattered most. He always looked on the positive side of any situation. But still, the loss of his family's farm had to be a great disappointment.

A glass of lemonade appeared before her on the smooth granite tabletop. She looked up. Jan wore an expression of determination.

"We must have lemons to make lemonade," Jan said, taking the chair directly across the table from Lia.

"You made this fresh?" Lia asked, examining the liquid in the glass. The color looked a little too yellow.

"No." Jan laughed. "It's out of a can. Frozen. I meant that we have to make a buzz about the theft and that may attract more people to the opening. The ones we sent postcards to will have seen the quality of your art. Maybe we can work some commissioned pieces out of this and capitalize on the loss."

"Opening of what? I can't reproduce a dozen paintings in two weeks. Eight landscapes? Not doable. And even if it were, I just can't magically conjure up four still- life paintings. Those take me even more time."

"I looked through the portfolio of your work

while the police talked with you. I believe there are ten, maybe twelve other paintings, I could show. They're good, but I won't lie, I prefer the ones I first chose. I like the idea of doing mixed media work. It will be unique. I've got a source that could take a print of your work and transfer it to canvas."

"But that's not original artwork," Lia said, shocked at Jan's suggestion.

"Just think about it." She reached over and patted Lia's hand.

"A collage? I worked with that in college. It takes even more time. I have to find the right details to add. Like the perfect piece of grayed, weathered board from an old barn."

"Give it some thought. In the meantime, I'll print the list of the paintings you have to replace the stolen ones. Only this time, make the trip without stopping, please."

"I'll hire an armed guard," Lia said dejectedly.

Jan flashed a half-smile, as though placating a temperamental artist and left the conference room.

Lia rose and paced. The more she tried to focus on a mixed media piece the more a fog seemed to settle in her brain. When the phone in her purse rang, it jolted her into a panic. Grabbing for the phone, she prayed the police had some news. A quick look at caller ID deflated her momentary hope. Lucas.

"Hello?" she tried to sound cheery. She couldn't handle a scolding from him. If she'd allowed him to bring her to the city, the theft probably would've never happened. Her conscience managed to heap continuous self-recrimination, but for how long could she keep the loss a secret?

"You made it okay? You promised to call me."

"I'm sorry. I was swept away when I arrived. The art gallery has expanded. The new wing will perfectly showcase my artwork." Had she successfully controlled the warble in her voice? "I didn't forget." She managed not to lie. At least she retained some measure of integrity.

"Well, let me know when you're back. I think we should talk about the argument Craig and I are having."

"Sure. As soon as I get back. I need to go. The gallery owner has some paperwork for me." She had to get him off the call. Hearing his soothing voice made it much harder not to break down and cry, not to share the misery of her loss.

"I'm taking that as a promise. Call me when you get back. As soon as you do."

"Promise. Got to go. Bye."

Jan walked back into the room and handed her the list.

"Thanks." She reviewed the list quickly.

"Let me know when you'll deliver the new set of paintings. The sooner, the better. Today?"

"I have a few at my studio here in town. The rest...I'll try to make it tomorrow," Lia said heading out of the room. She tucked the paper in her purse for a quick escape from the gallery.

Jack barked when she climbed in the truck. At least she wasn't totally alone.

"Good boy," she said turning around and stretching back to hug him. "Wish I were you right now. You'll always have a home with me. Good food and a warm place to sleep. And even if you can't run loose at the farm, there's a great off-the-leash park in the city. At least I can make you happy," she said, releasing his neck. Scrunching her eyes, she willed tears not to flow.

She made her way through the streets of Kansas City and over to the Crossroads Arts district. The first Friday of each month, all the galleries opened their doors to show off works of local artists. The free event pulled in big crowds, especially during the warm-weather months when restaurants offered free *hors d'oeuvres* and bands played on street corners. But with no crowds around, navigating the trailer proved to be easy. She pulled into a parking spot along the curb, next to the brick building housing her studio.

"Focus, Lia. You can't give up." She straightened her hunched shoulders. "The show will go on, just not an A-plus rated one." Never before had she worried about what critics might say about her work. This time, reviews would be crucial to her future. Local newspapers and magazines, online and in print, would carry opinions from the area's most acclaimed critics. What if they trashed her art? A lump knotted in her stomach. Humiliation would eat her alive. No one would buy her work, which would mean she couldn't make the expenses for the farm, which would mean...

Jack nudged her.

"I know. I'm spiraling down the rabbit hole."

"*Woof.*"

"You don't have to agree with me." She sighed. "You stay here and guard the truck," she told Jack. "I'm going to bring the paintings down on a dolly.

Then we're headed right back to the gallery." She hadn't thought to find a hardware store and buy another padlock. Luckily, only three of the paintings on Jan's request list were housed in the studio. She could load and leave promptly, unless something else went wrong.

Hiking up three flights of stairs, Lia unlocked the deadbolt and the door lock. She rolled open the large hanging, solid-wood door. The rollers creaked. She made a mental note to spray lubricant on them.

Sunlight flooded the studio, and she couldn't help but smile. Craig had provided her with a wonderful place to paint. Brick walls. High wooden beam ceiling. Open metal ductwork. Perfect lighting. Everything at her fingertips. She breathed deeply. The energy wrapped around her like a protective security blanket.

Sliding the keys into her pocket, she stepped inside, held out her arms, and turned a full circle. Maybe she needed to consider hosting an open house in her studio when she had new paintings to show. Invite a group of local gallery owners over for a wine and cheese tasting. Maybe that would generate some interest in her work...if Jan's show turned out to be a flop.

She pulled the list of paintings from her purse and scanned it. In her mind's eye, each painting appeared with perfect clarity. Her heart pounded. Grief. Joy. Love. Emotions she had experienced when painting. Then, her goal had been to capture those feelings on canvas. Now, reflecting on the artwork collection soothed her mind some, but her heart bounced as though jumping on a trampoline.

"*Maize Nocturne*," Lia said, flipping through the canvases in the storage rack. She grabbed it and leaned it against her hip. "*Daze of Maize. Fields of Folly.*" Once she had located all three, she placed a towel on the metal dolly before setting the paintings on their sides. The towel offered protection to the canvases. Since luck had abandoned her when she left Kansas, she took every precaution to protect her art.

Exiting the building, she approached the trailer from the rear. Jack barked like a two-alarm fire warning. The hair on the back of Lia's neck stood up. On the sidewalk, she slowly approached the truck on the passenger side. A man in a suit stood in the street attempting to put his hand through the barely open window. The very reason she left them open only a crack—so no one could harm her four-legged boy. Quickly she leaned the handles of the dolly against the truck.

"Jack, quiet! May I help you?" Lia asked, intimidated by the stranger. Did he want to hurt Jack? There had been reports in the news about someone feeding pets poison. The police surmised the culprit wanted to punish pet owners who left their animals in vehicles. The day had been bad enough, trauma to last her forever. If anything happened to Jack... Her anger shot up. No one would hurt Jack! Not here or anyplace else.

Snapping her fingers, she pointed to the backseat of the truck. Thankfully, Jack obeyed, and he laid down.

She kept the truck between her and the man, rather than going around to confront him. He had ten inches and at least fifty pounds on her.

"Do you need something?" She reached into her purse and pulled out her phone. "Is there someone I can call for you?" A quick glance up and down the mostly empty street let her know that unless someone watched from windows above, anything about to happen could be a crime without a witness.

Focusing on her phone, she hit the speed-dial button for Lucas. He would hear anything that happened. Besides, it wouldn't seem weird since Lucas was waiting for her call.

"I wanted to pet him. Handsome guy. I hunt." The man tugged on his suit coat. "I also raise Brittany Spaniels."

"Okay. Well, have a nice day." What else do you say to a stranger in a business suit loitering beside your truck?

"Hello?" Lucas's voice startled her from the other end of the phone.

"Oh! Lucas," she said, lifting the phone to her ear. Maybe the stranger before her would take a hint and walk away. She could hope. Her mind whirled with ideas about everything she'd learned regarding self-defense, but that didn't stop fear from making her nerves tingle.

When the man started toward her, she quickly darted her eyes from side to side to scan the area. She licked her lips. Her pulse raced. Her brain screamed, *don't show fear*.

"Lucas, you're coming to meet me? Five minutes? That soon?"

"Amelia? Are you all right?" Lucas replied.

The man reached into his suit coat. Lia wanted to unlock the truck, hop inside, and drive off. Missouri allowed conceal and carry. Did the guy have a gun?

"Sorry to interrupt your call, but here's my card," the man said. "I like the look of Jack. I'll leave you to your business. If you have papers on him, I'd like to talk with you about breeding. I've got a sweet female. Together, they'd make some very handsome pups."

"Lucas, please hang on a minute." Lia took the card. Robert Brooks. Realtor.

Her guard dropped a bit, her rising fear leveled off. She thanked him. "Sorry, but Jack's a tenor." All she wanted was the man gone.

As though he'd read her mind, he nodded slightly, crossed the street and walked down the sidewalk in the opposite direction.

The uneasiness swirling inside her had more to do with the earlier theft rather than the stature of the man and the oddity of their meeting. However, she didn't dare turn her back completely on him while continuing her call.

"Lucas, sorry about that. I'm parked on the street beside the building of my studio. A strange man was trying to pet Jack through the truck window. I got worried. I didn't know who else to call."

"Is he still there? Are you safe? Is there anyone else around?" Lucas's questions came rapid fire.

"He's gone now." Lia let out a deep sigh. "I confess I'll be glad to be home. As much as I love my studio space, I just can't live in the city anymore. I have an errand to run. After that, I'm going to start packing things up. I've got a proposition for Craig, one I hope he'll accept."

"You're coming back tonight?"

"No. Remember? I said I'd be spending the

night. I'll call you tomorrow when I get home." The less Lucas and Craig knew about what had taken place today, the better. "I'm on my way back to the gallery now."

At the gallery, Lia waited while Jan took photographs of the three pieces. They weren't her best, but better than some sold in the past.

"The colors aren't as bold as the stolen ones," Jan said matter-of-factly, inspecting the art resting against the white gallery wall. "However, the perspective is fresh."

"These were painted before my parents died. The ones you originally selected are mostly more recent works."

"I can't paint," Jan said. "But I'd love to collaborate with you and see what happens with a multimedia piece."

Lia paused. Not that again. Insulting Jan was the last thing she wanted to do, but mixed media wasn't her thing. Art speaks to people differently and trying to collaborate on the technical might work, but she could never take someone else's emotions, make them her own, and translate it into a painting. It just wasn't how she worked, not how she connected to the flow of creativity. "All I can say is maybe. It's been a rough day."

"Oh. Right. What was I thinking?" Jan said apologetically. "You've got to be in shock, so I hate to ask, but will you deliver the rest of the work tomorrow?"

"Before you close."

Lia flashed a half-hearted smile. The show had to be a success. Otherwise, lack of funds would mean closing the door to the history of her whole life and doing what Craig wanted all along—selling the farm.

While uncertainty had her in a chokehold, two things became crystal clear. One—she would take a risk, a big risk and show Lucas her heart. Two—the time had come to give up the lease on her art studio. She didn't need it as a safety net. No matter what happened with Lucas or with the farm, she wouldn't return to the city to paint, even if it meant living in a trailer in a sunflower field.

With her decisions made, she climbed into the truck and mentally compared the day to scaling a daunting mountain. She'd tumbled into a deep emotional bottom, free-fall style. The climb up promised a treacherous route.

She still had everything to lose.

Chapter 11

Votive candles blazed from every ledge in the art studio. Soft white light danced against the brick walls. Under other circumstances, the loft bathed in candlelight looked romantic. Now, dim lighting set the mood Lia needed for wallowing, indulging in a pity party.

"You've got until the sun comes up," she muttered, "to get on with life." She prided herself in being a glass-half-full sort of person. She had never ventured down the dark path of self-pity, not before or since her parents passed away. It would be like falling down the rabbit hole as Alice did in Wonderland, or waking up in Oz like Dorothy. There had to be something positive in the cloud of doom following her around. Many folks were worse off than she was. Poor Megan, for example, still stung from abandonment, and her parents lived only several states away, but to Megan it was as though they were dead. They claimed they couldn't bear losing the farm and breaking up the family, yet they ignored their teen-aged daughter? It made no sense. That had to be worse, right? But Megan was doing fine.

Love in the Britton household had been as plentiful as the kernels of corn on all the cobs in Kansas. She loved her parents that much and more. The ache of missing them beat stronger sometimes more than others. This was one of those times. While she was no longer the little girl who had climbed into her father's lap waiting for him to rock her pain away or who cuddled next to her mother and cried on her shoulder, she missed hashing out adult problems with them. They had always helped her find her own solutions, something Craig wasn't good at.

The scent of cinnamon drifted through the air, reminding her of her mom's famous cookies and breakfast rolls, the ones her mom made to cheer her up. Cinnamon equaled *Mom* in her memories. Stimulating her olfactory senses was the best way to connect with her mom. The pain of wanting her close thumped an echoing beat in the hollow emptiness of her chest.

Lia sat on the paint-stained wooden floor in old sweat pants and a worn t-shirt borrowed from Karen who'd sublet the studio. She painted black onto a small canvas, the color mirrored her mood. Tears dribbled down her cheeks. She brushed them away with the back of her hand. One escaped and dropped onto the painting, her rendition of grief. Having the show paintings disappear, brazenly stolen in broad daylight while she walked Jack only feet away, hurt as though someone had taken a box cutter to her heart. She cherished each painting and mourned their loss. Whenever a painting sold, she consoled herself with the belief that the person buying it had an emotional connection to it, loved it as she did, otherwise, they wouldn't be laying down cash. Buying art wasn't like buying a bathroom rug, something easily expendable.

Beside her on the floor, Jack raised his head and

bumped her arm. His soulful expression reflected her feelings. He rose and settled behind her, his side against her backside. He rested his head on his front paws. Her sweet four-legged boy always stayed close whenever she was sad.

Startled by the noise, Lia blinked when the door to the studio rolled open.

"Hi there! I was afraid I might miss you. Love the candles. How about some music?" Karen walked toward the armoire housing the sound system.

"Something happy," Lia replied. "My mom used to love Stevie Wonder. I need to get a grip and break away from stark and morose." Lia scanned the room, taking in Karen's art. "You've been very prolific here."

"It's the perfect place to paint."

Soft sounds of smooth jazz glided through the studio. Karen sat on a pillow across from Lia.

"I'm going to spend the night, Karen. Is that okay with you?"

"Technically, it's your studio." Karen cocked her head. "You don't look so good. What's wrong?"

Lia swallowed hard. "The dozen paintings for my show were stolen today."

"No!" Karen slammed her palms to the floor. "You called the police, right? Of course, you did. I'm so sorry. What are you going to do?"

"I took over three others I had stored here, but those paintings are several years old. I'm a much better painter now although the abstract, Five Seasons, won first place in the Plaza Art Festival five years ago. That was my first big regional win. Jan at the gallery wants a few I have at home. But this isn't the show I planned."

"Why don't you come home with me tonight?"

"Thanks, but I need to be alone." Lia shook her head.

Karen's frown deepened. "Again, I'm really sorry about your paintings, but this"—she pointed her finger at Lia and made circles—"goes way beyond the loss of some paintings. What's really going on?"

"It's complicated." Lia couldn't utter the words to share how hard-hitting and deep the loss of the paintings went, not without completely losing it.

"A margarita might help *uncomplicate* things," Karen said, gathering her purse and jingling her keys. "I need to deliver a gift. Girl, are you sure you want to spend the night alone here?"

"I've got Gentleman Jack. You go. I need to be alone." She hoped Karen would take the hint.

"Why don't I stay with you? I'll walk Jack. I'll run to the store and get some food for him. You won't have to worry about anything." Karen scooped up Jack's leash. "I'll open a bottle of wine. We'll drink straight from the bottle and munch on cheese and crackers. Very bohemian of us." Karen clapped. "Come, Jack. Want to go for a ride with me? You can meet my boy, Lucky. He'll want to play."

Behind Lia, Jack moved. He scooted around, resting his head on her knee, and stared with eyes so sad her heart seized. Who knew a dog could look so grieved. "Thanks, but Jack will stay with me."

"Seriously. Come with me, Lia. You can take my bedroom for privacy and cry your eyes out there, if you need to. I promise not to interrupt. I won't even hand you tissues. I'll worry if I leave you alone tonight," Karen said, her voice imploring.

As the sun began to set, it took Lia's resolve. The toll from the day ripped her defenses away like pulling a bandage off a festering wound. Lia stabbed the canvas with the paintbrush. "I just can't understand why anyone would want to steal my work."

"I know, sweetie. Tomorrow I'll start checking internet sites to see if they show up."

"Karen," Lia confided, "the police interrogated me. I felt so stupid. I didn't think to insure my work, which is the only reason they stopped their inquisition. Can you believe they thought *I'd* staged a heist of my own work for insurance money?" The insinuation by the investigating officer had shocked her as much as finding her paintings gone.

Karen let go of the leash and dropped to the floor again. "Okay, you win. If you won't leave, I'll stay with you."

"I'll be fine. This is, after all, still my studio. I've spent nights here in the past."

"But, not in the last year. You have two choices. I stay or you come with me."

Lia sat up straighter. "Please understand, I don't intend to be rude. I need to work myself out of this funk."

"And you can do it with company. If you were painting with blue, I'd agree, but you're painting black."

Bam. Bam. Bam.

The pounding startled Lia. She sucked in a breath. Karen jumped. Gentleman Jack jerked alert, barked, ran to the door, and then darted back toward her. Halfway, he turned again and barked at the door.

Bam.

Whoever pounded on the door meant business.

"Amelia?" The loud, muffled male voice on the other side of the door was unrecognizable.

Gentleman Jack barked louder.

"Jack, quiet," Lia commanded. "Yes?"

"Amelia, it's Lucas!"

"Lucas?" Karen asked.

Lia pursed her lips. Why had he come? She looked a mess, and her face had to be puffy from crying.

"Amelia, I heard Jack. I saw your truck. I know you're here. Open the door."

"Who is this crazy person?" Karen's quizzical expression reminded Lia that Karen was an art friend, one who knew little about her country life.

"Please let him in."

Karen slid the door open. Gentleman Jack squirmed into an attentive *sit* on the floor beside Lia. Though he was a bird dog, he often imitated a guard dog. One twice his size. She wrapped her arms around his neck, pulling him close for a hug. The last thing she needed was pity from Lucas. Jack would help her put on a brave front.

The moment the door moved fully aside, Lucas rushed in. Jack raced over and danced at his feet, following Lucas to her as if to say, *Thank God you're here. I don't know what else to do with her.*

"Are you okay?" Lucas pulled Lia to standing and wrapped her in a bear hug.

Lia nodded, unable to speak. Lucas had come to find her, something she'd dreamed about. But not now. Not like this. She swallowed hard. Her mind held up a red stop sign. The only thing missing was someone blowing a whistle and shouting, *Stop!* Stepping back, she put space between them, an invisible wall of protection around herself.

"Gentleman Jack, here," Karen called. "Ah, I'm going to walk him. I'll even get him some food before I drop him back here."

Jack cut his gaze to Lia, then pawed at Karen. He was ready to go. Lucas could handle things. Karen left the studio with Jack obediently heeling at her side.

"We'll be back in bit." Karen closed the door on her way out.

"How did you know where to find me?" Lia tried to keep suspicion from her voice. Wrapping her arms around her waist, she held her ground. Lucas was the only man who could reach inside and grab hold of her vulnerabilities. He and Craig might try to use the mess she'd gotten into against her.

"Shush." Lucas reached for her, running one hand gently from the crown of her head, down her back, down to her waist as if checking to ensure she was in one piece. "This had to be a hard day. Just let me hold you."

Never good at the *damn-if-I-care attitude* Zoë had perfected, Lia blanked all caution warnings from her mind and snuggled close to him. The heat of him comforted her. The bear hug offered shelter against the battles of the day.

"It will be okay," he whispered over and over again. Was he trying to convince her or himself?

Lia clung to him. The spot where her cheek

rested against his blue chambray shirt darkened from tears. She trembled. Had that whimper come from her?

Lucas held her tighter, his embrace an invitation to safety. Her heartache began to dissolve. Her spirits lifted out of the black hole, buoyed just above the surface, discovering warmth and light. He made her believe his words, now a mantra in her brain. Yet, resignation still clung tightly to her heart.

She sighed. "There's no reason for me to be upset. Tears won't change anything. I have to figure out how to carry on. Craig was right. I've failed."

Lucas cupped her face tenderly in his hands, his thumbs stroking away the remaining wet streaks on her cheeks. She searched his eyes for a stern *I told you so*, but didn't find the painful accusation. Instead, she witnessed an anguish she'd never seen before.

"You haven't failed," Lucas said with conviction. "I'll help you find a way to make it work."

"I can't take any help from you." She straightened. "I have to make it on my own. Otherwise, I have lost."

"Farmers help farmers. Neighbors help neighbors. That's the unwritten code. Your brother tried to help me, help my dad, but he couldn't pull a miracle out of his pocket. Craig doesn't want you to suffer what my family went through. His intentions are good, but his actions are a bit misguided. Know this, Amelia. *You* haven't failed."

"All I have left is a second-rate show with maybe ten or twelve old paintings. My crop. And a few more boxes."

"That's better than nothing."

Lia dropped to a cushion on the floor, sat cross-legged, and motioned for Lucas to sit on the one facing her. Hope danced a nervous cha-cha in her stomach. "I was so close, so close to turning the corner. Now it's as though all my dreams are scattering in the wind, blowing like dandelion seeds."

She remembered the morning she'd tripped and scattered boxes on the ground. Maybe it *had* been an omen. If not a foretelling of the future—that was Helen's department—it sure spoke of the past, one that kept inching into the present no matter how hard she battled. Had she run out of options? Had Craig won the war of wills?

Lucas took her hands in his. "I'll help you get through this. We'll find a way. Together. You must trust all is not lost. You still have the harvest."

"Thank you." Lia offered a half-hearted grin. "You're a good big-brother's best friend if ever there was one."

Lucas shook his head. "I'm not here because of Craig." He gently lifted her chin. "I'm here because of you."

The tenderness in his voice hooked her soul. She was a fish on the end of Lucas's line. Did he mean to reel her in or leave her dangling? He had for the last year. Rejection now would absolutely kill her.

Lia shrugged, hoping he couldn't see through her guise. "Old friend. Good neighbor."

"Right," Lucas snapped with an impatient growl. With one swift move, he pulled her close and crushed his lips against hers. Her surprise melted into hopefulness. She sagged against him. The warmth of his lips and the heat radiating through his hands warmed her and enveloped her in the softest of silk. All her worries floated away, drifting up as though carried on a hot air balloon. Lucas filled all of her senses.

When he broke their connection and frowned, Lia's eyes widened. He couldn't possibly lament the kiss. She chewed her bottom lip. She wouldn't allow him to think, only feel. There would be no regrets between them. The woman in her, not Craig's little sister, needed him. Leaning in, she teased his lips with the tip of her tongue. "I'm right here. Don't go away...neighbor." She added the last word to keep things light.

"There's nothing old-friend-like or neighborly about this." Lucas kissed her again. His warm hands drifted over her shoulders, burning a trail down her arms and resting on her hips. His kisses stoked a fire burning inside her, the heat increasing. She tensed her muscles, then relaxed into the delight of desire dancing in her heart.

Lia leaned closer, wrapping her arms around his neck. A magnetic current flowed between them and lit her up inside like an amusement park's night-light parade. The buried longing she had for him erupted into joy.

She pushed her fingers through his hair. Touching him zinged arousal to the core of her being. He was the one, the only one. She wanted only him forever.

Lucas pulled her onto his lap. Overflowing with anticipation, she wiggled into comfort. He reclaimed her lips, covering her mouth eagerly, hungrily. She shivered with pleasure. That feeling had no beginning or end…it just was…like floating on clouds in heaven with angels serenading them.

"Amelia?" Lucas whispered.

She hated it when he broke the kiss. She reached for him again.

"I think we need to talk about this before…" He kissed her forehead tenderly.

"*Talk?*" Trembling, she touched her lips where his lips had been, then leaning closer, she sought more nonverbal communication.

"Yes, talk." Lucas leaned back out of her reach.

Her blooming desire withered only a bit. Every ounce of her being wanted to rip away his clothes and make love to him. Wanton woman replaced nice girl-next-door. "No."

"We have to clear the air…before—"

"Lucas Dwyer, are you going to make me beg?"

He sighed with exasperation. His reaction shouldn't have surprised her. Lucas always wanted to do the right thing. This once she had to convince him now was perfect. "Kiss me again. No talking. Just kissing."

His eyebrows rose. He scooted back several feet, his back resting against the brick wall and his legs stretched out long. He laced his fingers together behind his head, and she wanted to believe the move was to keep himself from reaching for her. Clearly, he wrestled with some mental demon.

Then he patted the floor beside him.

"Really?" she groaned. Taking him up on the offer, she sat next to him, hip to hip, and waited. His kisses weren't chaste or brotherly. He had to see her as a woman. Waiting a minute more wouldn't hurt, but he wanted to talk *now*? The ache deep in her core said he better talk fast, otherwise her need for him would take control. For once, she wouldn't stop it.

When the silence grew, she folded and unfolded her hands, forcing herself not to touch. Her fingers itched to caress him. Another few seconds ticked by. She hummed and gently rocked. She folded her arms and held her elbows. Dread dropped like a brick in her gut. Maybe he didn't feel the same sizzle when he kissed her. Maybe he wanted a second chance to know his attraction to her didn't run deep. Or maybe he couldn't get past her being the *little sister*. If he regretted kissing her for one single second, it would leave a hole in her heart, one the size of the state of Kansas.

"Lucas?"

Lucas punched his fist into his open hand. The smack of skin against skin startled Lia. "This isn't what I had planned," he told her.

"You came with a plan?" There was nothing about any plan she wanted to hear. "Let's talk plans later."

"Amelia, let's take a moment here."

"How many moments?"

Lucas sighed and raised an eyebrow.

"Fine. We'll do this your way for now. How did you find me?" She rushed her words. She refused to hear regret come from his lips. He could have another thirty seconds. Only that long. Her lips refused to wait any longer. This could be her final chance to convince him of her feelings, and she intended to take it.

Whatever the aftermath, she'd deal with it later.

"Craig called." Lucas seemed to regain his composure. "Evidently, the police called him since the truck's insurance is technically in both your names. He's worried. Called me. Asked me to check on you."

"Craig. Craig. Craig." Lia pulled away. Anger welled in her chest, but need fought a good battle. A minute more and she'd use everything in her seduction arsenal to bend Lucas's will.

"So you're going play the big-brother card here?" Rejection pumped in her heart. *It couldn't be true. It couldn't be true.* "As you can see, I'm fine. I keep telling you and Craig. I'm a big girl now. In fact, I'm a grown woman. I can take care of myself. A few tears do not mean I can't handle things. You can report to him that all is A-OK."

Lucas flinched as if she'd slapped him. Maybe he had really come because of her. Not because she was Craig's sister? No matter how comforting his kisses and hugs were, she wouldn't accept pity. Especially from him. History would not repeat itself. She wasn't a rejected high-school girl or his best friend's grieving sister. She was a woman—who wanted a man, who wanted her—just for who she was.

"I'm sorry you had to come all the way here, only to turn around and leave. I'll be fine. As I said, I'm staying with a friend. Karen will be back with Jack in a minute." But she'd be darned if she would let him leave without truly looking at her like a man looks at a woman.

She rose and began to remove the ugly sweatpants.

"Are you staying here or at her house?" Lucas

choked out his words.

"Why?" She wiggled out of the pants and kicked them to the side. She prayed she had his full attention. Raising the old t-shirt over her head, she revealed her bra and panties.

"Because"—Lucas swallowed hard—"I brought a sleeping bag. I can stretch out here on the floor or on her couch."

"But—"

"You can't seem to get it through your head. I'm not leaving you alone tonight," Lucas growled, jumping up and reaching for her.

Lia grabbed his shirt and hung on. Planting her lips against his, she kissed him hard. His hands roamed her body. He rained kisses on her face and neck. Her heart danced pirouettes and high leaps in a ballet where she was a ballerina and Lucas, her cavalier.

"You need to get this through your head. I'm not leaving you alone tonight," she said huskily.

With a short hop, she jumped into Lucas's arms, wrapping her legs around his hips. His hands cradled her butt, and he backed toward the old chaise in the corner. When he sat, she straddled his lap and kissed his face, his neck, ignoring the slight scruffiness of his beard. Her heart pounded like a hundred drummers playing in a marching band. The first taste of joy lifted her spirits so high she could float all the way to the moon.

"Slow down, Amelia." Lucas's voice was low and full of strained emotion. It reminded her of warm honey, the way it soothed. Her heart beat faster. Sensations tickled her insides in new and delicious ways.

"This isn't exactly what I envisioned," he said, nibbling on her earlobe.

"Shut up, Lucas," she whispered back while unbuttoning his shirt, dying to feel the warmth of his flesh. "No need to talk. Just feel." She placed his hands over her breasts. It may have been an involuntary reaction on his part, but his slight squeeze produced a blooming of desire in her. She wouldn't let him turn back now.

She was waiting on an art show.

She was waiting on a crop.

She wasn't willing to wait a minute more to make love to Lucas Dwyer.

Sliding his shirt over his shoulders, the fabric fell, the cuffs still wrapped around his wrists. She traced fingers down his smooth, hard chest until she reached the top of his jeans. He leaned back against the wall, shoulders relaxed, allowing her full access. A sexy grin spread across his face. He didn't make a move to prevent her fingers from unbuttoning the single button. She playfully tugged at the zipper.

"I would've never taken you for a vixen." Lucas's body tensed. His fingers kneaded her flesh gently.

"Shhh. This is the only kind of talking I want to do." She stroked the hardness of his manhood.

Lucas scooped her up and laid her on the chaise. She glued her gaze to his body as he slowly, too agonizingly slow for her, unbuttoned his cuffs, and let his shirt drop to the floor. Like an experienced male stripper, he removed his socks and jeans. Lia stared at the man she loved. Lucas in briefs made her knees weak. Every inch of his body was lean and muscled, a hard-working farmer's body wearing a farmer's tan like a tattoo. Her insides clenched, craving to consummate and end the physical longing enslaving her body.

"Amelia," Lucas whispered, stretching long beside her on the chaise. She rolled on her side to face him. "There's something I want you to know," he continued. His fingers reached for the hooks on her bra and released them. He tugged and tossed the barely-there garment over his shoulder. Captivated by his eyes, his face, his lips, she barely heard his words. Her body hummed a symphony of desire.

"What?" she murmured, aching to feel the heat of his hands on her. She bent her leg and, with her foot, traced a line down his calf. As she reached to remove her panties, he slapped at her hands.

"There is only you and me"—he slid her panties down and they went the way of her bra, over his shoulder—"right now."

On her back, Lia stretched and arched her hips as he moved on top of her, his elbows bracing his upper body, the weight of the rest of him settled over her. His hardness pressed into her apex in a series of short thrusts. Her body contracted around him.

"Right now," she said, moving under him for the perfect fit. Leaning upward, she captured his lips. "You. Are. Mine."

Lucas groaned and crushed his lips against hers.

Their bodies rocked together. With each simple motion, her core craved more of him.

She'd waited so long for Lucas. The feel of him. Hard. Soft. Strong. Gentle.

Need shoved away desire.

She rocked against him faster. His thrusts matched hers.

Closing her eyes, she gave herself over to the sensations tingling every last nerve. Heat raced through her body. She arched her pelvis more, clawing at Lucas's back. All awareness dissolved. Only she and Lucas existed in a cocoon.

"Amelia!" Lucas cried. His body tightened.

"Oh," Lia groaned. "Heaven."

Fireworks on the Fourth of July. Skyrockets at midnight. Nothing compared with making love to Lucas.

He thrust harder.

She'd reached a peak, but then her climax shot higher.

Time had no meaning. Desire surged, pulsing steadily.

Lucas's body relaxed.

She floated back to earth, back to the chaise in her studio. She opened her eyes to find Lucas studying her.

"I love you," Lucas said, planting a kiss on her nose.

Her breath caught. Her chest tightened.

Had he really said it?

Her body vibrated from her head to her toes. "I lo—"

"Shhh, Amelia. Don't say anything. Let's just enjoy right now."

"But—"

Lucas silenced her objections, peppering kisses down her cheek, neck, and chest. He cuddled her into an embrace, snuggling her closer to him.

Later she would hear all about his plan. The future now shimmered with the light of a million stars. Hope surged through her and knitted fragile links between her and Lucas.

She'd make him understand just how much she loved him. She had a plan, too.

Chapter 12

Lucas grabbed for his jeans when he heard sounds echoing in the hallway. He managed the zipper and buttoned up as Karen slid the studio's door slightly open.

"I'll take Jack," Lucas said to her, leaning in the doorway, trying to appear casual, as though Karen was used to seeing a half-dressed man in the studio. He reached for Jack's leash. "I'm going to stay here with Amelia tonight," he whispered. "Anything you *must* have out of here before you can leave?" He hoped she took the less than subtle hint. The last thing he wanted was for Amelia to wake and awkwardness over his presence to fill the room and mar the evening he had planned.

With eyes wide as saucers, Karen shook her head and stared at his bare chest. He crossed his arms to cover himself from the woman's intense scrutiny.

"Nope. Not a thing." She winked. "Glad you're here." She turned and sauntered down the hallway toward the elevator. A few steps away, she turned back. "Lucky Lia." She whistled low.

Lucas slowly slid the door closed, but only halfway. He winced at the squeak and vowed to bring WD-40 from his truck to silence the noise. Pulling a blanket from the antique armoire in the far corner of the large space, Lucas covered Lia as she dozed. Jack jumped on the chaise and settled next to her. "Good boy." Lucas praised the dog. "Stay with her. I'll be right back." Jack rested his head on Lia's side as though he understood every word spoken to him.

Grabbing his cell and his boots, Lucas turned sideways to exit the studio through the narrow opening, then slid the door closed the rest of the way, hoping for a silent escape. Every sound from the building—the elevator, doors closing, and people chatting—echoed in the hallways ricocheted from every hard surface. The noises reverberated in his ears, ratcheting up the tension mounting in his chest. And the last thing he needed was for Craig to call Amelia and wake her up.

Lucas tucked his cell phone in his front pocket, backed to the hall's brick for balance, then bent to pull on his boots. Before he finished with the second one, his cell phone vibrated. He shot to standing, scraping his heel as he crammed his foot all the way into his boot. Pulling out the phone, he said, "Give me a few minutes. Let me call you back."

"Sure. But only five," Craig said.

Lucas ended the call. He walked on the balls of his feet to keep his boot heels from clunking against the concrete floor. "How do women walk in high heels?" he muttered.

Thirty steps later, he reached the elevator, feet cramping, but at least Amelia hadn't woken.

Once outside, Lucas let go of a deep breath. It was one thing to have a poker face, but quite another to have a poker voice. With Craig worried about Amelia, rightly so after the events of the day, Lucas considered the best way to express his feelings for

Amelia to her brother. To blurt out, "I love your sister," would be weird. True, he and Amelia had a brother-sister relationship in the past, but his feelings ripened into much more when he became a man, when he went away to war, and since he had returned home.

Opening the tailgate on his truck, he parked his butt on it, ignoring the few people passing on the sidewalk. Pulling out his phone, he contemplated exactly what news to share with his best friend. If Amelia were anyone else's sister, he'd be telling Craig how he loved her and wanted to spend the rest of his life with her. If not on a farm, at least in the country. Heaven knew, he'd never survive the city.

"If I say, 'I love your sister and want to marry her,' he'll laugh his ass off, or worse yet, when he finds out what just transpired, he'll want a duel at dawn. How did a man born and raised in the country come to equate vast open spaces, glorious sunsets, and fresh everything with an inferior lifestyle?"

"Are you speaking to me, young man?" An older man approached on the sidewalk. His cane tapped against the pavement as he walked.

"No, sir. Talking to myself."

"Crazy are you?" the man asked as he continued walking.

"Yep. Crazy about a woman."

"Continue on, then," the man said as he passed. "Try telling her about it rather than talking to strangers."

Lucas saluted the older gentleman, then pushed Craig's number, deciding to only answer questions asked, and not volunteer any additional information until he and Amelia had a chance to talk about what the future might hold. Maybe they'd begin their discussion over dinner tonight. Music, wine, and a meal at Tavern City down the street. Tonight, they'd make love. The studio had a romantic vibe, especially with all the candles. Lia clearly liked that.

"About time. Twelve minutes isn't five," Craig said, brusquely.

"She's fine," Lucas replied, trying to keep his voice even.

"You're sure? I know how sensitive she is. I hate that I'm not there. I'm glad you're my proxy."

Lucas groaned inwardly. He had not been the least bit *brotherly* with Amelia. He was going for *lover*. But he would stick to his plan. Only answer questions asked.

"She's obviously upset about the loss of her paintings. I'm going to take her to dinner—"

"That's a great idea!"

"I've to get some WD-40 out of my truck and lube up the squeak in the studio door."

"What do you think of the place? It's the perfect place for her to paint. By the way, the police called me back."

Lucas swallowed. An idea hit him and he didn't much like the impact. He hated to ask the question, but Craig had already lined up a buyer for the farm. With the paintings missing and the art show teetering on the edge of failure, the reality of Amelia's future had taken a one-eighty turn from what she wanted. If Craig had staged the theft or had anything, no matter how remote, to do with it, he'd probably have to kill him. At the very least, their friendship would be dead.

Linda Joyce

"Craig, tell me honestly. There's no way you had anything to do with the missing paintings, is there?"

"What!" Craig's outrage screamed through the speaker on the phone. "How could you even ask me that? Asshole! I would never—"

"Forget I asked. It was an errant thought. But I had to ask. We both know how much you want her off the farm."

"Why does everyone question my motives?" Craig shouted. "I only want what's best for my sister. Our parents are gone, and I'm all she's got. I'm here for her. I have to make her do the right thing, do what's in her best interest. You of all people should understand that."

"Craig," Lucas said, his voice low, calm, and even. "You're wrong."

"Really? About which part?"

"You can't make her do anything. Your intentions are admirable, but you have tunnel vision. Amelia is a strong woman. She knows what's best for her. And..."

"Spit it out. What else?" Craig roared.

"You're not all she's got. You haven't been here for Amelia for the last year. I have."

Silence hung between them. Lucas looked at his phone. Seconds ticked away. He'd spoken the truth. The ball was in Craig's court.

"What's your point, Dwyer?" Craig said dryly after a full minute of silence.

"How about talking with Amelia about all of this? Help her get what she wants. I'm not saying you should go into debt. But there are options neither of you have explored."

149

A text message from Amelia dinged on Lucas's phone. *Where are you?*

"I've got to go. I'll call you later," Lucas said.

"You do that," Craig said. "This conversation isn't over."

Lucas ended the call, grabbed the WD-40 from his tool chest, and headed inside the building. *On my way up*, he texted back.

When Lucas reached the studio and slid open the squeaking door, he noticed his shirt and the pile of clothes missing from the floor. He paused, considering what had transpired between him and Amelia. His whole world shifted. He'd made love to the woman he wanted to spend the rest of his life with.

Breathing in deeply, his chest filled with air sweeter than spring after a cold hard winter. His heart swelled with love. The longing buried deep in his chest thrummed through his body. Even if theirs had to be a long-distance relationship, he would find a way to make a relationship with her work. "Amelia?"

"Over here."

He passed Jack sleeping on the chaise as he walked to the far end of the loft and turned the corner in the L-shaped studio space. A small sleeping area was tucked out of view from the front door. A bed, a nightstand, a single lamp. An intimate spot.

"Join me, Lucas?" Amelia lay propped on several pillows. She wore his shirt, which exposed the shapeliness of her bare legs. His heart beat a quick two-step. His body wanted to clear the distance between them in less than that, but his feet remained cemented to the spot where he stood.

"I'm going to remove the squeak from your door." It sounded lame. His body craved hers and urged him to jump into bed and explore her body. His fingers clenched the can tighter, his other hand curled into a fist by his side. Restraint. His plan had been to wine and dine her and *then* seduce her at the finest hotel in Kansas City. Passion and need engulfed them, emotions so strong nothing short of a nuclear explosion could have stopped what happened earlier. But now... maturity had to rule their next encounter. He was more than a failed farmer running a harvesting business, and he would treat his woman right.

"Come closer, Lucas," Amelia whispered, motioning him with her fingers. Her web netted him, pulling him closer and closer, and against his better judgment, his feet moved, stopping at the foot of the bed. Though he maintained a poker face, his hunger for her exploded. His desire would no longer fit into the condensed spaces of his heart, the same way he couldn't *unring* a bell.

"Closer." Amelia gazed at him with half-closed eyes. Her grin changed from saucy to smug. She had to realize what she did to him, setting his thudding heart, and incited the growing hardness in his jeans.

When she sprang from the bed and embraced his neck, he dropped the can of lubricant. Hitting the floor, it clanged, before rolling off somewhere. His attention remained on the woman in his arms. She wrapped her legs around his waist. He cupped her butt. Firm. Round. Feminine.

"Why won't you let me tell you how I feel about you?" Amelia asked.

"I'm fine with words, but showing is always better than telling." Lucas strained against the ache building in his body.

"I'm not asking for anything except for you to make love to me."

"Now is all we have. The future is too uncertain." Lucas shifted and began lowering Amelia to the bed. "I wanted to take you to dinner. A little music, some wine, and then a view of Kansas City from high above the town."

"That can wait." Amelia scooted further into the middle of the bed. She reached for him, one hand embracing the back of his neck. "The hunger I've got has nothing to do with food."

Lucas removed his boots and crawled toward her on the bed. His hands rested on either side of her head and supported the weight of his torso. With his knees bent, he arched over her. "I like the way you think. We'll start with dessert." He kissed her softly. She deepened the kiss, her tongue dancing with his. She tasted so sweet.

He lifted and rested back on his heels. Before him, Amelia looked more than delectable, a nymph oozing with sexiness, her hair fanned out and her legs stretched long.

"Amelia..."

"Shhh,"

"I've got to say this."

She folded her hands and rested them primly on her stomach as though she might be a corpse in a coffin.

"Give a guy a break," Lucas moaned. "I just wanted to say it wasn't Craig's fault you haven't had much of a dating life. I take full responsibility for that, and, we're about to change everything."

"One. Two. Three..." Amelia began counting.

Lucas hopped back and removed his pants. He again settled next to Amelia, spooning her side and wrapping an arm around her, his hand covering her breast. His erection pressed into her hip. She wiggled against him.

"Ohhh," he groaned. "You feel so damn good."

"Let's take it real slow," Amelia whispered. "We have all night."

Lucas kissed her neck. His need rose. His control slipped. "I need you now, Amelia."

She rolled over to face him.

"Let your body do the talking." She nipped at his lower lip with her teeth.

A deafening sound exploded in the air. Lucas jumped.

Jack barked and appeared from around the corner. He launched himself onto the bed.

"What the hell?" Lucas shouted.

"Fire alarm. Grab your clothes and let's go."

"It could be a false alarm." Lucas reached for Amelia, but she slipped through his grasp.

"Maybe, but I don't want to take that chance." She ran into the other room.

"Bad timing," he groaned through clenched teeth. Tense, his body cursed the blaring alarm, but the loud noise killed any possibility of romance. By the time he slid into his pants and pulled on his boots, Amelia had reappeared, completely dressed, and shoved his shirt at him.

With her purse over her shoulder, she clipped the

leash on Jack. Together they raced to the door. "Get low," Lucas said before shoving open the studio door. The hall was smokeless. Other tenants filed out of their units and headed toward the stairs.

Lucas grabbed Amelia's hand, pulling her up. "Stay close."

When they reached the sidewalk in front of the building, Lucas pointed to a spot across the street. As they made their way through the crowd, a fire truck and an ambulance pulled up. A policeman stopped, lights flashing on his car, got out, and began directing traffic. "Everyone, keep moving away from the building. Move down the block."

A second police car arrived. Sirens wailed in the distance. Smoke billowed. Flames shot out from a fourth-floor window.

Amelia gasped. "Oh, no!" The terror on her face hit Lucas squarely in the chest. Was there nothing he could do to protect the woman he loved?

"Where are you parked?" Lucas asked. Standing around made no sense. If the whole building burned, they didn't have to watch the moment by moment, play by play, a cremation of what had once been a big part of Amelia's life.

"Parked?" Amelia trembled in his embrace.

"Amelia, look at me." He cupped her chin. "Where's your truck?"

"Around the corner in the pay lot. It was the only place with enough space for my truck and trailer. Why?"

"There's nothing we can do here."

"I can't leave!" Her brows furrowed. Her eyes bulged.

"Trust me. It's all just stuff."

Amelia shook her head as though in complete denial. She bolted and ran toward the building, dragging Jack alongside her. Lucas caught her just as one of the policemen stepped directly into her path. "Ma'am, you can't go in there."

"My paintings!" Amelia cried. "I need my paintings. The fire isn't on my floor. It's on the opposite end of the building. Please! Let me go."

"It's not safe," Lucas and the officer said in unison.

"I'll take care of her." Lucas turned Amelia around and gently guided her to the corner. The rising flames brightened the darkening sky. Dusk had rolled away, but ambient city light and the fire killed all opportunity to view the universe of stars he was accustomed to viewing in the country. Any thought he might have had about moving to the city to be with Amelia burned away same as the flames were incinerating the building.

"Let's go to your truck. Let's drop off the trailer. Then we'll come back and scope out the scene."

"No!" Amelia shouted. "You go. Take my keys. I'm staying right here."

"I can't leave you. It only makes sense for you to come with me."

Her shoulders slumped.

Lucas led her down the street, around the perimeter the police had created, and away from the burning building. They crossed over to the next block on the opposite side of the building. The illuminated parking lot sign guided them to the right spot. However, as they neared, additional police were cordoning off that side of the street.

"Could we get that truck and trailer out of there?" Lucas asked, with Amelia beside him, her gaze transfixed on the burning building. Water poured onto the fire, beautiful and destructive.

"Yeah, just head out the exit on the other side of the lot."

Close to midnight, Lucas had settled Amelia into a hotel room with a view of the city. The fire blazed many blocks away. Every news station in town reported on it. Avoiding the sight of the destruction was impossible.

Amelia curled up in bed wearing a robe taken from the closet. Her attention focused solely on the television. Jack huddled close to her, barely visible, white fur against white bed linens.

Luca stood at the window. The vision he'd carried about sharing a special night in this hotel with Amelia was ruined. The intimacy and closeness he dreamed of had been drowned out, just like the blaze drowning thanks to the firefighters.

When his cell phone rang, he grabbed for it on the first ring. "Yeah."

"I saw the news," Craig said.

"It doesn't look good," Lucas replied. From the bed, Amelia groaned when part of a wall collapsed on the building. Lucas stepped into the hall. "At least I know you didn't have anything to do with this fiasco." Lucas couldn't contain his sarcasm.

"I'll take that as your attempt at humor given the stress of the situation," Craig responded, dryly.

"We dropped the trailer at U-Haul. We're at Center City Hotel. I brought her here because she won't go home."

"You're sure she's alright?"

"Well, she's not happy, but she's safe."

"I talked to the police again," Craig continued. "That truck stop is a target for thieves. They'll steal anything they think will make them a fast buck. The police guestimate because she had so many paintings with her, the thieves figured the paintings were worth big money."

"Maybe they'll get them. Amelia's trying to maintain a stiff upper lip. She hasn't broken down or cried. She even called Gus knowing I was listening. He'll start harvesting the corn next week. You've got to tell her about your plans to sell."

"No, not yet. Besides, I can't sell unless she agrees to it, too. But the buyer's getting antsy. There are other farms on the market. I'll talk to her over the weekend. On Sunday, after her birthday party."

"What if she refuses?"

"Then I'll remind her that half of the crop is mine. I'll demand payment. Then she'll be forced into selling. With only a few boxes left, her paintings gone, a second-rate showing, and only half the crop for income, moving back to KC will be more appealing. There she can focus on her art."

"Only where will she go? The loft will soon be rubble."

The sound of a fist pounding a hard surface floated through the phone. "Dammit! The loft is completely destroyed?"

"I don't know about completely, but whatever the fire doesn't consume water will have ruined. Let's get through tonight and see how everything looks in the morning."

"Should I call her now? I want her to know I care." Craig sounded like a whipped man.

"Tomorrow." Lucas closed his phone. He understood Craig's position. Like him, he had a sister he wanted to protect. He'd made a mess of that on Sunday. Made Megan cry when she thought he was abandoning her like their parents had abandoned them for Arizona. However, unlike Craig, he wasn't trying to strangle the life out of Megan by making her live in a place she didn't want anymore.

Amelia wanted the farm. Wanted a life in Harvest. Would she accept his help to hang on to the farm? Could he intercede at the bank? He could put his equipment up for collateral and buy Craig out. One thing he'd learned in the military—patience. Wait for a clear shot. Then take it. He'd waited a full year for Amelia to live through her grief. It wouldn't have been fair to sweep her off her feet while sorrow wrapped her heart. He refused to use undue influence while she grieved. He wanted a solid foundation with her, not Fourth of July fireworks fizzling out in minutes. And while he admired her strength and gritty determination, Craig's concerns about her staying on the farm had some merit.

Was there a way for him to balance life and come out the winner of Amelia's heart?

Chapter 13

The next morning Lia woke and stretched. She blinked the room into focus. Uneasiness crept up her spine. Where was she? Looking around, it took a moment for her brain to register. This wasn't home or the loft...a hotel. The fire.

Lucas? Where was he?

Yesterday hadn't been a nightmare conjured up during REM sleep. Watching the fire destroy half of the building had kicked her feet out from under her and slammed her on her butt. However, Lucas's support had gotten her through the nightmare, which thanks to TV, was now emblazoned on her brain forever. While he'd held her tenderly, he'd so thoroughly captured her heart. Even through the darkest night, he brought hope shining into her world. She loved him. A warming sensation lessened her uneasiness. Her pulse fluttered. They had to find a way to make the relationship work.

Her mind raced. Thoughts spiraled up and down. Panic thumped a beat in her chest. She'd been so sure she could create the world she wanted after her parents' passing. The farm. Painting. Lucas. Yes, her parents' death had kicked her butt. In doing so, it had opened a new door, one that grounded her. Gave her comfort. Offered a new perspective on her well-ordered life.

Her mother had always pushed her to do more. Be more. Which had to be the reason Lia rejected the rebellious teenager times. She never got drunk. Never smoked. Never cut school. Never dated much. Painting meant everything. On canvas, she took risks. No bars on her emotions. No rules existed. That boldness garnered her local recognition and expanded to regional exposure. If she did nothing else, she had to paint. And she had to have a life with the man she loved.

"Lucas?" No response.

Where had he gone? She reached for Jack, but her hand came up empty. She leaned forward, tugging on the pillow beside her and stuffed it behind her back. A note fluttered onto the bed.

Taking Jack for a walk. Be back in a few. ~ L

What would she do without him? After last night, he probably thought she could play the Cowardly Lion in The Wizard of Oz. She lacked courage and had withdrawn into herself. Grunts and whimpers were her answers to any of his questions. Yet, ever gentle, Lucas put her needs first. He'd gotten her out of her clothes and into a robe and ordered hot chocolate to soothe her. He sat in bed beside her while the television blared about the two-alarm fire. She snuggled next to him after the news went off the air. He had held her until she fell asleep. He was right. Things would look different under the dawn of a new day. Now, with determination like Dorothy of Kansas, she wanted to go home, too.

A fumbling noise at the door drew her attention.

"Honey, I'm home," Lucas called in a sing-song voice. How wonderful would it be to hear his voice when she woke each morning and again before she went to sleep each night.

"I'm in here," she replied, joy pumping through her heart. Pushing all other thoughts aside, she wanted this time with the man she loved. Whatever might be happening beyond the hotel room, she didn't want to know.

Jack bounded into the bedroom of the suite. His stub tail wagged, shaking his entire back end. Lucas followed. Concern shadowed his halfhearted grin. Worry flickered in his eyes.

Lia opened her arms, intending to take Lucas into a hug, but Jack had other ideas. He jumped into her lap and squirmed. She petted him until he calmed down.

"Let's order room service." Lucas flopped onto the end of the bed. Jack rolled over and licked his face.

"I guess I'm *persona non grata* with Jack when you're around," Lia said.

Lucas stalked toward her like a tiger hunting prey. When they were nose-to-nose, he tilted her head and nipped at her earlobe. "I'm hungry, woman. I need food before I have you for dessert."

"Fine. Let's order." She giggled.

They scoured the menu and ordered enough eggs, sausage, muffins, and potatoes to feed several people.

"Yes, I want one hamburger patty, nothing on it. No salt or pepper or anything. Cooked well, then chopped up," Lucas said into the hotel phone. He winked at her. "Put that in a cereal bowl. And, I need a second bowl. Empty. Plus an extra bottle of water." Clearly, the room service person on the other end of the phone considered the request strange.

Concern flittered through Lia's mind. This might be the closest thing she'd ever get to a honeymoon with Lucas. Sadness plopped to the bottom of her stomach, making a splash. What did the future hold? With Lucas's departure for work out west looming, what would happen when he left for long periods of time?

She shoved the sad thoughts away and allowed contentment to flow. Taking a deep breath, she anchored those feelings in her heart. Allowing them to wash over her, she tingled. Love could lead her through darkness.

"Hey"—Lucas sat on the bed next to her, stuffed a pillow behind his back, and cradled her next to him, his arm around her shoulder—"Where are you?" He tapped her nose. "I see all sorts of wheels turning."

"There's a lot to talk about." She tilted her head, locking gazes with him. Would he see her love?

"And we will talk," Lucas whispered, stroking her cheek. "Let's just put that talk on pause until a little later. "I want to use sign language to communicate."

Lia signed, *I love you*.

Lucas chuckled. "I had something different in mind."

His hand left her cheek. His finger traced a line down her neck to the opening in the robe. He pushed it open and massaged her breast. When his mouth captured a tightening bud, he sucked, sending hot sensations straight to her core. Her body tightened. She slid flat on the bed. Her hand clenched the sheets. Her head lolled back as Lucas continued his tender ministrations to her wanton body.

She rolled on her side to face him and draped a leg over his. Reaching for the buttons on his shirt, she began to undo each one. Her breath grew shallow as she rocked her pelvis.

When all buttons were undone and she could finally smooth her fingers over his hard muscled chest, Lucas tugged on her robe's sleeve, freeing her from it. She sat up and finished removing the garment. Lucas followed her lead and, in a second, his clothes were tossed aside. Once again facing each other on the bed, Lia had full access to the body she had only recently been fully introduced to. She moved her hand tenderly over his arm, to his hip and down his thigh. To her delight, Lucas's manhood hardened. She stroked him and focused on his expressive face. A slight flutter of his eyes. A smile. A puckering of lips as his reached to claim hers. His kiss burned with intensity.

"Two can play that way," Lucas said, tweaking her breasts and running his hand down her abdomen to her legs. His fingers found her moist private opening. Her body tensed as her insides turned liquid.

"Now, Lucas. Now."

Sliding his finger into her wetness, he moved faster, but her words had given him the wrong direction. She pushed him flat, hurriedly straddled him, and quickly lowered herself onto him. He lifted his pelvis. She rocked against him. His hands covered her breasts and teased, shooting hot sensations to her core. He bucked. She rode, hanging on for the full ride. When a moan escaped her lips, Lucas quickened his pace. Her insides melted.

Hot.

Wet.

Wetter.

He sent her to heaven. Stars streaked. The world glowed.

Warmth bathed her body.

Lucas's body turned rigid. He moaned waves of deep and guttural pleasure. Together they melded. Heartbeat for heartbeat. Pant for pant. Thrust for thrust. Until they peaked, sliding off the edge of the earth.

Several moments later, limp and panting, she collapsed on top of him.

It was several minutes before she spoke.

"I've known you almost all my life. I didn't know you liked dessert before a meal." She traced a path from his jaw down his neck.

"If you're the dessert, honey," Lucas said, huskily, "I want it anytime I can get it."

Lia's forehead wrinkled. "I think we've wasted a lot of time. We could've been sharing dessert for years."

A knock sounded on the door. "Room service."

Lia hopped up and ran for the bathroom as Lucas grabbed a towel, wrapping it around his waist. She closed the bathroom door as he opened the door to the suite.

"Good morning, sir. Should I set this up by the couch?"

Lia couldn't hear the conversation after turning on the shower. When the water turned warm, she stepped in.

"Amelia, food will get cold."

"I'll be just a minute. Will you bring me the robe from the bed?"

"You don't need it. We might have dessert again." His tone was completely matter-of-fact.

Her cheeks flushed. Her knees nearly buckled. Leaning against the tile kept her from falling. The man made her feel utterly desirable. When she pulled open the shower curtain, Lucas offered a towel, and then held the robe like a valet offering a queen her mink-trimmed coat. Toweling off quickly, she slid her arms into soft terrycloth.

"Thank you." Another flush rose from her chest to her checks. Lucas stood before her completely naked.

"I won't ever deny you anything I can provide." He kissed the top of her head. "Now, food, woman. I'm starving."

She followed him to the sitting room and stood by the large picture window taking in the warmth radiating from the sun. Within her view, the Liberty Memorial surged upward into blue sky. Leaves on trees in Penn Valley Park shimmered in the breeze. The city skyline showed no hint of rising flames or traces of huffing black smoke. It was as though it had never happened. But it had. She needed to call Karen and console her friend.

Lucas pulled the coffee table out of the way and set the room service cart in its place. "Feast, Madame," Lucas said, raising the silver domed lids from the plates. Jack raced to his feet. Lucas placed a bowl of ground beef on the floor and filled a second bowl with water. "Jack, your feast." The dog wasted no time gobbling down his food.

Slipping into a chair, Lia reached for a slice of toast. She picked up silverware wrapped in a cloth napkin and unrolled it. "Which would you like first? Eggs or meat?"

Lucas cocked his head as though surprised by her question. "Eggs." She scooped some on a fork and held it out for him to eat.

"I could get used to this." He took the food.

"What exactly do you like about this?" She was fishing, but that was okay. A girl deserved some praise every now and then. Coming from the man she loved made it extra special.

"You, all to myself. Naked, or barely clothed." He reached and ran his finger from the hollow of her throat to the spot between her breasts. She shivered at his playfulness. "It gives me pleasure to see you smile. Watch the blush rise into your cheeks. Knowing it's because of me."

"If you don't stop that, we won't get through breakfast." She tapped his hand away when he attempted to untie the robe. "I am hungry. I need food."

Grabbing two strips of bacon, Lucas devoured them. He ate a few mouthfuls of eggs, picked at the potato hash, and buttered a slice of toast. His muscles rippled with each movement. Mesmerized, Lia ogled the man she wanted to spend the rest of her life with.

"Eat, woman. You need protein. Energy. I'm going to take you to bed again."

"Promise?"

"Guaranteed."

From somewhere in the bedroom, Lia's cell phone rang. "I need to get that, in case it might be

Karen. I should've called her last night." She found her purse on the nightstand. When she pulled out her phone, caller ID read, Craig Britton. "Lucas, it's Craig," she called out. She plopped at the foot of the bed to keep Lucas in her sights. The man was hot, and he made her hotter.

"Good morning, brother of mine."

"You sound awful chipper." Craig snapped.

"You're *not* having a good morning?"

"Are you okay? I'm really worried about you. About your future. We need to find you another studio space. Or maybe a large apartment so you can have an actual bedroom."

"So I can continue to sublet it to Karen?" she teased. It would push his buttons. She would not allow him or anyone else take the joy out of her morning.

"Amelia, be serious. I can't find Lucas. He hasn't answered his phone. I thought he was going home after he got you settled last night."

Her eyebrows shot up. Lucas hadn't mentioned any calls from her brother. Were they still scheming together trying to control her life? "Plotting again, are you big brother? Well, just so you know, I'm sequestered in a fabulous hotel suite enjoying room service. But it's Lucas you really want to talk with, right?" She rose and crossed the room.

Lucas's pensive expression gave her a bit of satisfaction. If there was any hope of a future with this man, he had to stop taking orders from her brother. "For the record, I'm a grown woman, Craig. I had dessert before I had breakfast." He wouldn't understand the significance of that remark, but Lucas would. She smiled devilishly. "Here's Lucas."

She handed over her phone. Lucas rose and took the call out in the hall. What the two men had to say that couldn't be said in front of her caused her some concern. She cinched the belt on the robe a bit tighter. A better plan came to mind. This one included Lucas, her farm, and painting...and not her brother. She would need Lucas's help. Could she find an enticing way to encourage him to agree?

Chapter 14

Lia dressed and gathered her purse. She folded Lucas's shirt and placed it on the arm of the couch. On the floor, his boots waited for his return. Picking up the bowls Jack had used, she placed them on the food cart. Plopping into a chair, she mused, only minutes ago she and Lucas had shared breakfast. Her to-do list was long, and she needed to get a start on the day. However, without her phone, she didn't know the time. If Lucas didn't return soon, she'd go in search of him.

"That's all I've got to say." Lucas's stern tone meant business. He entered the suite as he ended the call. "Karen called while I was talking to Craig." He handed her the phone. "I think she left a message."

"I'll call her in a few. Are there problems?"

"No. Not on my part."

"What did you tell Craig?"

"Amelia, you knew exactly what you were doing when you said what you did. I'm not about to go into detail with your brother, or anyone else for that matter, about how we spent our time alone. However, Craig guessed. I neither confirmed nor denied."

Her shoulders slumped. Creating more problems hadn't been her intention. Her brother wasn't the enemy. He did have her best interest in mind. But the days of him trying to rule her were over. She should've delivered the message in a more sensitive and mature way.

Lucas put on his shirt and buttoned it while Jack rested beside his feet. He sat on the couch and put on his socks and boots. How a man could appear so sexy doing the most mundane things? Lia shook her head to break the spell Lucas wove around her whenever he was near. Never had she had a single-track mind, but with Lucas it wasn't hard.

He walked toward her, crouched down, and lifted her chin. "That's a cute little grin. What are you contemplating?"

"How do you know I'm thinking about something?"

"I know when the wheels turn in your head."

"Would you be happy to know I'm thinking of you?"

"Well, that deserves a kiss." Lucas brought his lips to hers, his lips seducing hers. She gave into his insistence. Surrendering not only her lips, but her willpower. Heat lingered when he pulled back. She blinked and lifted her face begging for more. Lucas kissed her nose. Picking up Jack's leash, Lucas hooked up the dog. With Jack in tow, he held out his hand to her. "We've got to start the day now. Lots of things to do. Like swinging by to pick up my vehicle. Maybe we can get a look at the building's damage. The whole thing didn't burn."

"You're right." She took a final glance at the room. She would cherish the memories they'd created all night, last night.

"Want me to drive?" Lucas asked when they entered the parking garage.

"Thanks, I can manage."

Jack hopped in when she opened the back door. Lucas climbed in the passenger side. She put the truck in gear. Having Lucas beside her was the most natural thing in the world.

Blocks away from the hotel, she turned the corner and the building she'd stared at most of night on the TV appeared.

She gasped. "It looks like it's been bombed, like pictures I've seen from World War II." Crumpled brick. A skeletal iron structure visible through shattered windows, now appearing as ugly eyes of a dying monster. Sourness filled her mouth. She fought to keep her breakfast down. Her eyes watered. She wouldn't accept defeat. Couldn't allow this to break her.

Lucas shook his head. "It doesn't look any better in daylight." He squeezed her arm gently. "It will be okay. No one got hurt. What's left is stuff."

She stopped her truck in the street at the barricades. A police officer walked up to her window.

"Lady, were you a tenant?"

"Yes. I want to see if there's anything left of my studio. It's not in the burned-out section."

"Sorry. Fire marshal is still inspecting along with a team of experts. The building isn't safe. I'm not sure if you'll ever get inside. This place may be bulldozed as it stands."

Lia shook her head. The magnitude of her loss hit like a smack of a two-by-four. The blanket her mother had knitted, the antique floor mirror her father had given her, and her grandmother's armoire would be bulldozed? No. That couldn't be true. "Please. I can take the stairs over there." She pointed to the entrance at the opposite end from the damage.

"I can't let you in. We have a list of tenants from the landlord. *If* it's determined to be safe and *if* anything is salvageable, you'll get a call. But don't get your hopes up."

"But I have family treasures there. I must talk with someone about this. I can't leave without getting my things."

"Can't let you in. Sorry. Again, if there's a safe way for items to be removed, the fire marshal will be in contact."

"Amelia Britton," Lucas interrupted the conversation. "Officer, her name is Amelia Britton. Please take down her name and give it to the fire marshal. There are some valuable items in the studio."

"I can remember Amelia, like Amelia Earhart."

"Yes, I'm named after her," Lia said. She managed a grin hoping to make a good impression. Maybe if he remembered her, he might be more helpful.

"This is what I'll do. Here's my card. Call me if you don't hear anything in a week or so. But I'm not making any promises."

"Thank you."

"I need my truck. It's over there." Lucas pointed across the street to the barricaded area.

"Sure. I'll make it so you can get out."

"I'll follow you home in my truck," Lia told Lucas. "Don't drive like a crazy man."

"That would be your brother in his fancy BMW."

Allowing Lucas to lead gave her a sense of

comfort. She rode in silence through the city, then remembered Karen's message. After listening to it, she relaxed a bit. No further need for panic. Karen figured Lucas had everything under control, but she did need to talk about what insurance might cover for the loss of their things. As a result of Karen's calmness, Lia resolved to not allow thoughts to overwhelm her brain.

After exiting the interstate and picking up the county road west to Harvest, Lia turned on the radio to the community station, KKFI, to sooth her racing nerves. Thoughts ran laps in her mind, round and round. Exactly what and how should she bring up the subject with Lucas? Before she launched into any one topic, she had to get him to open up and let her know if he saw a future for them. She didn't want to take things slowly. She'd been on pause with that man for nearly ten years.

With the radio cranked loudly, Lia lost herself in the bluesy guitar of Tab Beniot. Her phone rang during a pause between a line and the chorus. If not for the break in the music, she might not have heard it.

"Amelia, I've got to veer off. Megan's been in some sort of accident. I'm heading to Manhattan to check on her."

"What kind of accident? At school, in a car, or what?"

"Car. She was rear-ended. I think she's okay, but she's shaken up."

"Call me later and let me know. If she needs me, I'll drive up, too."

"I'll keep you posted. And Amelia..."

She waited for him to finish what he intended to say.

"Accidents can happen at any time. The fire last night, now this with Megan..."

"Lucas, what are you trying to say?"

"I love you. That's what I'm saying. To you and everyone else. I love you, Amelia Britton."

Her heart melted, oozing like warmed honey. Her foot let up off the gas for a moment as her body relaxed. She gripped the steering wheel because she couldn't grab hold of the man and kiss him silly. Hitting the gas, she raced on the long, lonely stretch of highway.

"Amelia?"

"Lucas Dwyer, I love you, too! Now get over to see your sister, and then come home to me. We've got a lot of talking to do. I most definitely want dessert again."

****

Arriving at the college, Lucas parked and ran in a full sprint to his sister's dorm. A student was leaving the building and before the door closed, Lucas jerked it open. He entered against school policy, but he had no time to waste. Until he saw Megan, he couldn't truly believe she was unharmed.

Running up two flights of stairs, he located her room and pounded on the door. It opened before he could pound again. Megan launched herself at him, reaching her arms around his waist, and broke into a sob.

"I'm so sorry," Megan wailed.

"Let me look at you." Lucas's voice rang out louder than he intended. Fear had a hold on him. He held her from him for a better look. He felt up and down her arms as if they would give him clues about her injuries.

"I was checked out at the clinic. A little bit of whiplash maybe, but I'm okay. They kept asking me if I hit my head or if I was knocked unconscious. I wasn't. But Lucas," Megan wailed. Her eyes teared up again. "My car is a total loss. They towed it way. The cop called it salvage." She sniffed. "It's the only present Dad ever bought me without Mom's approval."

His heart thudded like a bass drum in his chest. His brain failed to believe she wasn't hurt. "The car is just a car. You're important. I understand you're upset, but I need to be certain you're not injured. Why did they keep questioning you about a head injury? Did you hit the windshield or the side window?"

Megan shook her head.

"Do you want me to take you home and make a doctor's appointment?

Again, Megan shook her head

"If you're sure you're fine... Did you get all your stuff out of the car?"

Megan shook her head again.

"I'd feel better if you'd come home and let me take you to a doctor who knows you." He pulled her close for another bear hug.

"I'm fine. I'll be sore, but okay." He accepted her decision reluctantly and released her.

While he looked for signs of injuries on Megan, a few students had opened their dorm doors and a few more hung out in the hall eavesdropping on their conversation.

"Where was the car taken?" Lucas asked.

"I don't know exactly." Megan shrugged.

The crowd of students moved closer.

"Dude, are you bothering her?" One male student stepped forward.

Megan turned to face the guy. She shook her head at him. "He's my brother."

"How about we go inside and talk about this more?" Lucas asked.

Megan let him pass into the room, then she followed him in.

"There's a card on my desk." She plucked it from the mess and handed it to him. "Information," she said, collapsing on the bed.

"If you're up to it, let's go over to the tow lot and remove your personal things from the car. We have to get the tag, too, if the car is, in fact, a total loss."

"The car behind me pushed me into a truck with a tow hitch that inserted itself into my radiator. My poor car looks like an accordion."

Lucas pulled out the chair from desk and sat. He rubbed the back of his neck. The car was just stuff. Same as the remains in Amelia's loft in the city. Same as Amelia's paintings. Stuff. Okay, valuable stuff, but still replaceable at the end of the day. The woman he loved was unharmed. His sister, slightly bruised, was fine. A lot of trauma in twenty-four hours to the women in his life. What more could he do to keep them safe?

"Megan, let me give you a hug. I'm so glad you're okay. I worried all the way here. I was following Amelia home from Kansas City..."

"You spent the night in KC with Amelia?"

Lucas nodded. "She says if you need her, she'll come."

"Does this mean what I think it does?" A smile wiped away all traces of Megan's earlier discomfort.

Lucas shifted his weight and eyed his sister warily. "What does what mean? Is that some sort of female speak?"

"You're in love with Lia."

Lucas frowned. Did his sister now read minds and hearts?

"Oh, big brother, it's been obvious for months. The question is, when will you finally do something about it?"

How had the discussion turned on him? Megan seemed to quickly forget she'd been in a car accident.

"Let's go check out the car." He didn't intend to discuss his relationship with Amelia until it was clearly defined in his own mind. He started for the door. "Grab your purse or whatever you need, and let's go. After we do this, I need to get home, that is, if you're sure you're okay."

Megan grabbed a small purse and tugged on his hands. Once outside, she raced down the stone steps. Her youthful exuberance baffled him. Tears one minute. Smiles the next.

"Come on. Let me explain the facts of life to you."

Lucas bristled. "I hardly think so, little sister."

"Which way's your ride?"

Lucas pointed across the lawn to the far parking lot.

"Don't try to pull on me what Craig Britton pulls on Lia. By the way, why is it the two you are the *only* ones who still use her full name?"

"Wait, what do you mean about Craig? And what does she want to be called?"

"Lia. Don't you ever listen? As for Craig, he's a controlling tyrant."

"He means well." Now he was defending Craig to his little sister? He might very well behave like Craig with Megan. He wanted only the best for his little sister.

"Forget about Craig. Focus on Lia. Who does she want?" Megan thumped his chest. "She wants you! Can I help you pick out her ring? When do you think you might get married? Can I be in the wedding party? Where will you live after you're married?"

"Slow down. Things are not that simple or moving that fast."

"Why not?"

"Why not, indeed," he muttered.

When they reached the truck, Lucas held the door for his sister. He went around to the driver's side and climbed in.

"You didn't answer the questions. All you need to do is ask her to marry you. She says, yes, and you live happily ever after. On her farm. Simple."

"Megan, stop." Lucas started the engine.

"But—"

"Amelia could lose the farm." He tapped the address for the tow yard into the GPS. "Craig wants to sell," he explained. "He's found a buyer. Craig's plan all along has been to move Amelia back to the city to paint. She had a studio there."

"Had?"

"Guess you didn't see the news about the burning

building in KC yesterday?"

"Lia's studio is gone? What about her paintings and stuff?"

"We're not sure yet. The fire marshal won't let anyone in."

Megan slumped in the seat like a deflated balloon. The news popped her momentary bubble of enthusiasm.

"You could get married and live in our house. It's not nearly as nice as Lia's, but it's better than nothing.

He patted his sister's shoulder. "That's a generous offer, but no."

"Why not?" Megan demanded, sitting squarely in the seat. Her determination had rematerialized.

"Because the house will be yours when you graduate from college."

"Lucas, the house belongs to both of us."

"Yes, and we see where that arrangement is getting Craig and Amelia, so I have decided, the house will be yours. You will always have a home. You will never face the worry Amelia is dealing with now."

"You sound like Craig." Megan pouted. "What if you and Lia got married and lived in the house until I graduated? If I go to graduate school, I'll be away for another five to six years."

Her eagerness to fix his problem touched his heart. "A nice offer, sis. But bringing a wife home to my sister's home...just not manly. I want to give my bride a home of her own."

Megan crossed her arms. "Well then, Lucas, you'd better find a way to keep Lia on her farm."

"Yep," he agreed. A new plan began to form, but would Craig agree? Even if he did, could Lucas pull it off?

Chapter 15

Since returning from Kansas City several days ago, she'd painted like a fiend, surviving on catnaps and nourishment from Helen's daily delivery. The spunky woman came laden with food and a lecture, yet she hadn't demanded to read Lia's palm again. Helen's harangues were worth the pain in exchange for chicken potpie, fork-tender roast beef, and barbecue. Helen tried to entice her into admitting she now had a man in her life, which Lia wouldn't confirm or deny. She had zipped her lips and shook her head under the heat of Helen's scrutiny.

"Amelia, hurry!" Craig hollered.

"I'll be down in a minute." She turned off the light in her bedroom and trudged down the hall to the stairs.

'The truth is in your eyes,' were Helen's final words yesterday.

Would Harvest be shocked to learn which man claimed her heart? Was Helen spreading news, gossiping around town?

She smiled remembering Lucas's visit. Dessert in bed.

Lia picked specks of paint from around her nails while taking stock of her efforts. Three paintings. Only three. Even after working around the clock— halogen work lights producing a daylight effect in the middle of the night, lighting the night so brightly coyotes ran in the opposite direction. Anyone taking pictures from space surely spotted the farm.

At the top of the stairs, Lia paused to gaze at the undulating green hills beyond the window. Even overwork and exhaustion didn't negate her delight of the view. The lingering rays of sunlight cast shadows across the yard.

"How can anyone not love this?"

She and Karl would catch the sunset from the windows of the restaurant. No other place in the world lifted her spirits and plugged her into creativity like the Kansas countryside.

She'd been painting since returning from Kansas City, but inspiration didn't appear with a flip of a switch. She couldn't just duplicate the stolen work. Art had to flow from her heart to her hand, then to paint on canvas. However, the remarkable thing about being in love—it provided new inspirations. That morning before dawn when she examined the three paintings in progress with a critical eye, she spied a newly honed depth in her artistic voice. She credited Lucas with the change, which made her date tonight rather awkward. But she wasn't prepared to share her good news about Lucas with the world even though it brought joy to her heart...made her so happy she could float away like a feather on the breezes of the Kansas plains.

She and Lucas hadn't yet gotten around to *the talk*—life kept yanking their collars, pulling them in different directions. Canceling on Karl at the last minute would be rude. Besides, there was nothing wrong with getting to know the man who made Zoë's heart skitter like water popping in a sizzling pan. She smiled at the thought of her friend's heart all tied up in knots. The always *love 'em and leave 'em* woman had come to a screeching halt.

Descending the stairs, Lia sighed. So far, the police had no new clues about the thieves. But the show must go on.

With less than a week before the exhibit, her hopes of recovering the paintings chipped away each day. The art world could be a risky business. As Heidi Klum, host of *Project Runway*, always said, "One day you're in—the next, you're out." Lia's three new paintings might salvage the show, along with her reputation.

She feared letting down Jan and the show's success slipping away just like the stolen painting. Yet, she had to admit, as bad as life had abused her, the incident had gifted her with a previously unseen benefit—Lucas. If not for the stolen paintings, he might not have known he'd stolen her heart. He wouldn't have come to her rescue in one of her darkest moments. Her heartbeat quickened at that thought. A flush raced from her chest to her cheeks and lifted her mouth into a grin. Love had invincibility pumping through her veins. She believed it when Lucas had said, "Everything will work out perfectly." She'd stake the farm on it.

"You look nice," Craig said when she crossed into the living room.

"Why, thank you." She wobbled on the carpet in black heels. She'd decided on a black pencil skirt hoping for sophistication rather than the country look. The pearls her father had given her for her sixteenth birthday gleamed against her soft, dove gray, silk blouse.

"Happy Birthday, Amelia." Craig sprang from the couch and ran to the dining room table. He returned toting a medium-sized package wrapped in shiny paper with a lacy bow the size of a large zinnia blossom. "Since you don't want to celebrate your birthday with me, here's your present."

"Oh, Craig," Lia said softly. "It's not that I don't want to celebrate with you. It's just that I need to do something different after twenty-nine years."

"Mom and Dad would be really proud," Craig told her. He shrugged. "I had wanted to celebrate with you, like we always used to."

Lia hugged his neck. "We'll have cake when I get home. I think it's sweet that you're going to hang out with Lucas and Megan tonight. I'm expecting them to be here for the cake cutting."

"Open your present," Craig said, his voice low and serious.

Lia paused. Whatever it was, she wanted to share it with her family—Craig, Megan, and most importantly, Lucas.

"Would you mind if I waited until I get home? Karl said the reservation is for seven. I imagine I'll be home by ten at the very latest." Sentimentality pulled at her heart. She would be a reluctant date. After celebrating every single birthday of her life with her brother, except last year, the tradition was hard to break

"Hey, it's your birthday. Whatever you want." Craig leaned in and kissed her cheek. The simple action dissolved her remaining tension over the tired argument about the farm. Surely, Craig would help her keep it. He did have her best interest at heart. Lucas had reminded her of that.

The doorbell rang, interrupting their moment. Jack barked and bounded down the stairs. Craig jogged to the door. "Let me intimidate the prospective suitor. Wait here." He grinned wickedly, reminding her of the Wolf in *Little Red Riding Hood*. He hadn't broached the subject of selling the farm again, even though the year was up tomorrow. She wanted to believe he wasn't just waiting for the right opportunity to strike. For the reprieve, she was thankful. It was the birthday present she truly wanted. After tomorrow, they could argue about what came next for the farm.

"Lia ready?" Karl asked.

"Enter," Craig said, stepping aside.

Lia crossed to the foyer. "Hello, Karl. I'm looking forward to the evening."

Karl looked her over. For a moment, she thought he might whistle. She didn't miss the appreciation in his wide grin.

"For you," he said, offering a bouquet of pale pink flowers and greenery.

"So, Karl, what are your plans for the evening with my little sister? We haven't gotten to know you very well. And since my father's gone, it's my duty to stand in for him."

Lia took the flowers. "Thank you. These are lovely." She turned and shoved the bouquet at Craig. "Put these in water in mother's crystal vase and set them on the dining room table." Turning back to Karl, she tugged on his hand, leading him back out the front door. "Bye, brother dearest. See you later tonight."

Once in the car, Lia turned to Karl. "I'm sorry about that. He's a little overprotective sometimes. In the future, just ignore him."

"He's kind of hard to ignore," Karl chuckled. "Your brother is a well-respected man around these parts. His word carries a lot of weight. I wouldn't want to be on the wrong side of him...or Lucas."

Did she detect a hint of concern in his voice? Was it over Craig or Lucas?

"Tell me, how are you liking Harvest? A big change from where you're from."

She listened while he talked and tried to keep her mind from wandering to Lucas and memories of him in her bed. When she returned home tonight, after the cake cutting and tasting, she planned to walk with Lucas in the moonlight down to the creek and show him the spot on the tree where she'd carved their initials all those years ago. Back when she was young and had her first boy crush...on him. Dessert could be sampled anywhere.

"If you don't mind, I need to stop by the Sunflower Café before we go to dinner," Lia told Karl as town appeared. The ride to Atchison took them through downtown Harvest. Most of the stores were dark and locked up for the night. Brick and stone buildings, with a few old wooden ones, gave the town a quaint antique feel. Shops with large picture windows showed off colorful displays. Only one business still had lights on, and she instructed Karl to park in front.

"I have to pick something up from Helen. It'll

take just a minute." Lia scooted from the car.

Chimes tinkled when she pushed the door open. "Helen?"

"Back here."

Lia's heels clicked against the aged, polished wooden floor. The empty café exuded serenity with the lights turned low. Lia made her way toward a well-lit kitchen. Helen appeared from behind the old saloon swinging doors separating the dining and cooking spaces. Backlit by the bright kitchen light, Helen appeared to glow. Lia blinked. The woman had great psychic abilities, but was she actually an angel?

"Happy Birthday, Amelia." Helen tilted the cake she held in her hands.

"Oh. Helen! It's beautiful. But you know, no one calls me that anymore."

"Your mother called you that. Your father called you that. Your brother still calls you that. I've known you since the day you were born. I'm sure if we did that genealogy thing, we'd at least be kissing cousins. And since your parents are gone, I've claimed you and Craig as family."

"Well..." Lia's mouth began to water as the aroma of chocolate hit her nose. "I don't care what you call me if this cake tastes as good as it looks and smells. It's not the German chocolate I ordered, but I'm so glad you didn't listen to me."

The round three-layer cake, decorated in pink fondant and embellished with piped white icing resembling delicate lace, displayed a painter's easel perched on top. The easel supported an exact replica of one of Lia's abstract paintings. Her heart lurched. The painting had been one of her best ones from the stolen batch.

"I received a post card from that gallery doing your show. I reduced it and copied it onto edible film." Helen beamed.

"I'm awed. You've outdone yourself."

Helen put the cake into a custom-made box and set it on the counter. When Lia reached for the box, Helen grasped her hand.

"Palm reading time."

"Oh, no. That's okay. I appreciate all you've done. The cake is enough."

"I didn't listen to you when you ordered the cake. I'm not listening to you now. Instead, I'm listening to voices that have a message for you."

Helen held tight to Lia's wrist until she relaxed and opened her fist.

"Stop human-doing and start human-being. What you seek, you already have."

Perplexed, Lia turned the phrase over in her head. "What does that mean?"

"I don't know. I'm just the messenger. But if you're seeking something, you're wasting your time because you already have it. Best to figure it out what it is."

Something in Helen's voice shook her. Thoughts raced through her brain like a computer processing on overload, but no significant thought stood out. She had no idea what Helen was talking about.

"Okay. Thanks again for the cake." Troubled, she quickly left the shop. When she crossed the threshold, she vowed to tuck away all worries until tomorrow. Tonight was for fun, and she intended to enjoy her date. However, going home and knowing Lucas would be waiting had her spirits dancing on clouds. They would have the talk that had been shoved aside by other pressing things.

Yet, Helen's words haunted her. The unsolved puzzle would drive her crazy. Maybe Lucas could help find the answer?

Once she and Karl set out on the final leg of their journey to the restaurant, Lia searched for a subject of conversation.

"I don't mean to pry, but do you think your time in Harvest will outlast that of your cousin?" she asked.

"He didn't last long, did he?"

"Country life isn't for everyone. With cold winters, wind chills reaching well below zero, and the dry hot summers, in excess of a hundred degrees, Kansas isn't for the faint of heart."

"I assure you, I've got a big incentive to make this work."

"Something you care to share?"

"Well, first, tell me more about your friend Zoë. That might make all the difference in the world."

"Zoë? Hmm, let's see. She's funny. Full of ideas to make money. She's smart, but tries to hide that fact. A good horsewoman. She used to barrel race as a kid and has trophies."

"Romantic interests?"

Lia raised her eyebrows and stared in Karl's direction. "Interesting question. That, sir, is something you're going to have to find out for yourself."

Karl frowned. "I thought ladies liked to gossip."

"Gossip is one thing, prying into someone's love

life—a different matter altogether."

Karl cleared his throat. "I'm not above gossip. Helen told me you definitely have a man in your life. If it was me, I think I'd know. So, do you want to share?"

Lia blurted, "No. Absolutely not."

Chapter 16

Lucas climbed up the wide wooden stairs and scanned the ballroom. Anticipation danced a samba in his gut. He made fists, then slowly unclenched his hands. If ever he wanted a party to be a success, this one was it. A big *hurrah* for Amelia. Tonight would forever remain an etched memory of happiness.

"Lucas, glad you're finally here. Start lighting all the candles," Zoë called to him while she placed napkins on the tables. "Matches are in that bag on the side table."

He grabbed a box and began his assigned task.

"Hey!" Craig called. "Get to work! You're late. Not much time before Amelia arrives."

"With Karl," Lucas muttered. "Got it covered!" he called back.

Overhead recessed lights had been dimmed. Strings of tiny white twinkling lights striped the walls, illuminating the room with a magical ambiance.

Zoë had forced him and Craig to review a decorating magazine in order to be more help with the party. She decorated each large table with a centerpiece of miniature pink roses, one of Amelia's favorite flowers. Three cut-glass votive holders surrounded a bulb-shaped flower vase. He'd voted for cinnamon candles, but Zoë reminded him how they brought back strong memories of Lia's mother, and she had nixed that idea. They all agreed sadness needed sweeping to the shadows.

Instead of cinnamon, Zoë selected coconut, mango, and ocean fragrances. She jokingly said she hoped those scents didn't somehow entice Lia into a seduction she'd regret. It took tensile-steel strength on Lucas's part not to set her straight about Amelia's private life. He wanted to shout, *She's mine*, but he'd had a few days to think and his future with Amelia now seemed bleak.

The hard cold facts—she would lose the farm. Then leave him.

He'd had an idea, but needed time for further investigation, especially after his meeting yesterday. He had one last idea to research, but it was a long shot.

Amelia needed cash. The boxes bringing in extra income wouldn't last her through the end of the year. The art show might bring in money, maybe enough to pay for the spring planting. The only remaining income source was the harvest, which wouldn't net enough after the mortgage payments and expenses to buy out Craig's entire share of the farm.

The inevitable had only been delayed.

Amelia would have to bend to Craig's decision and sell.

Maybe Craig had been right all along. Amelia belonged in a loft in the city. He'd checked into suitable places for her and compiled a list of five with living space. He planned to offer to studio hunt with her. Above everything else, he had to know she was safe no matter where she lived.

Over the last few days, he'd suffered like crazy. Grief descended on him when the reality of Amelia's future became clear. His heart hung down to his knees. He'd faced battle and come out alive. However, a life without the woman he loved would be no life at all. He even considered moving away from Harvest after Megan graduated from college. The pain of being so close and yet so far from Amelia would kill him. If she found someone else to love, another artist or someone in the city, a man like Craig wanted for her, he'd die another death.

But tonight...they would have tonight. That would have to be enough.

Lucas walked over to the leader of the band. "Sounds good," he said. "Remember, I want the third song to be *When a Man Loves a Woman*."

"Sure thing," the guitar player said. The drummer gave a thumbs up.

Across the room, Craig tugged on a string. Pink and white helium-filled balloons floated upward and hugged the ceiling. Silver stars dangled from various lengths of white ribbon, replacing the confetti Zoë had wanted everyone to throw when Lia arrived. The owner of the restaurant put the kibosh on that idea, saying it made too much of a mess.

"You okay, man?" Craig asked. "You're dragging. Not in the party spirit?"

"Lot on my mind."

"Amelia is going to be surprised. I look forward to seeing happiness written on her face."

"Me, too." Lucas nodded, forcing a smile. "I want her to be happy."

After Lucas finished lighting all the candles, he

paced from the small stage to the window overlooking the parking lot, then back again. Guests began arriving. Zoë stood at the top of the stairs and acted as the greeting committee.

Craig stepped behind the antique bar running the length of one wall. "Want a beer?" he called out to everyone, hoisting bottles in each hand. "Boulevard beers. Best beer from Kansas City." Several of the guests headed in Craig's direction.

Lucas continued to pace. As he approached the window again, he caught Zoë's stare. She scrutinized him as though scanning his mind to read his thoughts. Lucas bristled. Harvest didn't need another psychic.

"Lucas." Zoë waved him away from the window. He joined her, smiling and greeting the next guests ascending the stairs to Amelia's surprise birthday party.

"If you pace like an expectant father, she might see you through the window. Karl said he'd text me." Zoë chuckled. "Karl said, 'the one-if-by-sea or two-if-by-land signal went out with the last century.' He'll excuse himself and text me when he and Lia are finished with dinner."

"I want tonight to be perfect for her," Lucas said. "She's had a run of bad luck. And, to make matters worse, I checked the weather reports—you know I'm heading out Monday—there's strong speculation about a storm headed down from the northwest. Blowing hard. That could hurt her crop—and everyone else's—in a bad way."

"You sound like the voice of doom. Think about that tomorrow. Not tonight. No worries now. By the way, what's up with you and Craig?"

"Nothing."

"Really? Tonight's the night you've decided to start lying? Usually the two of you are thick as malt at the drive-in diner. Now you're here. He's there, knocking back a brew."

Lucas shook his head. "We're not on the same page about something."

"I'm guessing that something has to do with Lia."

"Yeah, but you're going to have to pry the information out of Craig. I'm trying to protect Amelia, only Craig doesn't see it that way."

Zoë eyed him hard. "I think you like her. In fact, I'm a gambling woman. I think *love* is a better word."

Lucas frowned. "So Harvest now has two mind-reading women? Is there something funny on those postage stamps you lick each day that's making you hallucinate?" He refused to confirm or deny her probing. The less he said the better.

Zoë smiled. "Play it your way. Is it possible for two hardheaded mules to close their eyes, shut out the past, and join forces?"

"Mules?"

"I intend to give you and Craig a big shove. You need to step up for Lia and join forces with her against Craig. I'm going to find out what's brewing with Craig besides what he's drinking."

"I think the truth is going to carry the stench of a pig farm."

Helen entered the downstairs foyer and ascended the stairs toward them.

"Helen, I need your help. I need a minute with the guys. Will you greet the guests and let them know

195

they can take a seat?"

"Oh, my, Zoë. What a magical setting!"

Zoë winked. "Thanks, Helen. That's what we're going for. Excuse us, please."

Lucas looked down where Zoë had linked her arm with his. "Now, I can handle the truth. Unlike Lia, I *will* fight dirty. Come with me."

Warily, Lucas marched beside Amelia's best friend. Somewhere over the years, the hellion had become a savvy woman. They crossed the ballroom to the bar where Craig played barkeep.

"Craig, how did Lia like the birthday present you got her?" Zoë asked, parking herself on a tall stool. Lucas moved behind the stool next to her and remained standing.

"She was in too much of a hurry to get out the door with your boy Karl. Never opened it." Craig held up a longneck bottle. Lucas shook his head.

"Is that what's got you twisted tight?" Zoë asked.

"Twisted how?"

"What's up with you and Lucas? Why aren't the two of you hamming it up with the band? Or singing your college fight song, or whatever other crazy male-bonding things you do when turned loose in town for the night?"

"It doesn't concern you," Craig replied quietly.

"If it concerns Lia, if it's something that's going to hurt her, it concerns me. I'm her best friend. You've had Lucas doing your dirty work for the last year. You better come clean."

"What did Lucas tell you?" Craig eyed Lucas suspiciously.

"A little of this. Some of that. I'm giving you

the chance to tell me your side of the story. Maybe I can help."

"Lucas told you!" Craig shouted. Zoë jumped. Lucas glanced around. It appeared no one else had heard the exchange over the band's warm up.

"Well…" Zoë paused.

"Selling the farm is in Amelia's best interest."

Zoë pounded her fists on the bar.

Lucas stepped aside when shock hit Zoë full force. He'd warned her, but now wasn't the time to remind her of that.

"Sell? The hell you say! You trying to kill your sister?"

"She can't make it. She's not superwoman, no matter what she thinks."

"Have you told her yet? Tell me you haven't ruined her birthday."

"I'm not that callous. Tomorrow morning I'll tell her. I've got a buyer waiting."

Zoë stood on the rungs of the stool, reached across the bar top, and slugged Craig in the arm. "You'll crush her with the news, then run back to St. Louis. When did you get so cold and cruel?"

Craig scowled. "I'm not cold or cruel." His voice was deadly calm. He planted his palms on the bar and leaned across, pinning Zoë with a stare. "I promise you, I'm trying to keep her from what happened to the Dwyers. I couldn't bear it if she lost the farm. That would be a shame she couldn't live with. Best to sell before it's ripped away. Better for her to transition back to the city."

Zoë sputtered. "You—" She jumped down from the stool. Her heels clacked on the wooden floor. She stormed away, but suddenly turned and shot a piercing glare at Craig. "Lucas, you can't let this happen."

Lucas nodded. Zoë lifted her chin and squared her shoulders as she headed in Helen's direction.

"I want to be there when you tell her," Lucas said to Craig.

"Sure."

"One more thing. You have to put it off until Monday evening."

"I'll be back in St. Louis. Nope. Tomorrow. I can't do this over the phone. That would be cold and cruel. You know I have Amelia's best interest at heart."

"For the sake of our friendship, I need until Monday evening."

"Our friendship is on the line? What are you saying?"

Zoë raced up and interrupted. "Karl just texted. He's walking Lia over in ten minutes."

"Everyone, quiet," Craig hollered, coming around from behind the bar and standing next to Lucas.

Lucas gave the band a kill-it sign, and the music faded away.

"Lia and Karl are on their way. Remain quiet," Zoë called to the crowd. "Wait until she's at the top of the stairs and removes the blindfold before yelling surprise!"

Lucas nudged Craig with his elbow. "Before you tell Lia about the buyer, I have something important I need to share with her."

"What?" Craig shook his head. "This is all too

cloak-and-dagger for me. What's up?"

Lucas scanned the room. Footsteps in the tile foyer below echoed up the stairs. More guests appeared. Any minute now, Amelia would arrive. This was his chance.

Lucas held out his hand to shake Craig's. "Put it there," he said. "We're going to be brothers-in-law."

Craig's mouth gaped. Lucas slapped him on the back. "I love your sister. I can't let you take the farm from her. I'm going to ask Amelia to marry me. Together, we'll fight you."

Chapter 17

At the restaurant, Lia opened her menu, but before ordering, Karl took over. He requested the most expensive items on the menu, never bothering to ask what she might enjoy. Good thing she wasn't allergic to peanut sauce on her salad or blue cheese on her filet. He did, however, have a fine palate for wine and ordered a highly ranked bottle of California cabernet.

Lia glanced through the window. Lavender, pink, and orange shone against the sky's pillowy clouds. Streaks of silver shot upward, fanning across the horizon as the sun trailed a path toward dusk. The grandeur of nature teased the eye with ten shades of green in the fields. The river darkened as light disappeared. Lia itched to paint as Karl chattered on like a streaming news banner on CNN.

She shivered from the air conditioning blowing down the back of her neck and pulled her wrap over her shoulders. Bringing her attention back to Karl, she smiled and nodded in all the right pauses during the non-stop monologue, and remained utterly polite after realizing the man's genuine fascination with her best friend. The date with Karl would be over soon. Yet, for a reason unknown to her, every time she tried to suggest they leave, Karl started in on another question about some obscure fact about Harvest.

"Yes, Zoë can trace her roots back to the covered wagons rolling along the Santa Fe Trail." Lia dabbed the corners of her mouth with a cloth napkin.

"She's got a great sense of humor." The man actually beamed.

"Our Zoë is a tickle a minute." Raising her wine glass, Lia waited for the last drop to dribble into her mouth. "Thank you so much for dinner, Karl. Let me go to the ladies' room before we depart." Without being rude, she couldn't have been more direct. She rose and left the table.

On the drive to the restaurant, Karl had spoken excitedly about his new afterschool basketball coaching responsibilities and how much he enjoyed getting to know the farmers and townsfolk. When he took a breather, he asked about her art. It seemed Zoë had mentioned it to him. When Lia finished her first sentence, he dove in, explaining he didn't understand art critics. Instead, he took a like-it-when-I-see-it approach to things he hung on his walls. His tastes, he confessed, tended to modern abstract. Bold colors. Decisive lines. He had even tried to impress her with his explanation of energy art. Then, he'd asked, if she would consider painting a mural on the side of the farm store. He had in mind a colorful checkerboard of different species of roosters. He couldn't pay her, but advertising her work could be their trade.

She contemplated his offer momentarily, not wanting to offend, before replying, "I'm not sure I'm qualified to tackle that type of project. I've only painted the side of a building once. Someone with more experience would probably better suit your needs, but thank you for thinking of me."

His dismay lasted barely a second before he changed the topic of conversation. She had helped herself to more wine while he talked on—the subject remained everything Zoë.

He'd shared his collection of sort-of-dates with Zoë. He recounted her impish smiles and girlish giggles and other angelic qualities, most of which she had rarely witnessed in her friend. However, what hooked her attention was how his face lit up whenever he mentioned Zoë's name. It didn't take a Saturday sportscaster to give her the score. Karl had it bad for her best friend. Over the top. Intense infatuation. Maybe even falling in love.

"Who am I to interfere with the course of Cupid's arrow? Karl and Zoë would make a cute couple," she said to her reflection in the mirror as she washed her hands.

But Zoë hadn't said a single word about any dates with Karl. Was it because of tonight? Because she'd asked out Karl before Karl had a chance to experience Zoë's farm-girl charm? She couldn't wait to call Zoë for a chat.

"Sorry to be so long," she said returning to the table. Karl rose and tried to pull out her chair for her, but she stood behind the chair with no intention of sitting again. Through the window, the gas streetlights flickered on around the memorial commemorating the Lewis and Clark expedition stop along the Missouri River. Lia blinked and looked again. Her brother stood by the river, his hands shoved in his pockets, rocking back and forth on his heels. She'd never been happier to see him. She wanted to run to him and demand he take her home.

"Karl?"

"Oh. I'm sorry, I'm hogging the conversation. Tell me when you and Zoë met."

"Could that wait? I think I see my brother, and I'm concerned about him. Craig said he had no plans to leave the farm. Lucas and he were going to hang out. I'll be just a minute. I'm going to speak to him."

"No." Karl's sharp tone surprised her.

"Excuse me?"

"Ah. I mean. I'll join you."

"I'll only be a minute."

When she reached for her purse, Karl locked his hand around her wrist. "It's safe with me." Uneasiness slid down her spine. She nodded. He let go. She grabbed her purse, and practically sprinted for the front door with Karl hollering after her, "Wait!"

Out the door and down the sidewalk, she crossed the street before calling out to her brother. "Craig!"

He turned, folded his arms over his chest, and huffed out a breath. "What are you doing here?" he demanded.

After a few quick steps, she slowed and walked. "I could ask you the same thing."

"Did you ditch Karl?"

"How did you know?"

"We have to go find him. He's got your birthday cake."

Lia twisted her mouth to one side, cocked her head, and closed one eye. "What are you up to?"

"Nothing."

"Liar. How did you know about the cake?"

"Helen phoned me."

"Great! You find Karl. Get my cake. I'm going to

the Rooftop for a drink. Maybe two. Then, you, big brother, can be the designated driver and take me home."

His shrug and nod made her more suspicious. His robotic behavior worried her. Something was wrong, but he'd shut her out. "Where's Lucas? I thought you'd be with him."

"He's...I don't know where he is this minute."

Lia paused. No music filtered down from the Riverview's Rooftop lounge. "Is there a band tonight?" She pointed to the rooftop. "I don't hear any music."

"I'm sure something is happening there. Go on up. Meet you there in a few."

"I'll have one drink and then we'll go, but promise to keep Karl away from me. He's infatuated with Zoë, but he's a bit odd for me."

"Let's go." Craig wrapped his arm over her shoulder and walked her in the direction of the restaurant. "Since I'm a great brother, I'll do your dirty work. I'll be up in a minute to collect the birthday girl."

As Lia climbed the inside stairs to the ballroom, a band struck up a fast-paced tune. The lights and decoration came into view before she reached the landing. Taking it all in, her breath caught in her throat. Balloons, ribbons, dangling stars, tables draped in white linens. This wasn't the Rooftop's usual Saturday-night band jam. This was a party, someone's private event.

"Surprise!"

People popped up from behind tables like jack-in-the-boxes. The band played *Happy Birthday*.

Everyone sang. Stunned, Lia froze in place. Friends and neighbors followed up with *For She's a Jolly Good Lady* and concluded with *How Old Are You Now?*

Folks began calling out, "Happy Birthday," and the band began to play again.

Lia turned when warmth caressed her shoulder. Lucas stood behind her with Craig next to him holding her cake. Karl grinned from ear to ear and scanned the room. When he apparently found his target, he held up his arms as though shooting a bow, pointed at Zoë, who played along and took the arrow to her heart. Next to her stood her brother Seth scowling. Lia waved to them and blew a kiss.

"Surprise, Lia! Happy birthday," Zoë shouted. When she applauded, everyone else joined her. Megan whistled loudly.

"Thank you. I'm very touched," Lia tried to shout above the roar.

"Happy Birthday, Amelia," Lucas said, pulling her into a hug. She stiffened for a moment. Lucas's display of affection would set ears burning and tongues wagging, but that didn't stop warmth from rippling all the way to her toes. When he didn't quickly release her, but hugged tighter, she hugged him back. There was no reason the folks of Harvest couldn't know she was in love.

Lucas kissed her forehead. Lia blinked back tears. "Thank you," she managed to say without her voice breaking.

"Speech!" everyone cried.

Lia groaned. "I'm speechless. Thank you! Thank you for coming out. Let's party."

Craig stepped forward with the cake and addressed the crowd. "Check out this cake Helen made." Craig pointed to it. "Thank you, Helen, for all your help. The buffet is now open. Let the bartender know your brand of poison. Thank you for coming. Please enjoy. And, happy birthday, Amelia!"

The band began a slow ballad, and folks began to mingle. Lia gazed at the group, dumbfounded. Happy didn't capture her pulsing emotions. A little guilt rubbed her conscience over her rudeness to Karl, but she figured he'd forgiven and forgotten her when he pulled Zoë to the dance floor.

"I'm claiming the first dance," Craig said. "Let me put this cake down. I know Dad always did the first dance, but I'm here instead."

Craig led her in a country two-step.

"It smells so good in here," Lia said taking in the tropical scents. "I'm sure Zoë had a hand in this."

"Yep. Listen, I've got really good news to share with you tomorrow before I leave. Tonight we celebrate you and your future."

"What are you talking about?"

Craig flashed a boyish grin. "Relax. Have a great time tonight. Zoë, Lucas, and I worked hard to pull this off. Okay, Zoë did most of the work, but I paid for it. You were surprised, weren't you?"

His eagerness made him appear more at ease than she'd seen him in the last year. Although an uneasy suspicion tickled the back of her neck, she wouldn't purposely hurt Craig with a catty remark. "A complete surprise. Thanks. It means a lot."

As the band ended the song, without missing a beat, they launched into Reba McIntyre's song, *You*

Lie. Karl cut in.

"I'm sorry for the deception, but Zoë and the guys recruited me."

"Was that before or after I asked you out?" Lia asked, wondering why Zoë was so infatuated with Karl.

Karl didn't respond right away. He swung her into a twirl. "After. Right after we set up our date."

Seth approached. "I'm cutting in."

Lia waved at Karl and smiled at Seth. "I'm glad you came. How's the home visit going?"

"Let's just say I'm glad I'm leaving tomorrow. I don't miss harvesting. I wanted to wish the birthday girl good wishes." Seth leaned in and kissed her cheek. "I hope the coming year delivers your heart's desire."

"Thank you. Don't be mad when I say you've grown into quite the gentleman."

Seth winked. "I try. Let me get you a drink. Zoë brought a bottle of champagne. How about a glass?"

"Wonderful," Lia murmured. She and Seth moved off the dance floor. Standing back, she gazed at the people, all of whom were woven into the fabric of her life. Most of them had known her since she was a small child, or at least as far back has her memory allowed. She could never leave Harvest. Her past, present, and future could be found at only one address.

A hand on her shoulder startled her from her thoughts.

"Were you surprised?" Lucas whispered. He stood behind her. Heat emanating from him warmed her, sending a shiver of delight through her body. Her thudding heart beat double time to the beat of the band. Lucas tangled his fingers in hers, guiding her to the dance floor. The band hit the first licks of *When a Man Loves a Woman*. He pulled her close, and she relaxed, laying her head against his shoulder. They swayed together. People moved off the dance floor until only she and Lucas remained. A mirrored ball turned and cast prisms of white light around the room, making the hanging silver stars glow.

Contented, Lia sighed. She floated like one of the balloons.

Lucas squeezed her hand. "Happy Birthday, Amelia. *I* have a special surprise for you later."

"Lucas, I have a special surprise for *you* later, too."

Chapter 18

The band played a final song while Lucas stood with Amelia at the top of the stairs. Only a few more minutes and he'd have all of her attention. In the meantime, his face hurt from smiling. Standing still took all his concentration. He wanted to scoop her up and whisk her away. Instead, he remained glued to the spot beside the woman he loved while she thanked each departing guest for sharing her birthday.

"I'm so glad you came."

"Thank you for the dance."

"Yes, I'll come into town, and we'll have lunch next week."

Whiffs of smoke trailed upward and curled, creating a slight haze in the room as Megan blew out all the candles. Craig opened a few of the tall windows to clear the air. Lucas stiffened when Zoë headed in his direction.

"You go on with Lucas." Zoë shooed at her like she might shoo chickens. "Craig, Karl, Megan, and I will clean up. Craig said he'd drive Megan home. Helen will take the leftover cake and box it up. I'll drop it by the farm tomorrow after Seth leaves."

"You're so great." Lia hugged her friend. "Fabulous party!"

"I'm hoping you two are off to have a private party of your own," Zoë said, kissing

Lucas's cheek.

Lucas rolled his eyes. Girl-talk made him squirm inside.

Zoë's eyebrows lifted. Her smug smile stretched as wide as the Missouri River.

He gritted his teeth at her teasing. She understood full well his discomfort and held back a snort. Before the conversation delved any deeper into his private longings, he had to get Amelia away.

"Mr. Dwyer, will you give a woman a lift home?" Amelia asked, wrapping her arm around his. The gentleness of her touch soothed his tension. If he managed to hold on a few minutes more, his reward was the rest of the night with Amelia.

"Let's go." Lucas linked fingers with hers and led her downstairs. His mind drifted to the memory of when he and Amelia had last made love—in her bed. She surprised him the other day. A private party that showed him how much he meant to her. His hands now tingled with longing to caress her creamy, smooth skin. A few kisses wouldn't be enough. He had to have more. If she agreed, he planned to share the night, the refreshing outdoors, and the stars, while camping in the back of his truck in the middle of one of her fields. He'd dropped off the cleaned pickup at Amelia's farm before heading to the party earlier.

"Look!" Amelia pointed upward.

"An image burned in my memory," Lucas told her. Amelia, radiant against a dark sky with stars shining like a halo around her. He had relied on memories of her to get through the worst days when he fought overseas. This one, he'd never forget.

Lucas tugged on her hand, leading her to the

parking lot across from Rockets.

"Whatcha thinking?" Amelia asked.

"I drove Megan's car. It's over there." Lucas pointed.

Once inside the car, away from possible prying eyes, Lucas reached over, captured Amelia's face, and stroked the smoothness of her cheeks. "I'm bigger on showing than telling." His lips met hers, soft and pliant. Kisses from her were his lifeline to love and contentment. He wasn't a man with big ideas or fancy cravings. Solid. Simple. True. It was how he lived his life. Those three words were ones he wanted carved on his headstone. The way he wanted to be remembered.

Raining kisses on her cheeks, nose, and forehead, he savored the sweetness of her. When he let go, Amelia melted into the car's seat. "Ahhh."

Her purring over his kisses boosted his spirit and his anticipation. And with a few more, he might be able to wind her up the same way she did him, full of naked desire.

"Take me home, Lucas." Her voice seduced him. She buckled her seatbelt and rested her head back. Her eyes remained closed. She licked her lips. Maybe it was a subconscious action, but he wanted to believe it was because she savored the taste of his lips.

Putting the car in drive, he sped from the parking lot, traveling familiar country roads. He slowed when he recognized a deer by its glowing red eyes by the side of the road.

Amelia reached across the console and rested her hand on his forearm. Excitement shot through him. He loved everything about this woman. The caress of her touch. The softness of her lips. The smoothness of her skin. He reveled in her passion for her art, for her farm, for her family and friends. She was strong. Determined. Optimism was truly her middle name.

"I have a private party to attend tonight," Amelia whispered, her eyes still closed. She appeared completely relaxed in the seat beside him. "Only, I'm not the guest of honor...you are." He felt her squeeze on his arm. She stroked her hand up and down.

He forced himself not to press the accelerator harder, but imagined metal bumping the floorboard. Lia wanted him!

It might be her birthday; however he would be the recipient of the best gift of all. Amelia. Her heart and her body. That made him the richest man in the county.

Turning right, starting up the hill, his gazed scanned the horizon. It appeared to slip beneath them. Before them, only an endless sky with stars shimmering like jewels.

"Amelia, look," he said quietly, slowing to fully appreciate the view.

"Oh, Lucas, I'm going to emboss this moment in my memory. It's totally perfect."

"Look!" Lucas pointed. "A falling star."

Amelia squinted her eyes tightly before opening them. "I hope my wish comes true."

"*I'm* wishing your wish comes true."

Amelia leaned over. Her kiss on his cheek filled him with surging anticipation. He hit the gas. Tires spun on the dirt road. The car shot forward. "I have a surprise for you. I intend to make this a very happy birthday, Amelia."

They reached the house in a flash. "Go change. Something comfortable," Lucas ordered. "We're going exploring. You get to discover your birthday present from me."

A glowing smile lit Amelia's face. She dashed from the car to the house. When she opened the door, Jack shot out. He ran straight for Lucas.

"Come with me, boy," Lucas said. He leaned down to pet Jack before opening the trunk. Pulling out rolled up jeans and a t-shirt, he said, "You can go with us tonight, but you have to stay in the cab of the truck." The dog followed him into the house. Lucas helped himself to the downstairs bathroom where he changed his clothes. When he entered the hallway, Amelia waited for him wearing a smile that radiated tenderness. He loved this woman fiercely. Her loveliness wrapped around his heart.

"I'm ready," she whispered.

"Let's grab an extra flashlight." He headed toward the pantry where the Brittons always kept theirs.

"Come on." Amelia tugged impatiently on his hand. Excitement danced in her eyes. "I see you've recruited Jack to join us."

At a trot, they followed the path from the house toward the creek. Lucas loosened his grasp on Amelia's hand, but she grasped his tighter. The cool breeze hinted of fall. Wind chimes harmonized, their music floating across the fields. Frogs croaked, deep and low, like the bass in a jazz combo. Rustling corn whispered a lullaby. Scents of freshness and rich, dark earth mixed with hints of honeysuckle. As they drew near the creek, a symphony of sounds stirred around them while Jack ran on ahead, disappearing beneath the cover of draping tree branches.

"I want to show you something," Amelia said. She slowed as they neared the wall of branches blocking the path to the creek.

Lucas pushed foliage aside, and Amelia stepped through to the shelter of an umbrella of greenery. He followed her into a creekside cocoon where Jack chased fireflies.

"Look." Amelia lowered her chin, and she peered up at him shyly. "Here." She pointed to a post on the bark of the ancient tree. It was old when they were kids, surviving years of changing seasons, creek flooding, and ice storms.

He leaned in closer for a better look, then focused a beam from the flashlight on the spot. Carved into the bark of the tree, an old wound, scarred and healed over, were the initials AB + LD encased in a heart.

"Amelia Britton plus Lucas Dwyer," he whispered.

"I was fourteen."

"We were both kids."

"But I knew. Lucas. I knew I loved you."

Lucas reached for her, pulling her close. Her breath hitched. When she relaxed, he folded his arms securely around her, joy folding around his heart. Holding her close, he rested his chin on top of her head. "I've waited a long time to say these words to you. I wanted the timing to be right."

"Shhh."

"I love you, Amelia. Only you." He lifted her chin and kissed her nose before claiming her soft lips.

Her arms circled his neck, and she clung to him as her kisses turned deeper, more urgent.

"I love you more," she whispered back before kissing him again.

His heart swelled. Delight shot him to the sky, and there he joined the brilliant stars. He leaned against a low hanging branch to steady himself, never breaking contact with her. She pressed her body closer to his. There was no way she could miss his hard bulge between them.

"Wish I had thought to bring a blanket," Amelia said, taking a breath. She tugged on his bottom lip with hers and rocked her pelvis against his. The grass might be soft, but not a place for making love with her. His need for her hit a fevered pitch.

"Come." He pushed through the brush and led her along the path with Jack nipping at their heels. Jogging slowly so she could keep up, he made several turns to keep her off track.

He cut through a cornfield to a field of sunflowers visible under the moon's glow. After several minutes, which seemed like an hour, the final destination came into view. Her surprise waited around the next corner.

At the top of the rise, they stood together bathed in the moonlight. Below them, a field of sunflowers, surrounded by acres of tasseled corn spread out like the train of an evening gown. His truck sat in a small clearing where he'd parked it to capture the view. A royal blue tent, the center pitch high enough for them to easily sit up, covered the bed of the pickup. He held his breath waiting for her to speak.

"I don't understand." Amelia stopped beside him.

"A night under the stars."

"Alone? The two of us?" she asked eagerly.

"Well, I promised Jack he could stay. I'll put him on the backseat and open the window so he won't feel left out."

Amelia made her way to the rear of the pickup and hoisted herself on the tailgate. "An air mattress, sheets, pillows, *and* a quilt. Soft lights and music. You are a man with a plan." She grinned and batted her lashes. "I like that about you, Lucas Dwyer." She opened her arms. "Now come over here and let me show you how much."

Her flirting set off more flares of desires. He hugged her tightly.

"Let me get Jack situated," he whispered, hating to tear himself away from her. He opened the back door to the crew cab, and the obedient dog hopped in. By the time Lucas walked back to the rear of the truck, he discovered Amelia had peeled back the bedding. He remained very still. Silhouetted by the beam from a flashlight, Amelia with her back to him, knelt on the air mattress clothed in only her bra and underwear. His breath caught in his chest. When she reached behind and unhooked her bra, it was the sexiest move he'd ever seen.

Tossing the bra aside, she turned and glanced over her shoulder at him. He caught sight of her slender shape and full round breasts. Every muscle in his body tightened.

"Don't tell. Show." She crooked a finger in his direction.

He backed up. With a step and a hop, he landed on the tailgate. Kicking off his shoes, he jerked off his jeans before dropping to his knees. He tossed his t-shirt in the corner.

"Woman," he thundered. "I want you. I love you."

"I'm yours."

Amelia relaxed into the bed and stretched her legs long. Raising her hands over her head, she laced her fingers together. This Amelia was seductive and wanton. He intended to satisfy her every need. Running his hand down her arm, around the curve of her jaw, drawing a line from the hollow of her neck to the spot between her breasts, he stroked her skin.

Moving on to removing her panties, sexy and silky, he never imagined the always-proper, ever-decent, perfect girl-next-door, Amelia Britton owned such things. He smiled hoping for many days of opportunity to remove more of them from her body.

She surprised him when she lifted up and pushed on his chest, forcing him back against the mattress. Just as he had done for her, she gave back to him. Her soft warm hand stroked from his arm to the curve of his jaw. Only after she reached the hollow of his neck, she traced a line all the way down to his erection. When her soft hand cupped him, he groaned. She removed the barrier separating them, tossing his briefs aside.

"Amelia, I can't take much more, honey."

"Lucas, darling, there's no more waiting."

He arched over her. His entry to the heated softness between her legs was sweetness beyond his dreams. They fit together perfectly, like jigsaw puzzle pieces.

He nipped at her breast. She squirmed beneath

him, undulating her hips. Together, they moved. She matched his pace. A slow rock. The pace quickened.

"Oh, yes," Amelia moaned. Her eyes closed. She licked her lips. Her expression spoke of focused intensity. Her body nudged against his faster and faster. Her writhing drove him crazy. He matched her pace, quickening each thrust.

When Amelia moaned again and grabbed his butt, he let out a moan of pure pleasure.

Heaven wrapped around them. Physical sensations shot them through the universe.

Expressions of love, lust, and desire culminated in a long guttural moan, their cries melding just as their bodies had. Floating back to earth seemed a crime.

Being with a woman had never been like this. Amelia wasn't just any woman.

"Love you," Lucas said, when his breathing allowed him to speak. Amelia's reply came as a deep and satisfying kiss. He locked his fingers in her hair. Silk thread couldn't feel any more luxurious.

When his breathing slowed a bit more, he rolled beside Amelia and propped on his elbows. "I can't recall a more perfect evening. Happy birthday, Amelia."

"Thank you," she whispered almost shyly. "It's been the best birthday." When she didn't reach for the sheet to cover her body, it pleased him in a way he'd never considered. His woman was comfortable with him and their intimacy. Society's propriety remained parked at the door.

He sat and reached for his jeans. From a front pocket, he pulled a small box. "I've waited a long time to give you this." He opened the box for her. His gift nestled in velvet.

"Oh!" Amelia cried. "It's beautiful."

Lucas lifted a solitaire diamond pendant hanging from a chain. She hurriedly motioned to him to put it on her. It hung in the middle of her chest. She stroked the length of the chain as though it might bring her good luck, or maybe a genie would appear and offer three wishes.

"I don't want to rush things, or rush you. I love you. Amelia, I want to marry you."

Her eyes widened. A smile spread across her face. She brought both hands to her heart and clutched the diamond pendant. "I want to be with you."

"When you're ready, we'll find a setting for the diamond, and it will become your engagement ring."

She kissed him tenderly. "You mean the world to me. But my future is so uncertain. Are you sure?"

He'd do everything to ensure her happiness, including convincing her brother of the rightness of their relationship. Amelia was locked in his heart forever. His.

"Woman, let me show you how certain I am." He pulled her close. "Actions always speak louder than words."

She giggled. He loved the lightness of her laugh, the unjaded way she lived and loved. He'd make love to her until dawn.

"Talk away," she teased.

He tried to shove away the niggling thought working on a foothold in his mind. It would break his heart forever if she had to move back to the city to fulfill her artistic needs, something he could never give her. Everything in her life, and now his, rested on the crop spread out before them. It was only gold when harvested and money from the sale deposited in the bank. Then she could claim the independence she craved.

He still had a plan to save her farm.

Chapter 19

Dawn lifted the sun upward over the horizon as Craig paced the length of the back deck. Last night, Amelia had never opened her birthday present. Last night she never came home. Last night she changed before his eyes from a younger sister to a woman in control. She carried herself with grace and dignity, displaying a poise he'd not seen before.

He should be happy. A grown-up confident woman would understand the realities of life. He wouldn't have to sugarcoat anything anymore. But at six in the morning, his sister still hadn't appeared, and Megan's car remained in the driveway. Lucas had to be with Amelia, but where were they?

Lucas. He wanted to blame him and thank him.

Amelia had danced with him once, but the rest of the evening, she danced with everyone, especially Lucas. At first, their closeness bothered him. Then it surprised him. When the two of them made the rounds to greet the guests, no one but him seemed fazed that Amelia and Lucas were a couple. A couple!

In the beginning, his friend had shown *brotherly* attentiveness, and he reasoned it was because Lia was the birthday girl. When he spied Lucas tilt Amelia's chin and kiss her, reality struck hard. Lucas had fallen for Amelia. His feelings about his best friend and his baby sister whirled in his heart like a spinning propeller. The emotion, not exactly disbelief, well, maybe that mixed with anger and possibly betrayal...but why?

His mind couldn't circle around the idea of the two of them. Since high school, he had dissuaded Lucas from any relationship with Amelia after she'd declared her love. Even last year after the funeral, he'd cautioned Lucas to keep his distance, insisting Amelia needed time to grieve the loss of their parents.

Unable to wait any longer for his sister to appear, Craig pumped his fists and jogged down the steps to the backyard. Gentleman Jack came to greet him bearing his toy pheasant in his mouth.

"Hunting season will open soon. We'll go this year, I promise. Where's Amelia?"

Jack ran off toward the creek and Craig followed. The dog came from excellent pedigree, the progeny of many world champions, but his breeding made him a pointing bird dog, not a human tracker. His gaze followed Jack as he shot through the low hanging branches obscuring the view of the creek. As a kid, it was Amelia's favorite place to hide. When she was about seven and going through her princess stage, she ordered him and Lucas to stay away from her castle.

Nearing the creek, he walked along the tree line, then slipped between the tree branches as Jack had done. There he found the Brittany spaniel hunkered down and panting near the water's edge. Craig squatted next to him. Morning sun filtered through the limbs and leaves, hitting one particular spot. He noticed something carved into the trunk of a tree. Scooting along the thick branch, he jumped down on the opposite side of the creek and stared at the letters,

Linda Joyce

tracing the carvings with his finger.

A heart with the initials L & L inside. The carved letters had to stand for Lucas and Lia.

His heart sank. What had he done?

Below the heart, a date. He counted back the years. Amelia had been a senior in high school. Back then, she demanded to be called Lia. Her friends complied, but their family had always used her proper given name.

Had his sister carried more than a schoolgirl crush on Lucas all these years? Did Lucas know? If so, then why had Lucas gone along with the plan to get Amelia to move back to the city? Maybe the man loved her—which might explain his angry rant in the barn before when he'd stormed away.

Craig scrunched his forehead. Confusion swirled until his head hurt. People and their love lives...it complicated life in a way he wanted no part of. He would forever be a bachelor. Certainly he enjoyed the company of a smart, sexy woman, but he liked women who loved their careers more. That kind of woman he understood. A nice time. A little companionship. No lasting entanglements to cause complications.

After crossing back over the creek, Craig squatted to pat Jack. "Where can I find Amelia? Jack, find Amelia."

Jack bolted. Craig ran wide open to keep up with the dog. The paths they ran turned like a maze. He halted when a tent came into view. He slowed his pace, turned a corner, and approached Lucas's truck from the front. Jack shot past him, heading back in the direction they had come from as though to say, *I*

223

did my job. This is in your hands now.

No sound came from the tent perched above the truck bed. The hair on the back of his neck rose. Silently, he made his way alongside the truck. All quiet. He grimaced and paused before peering around the corner. If there was anything to see, anything at all, he wouldn't be able to un-see it, like a bell that couldn't be unrung. Sucking in a deep breath and squaring his shoulders, he marched the last several steps to the open tailgate.

The scene before him burned in his brain. Squinting into the darkened tent, his eyes adjusted. Amelia and Lucas. It was like watching a train wreck and being unable to look away. He shook his head in denial. "No!"

Inside the tent, Amelia and Lucas were lay tangled together. She on her side, one bare leg exposed all the way to her butt. Thank God, her chest was covered. Lucas lay on his stomach, his entire bare backside visible.

"What the hell!" Heat flooded Craig's face. He put his hands over his ears to be sure his exploding blood pressure wasn't spurting blood from there. His sister naked in bed with Lucas? Crushes and puppy love were one thing. This was just... just... mind-blowing.

"Amelia, wake up! Have the decency to cover your ass!" he snarled. "Lucas! Christ, man, what the...did you do? My sister?" He yanked on the quilt, and Amelia grabbed it from his grasp.

"Stop this craziness," Amelia chastised.

His sanity fled. He wanted Lucas to climb out of the truck and fight.

"Lucas, have you lost your mind? Get out of there!" Craig yelled.

Lucas rolled over and pulled a sheet to cover himself. He yawned. "Screaming like a girl doesn't change anything. We'll be up to the house in a little while. How 'bout some privacy?"

Craig locked his jaw and slammed his fist on the tailgate. "Get your ass out of bed. Away from my sister!"

"Stop it!" Amelia demanded. "You're acting irrational. You're not my father. I'm not a wayward teenager. Get the heck out of here. We'll see you at the house in a little while."

"No. Now."

Lucas eyed him. "Please respect your sister and leave."

"I'm not going to stand here and watch you dress. I'll be waiting. I expect you in fifteen minutes," Craig snapped. He stalked away, certain if anyone saw him, they'd see fury rolling off him and have the good sense to stay away.

"We may be more than fifteen minutes," Lucas called out, his voice full of sleep and laziness. Amelia giggled.

Sweat broke out on Craig's brow. He burst into a full run as if chased by hell. Whatever might happen next in that makeshift bedroom, he could imagine, but didn't need or want confirmation. The sooner he got away, the better.

But he'd be waiting.

With a shotgun.

Lucas Dyer was about to get some old-fashioned coaching.

Chapter 20

An hour later, around the breakfast table, the most important people in Lia's life, minus one, laughed and scarfed down scrambled eggs, home fries, bacon, and toast. The kitchen was made more homey by aromas from frying applewood-smoked bacon, Craig's favorite. But he was nowhere to be found. With his car still in the driveway, he couldn't have gone far. Lia poured orange juice into glasses and mussed with Megan's hair as though she were a small child rather than a college student. Maybe one day, the two of them would be sisters-in-law. Giddily, she fluffed Megan's hair again.

"Coffee?" Lucas asked.

"Coming right up." Lia's heart sang a melody, part Irish jig and part down-home blues. How she loved Lucas! The man was a package and then some. A tender and thorough lover. A solid man, always wanting to do the right thing for everyone in his life. He worked hard, kept his word, a handshake his bond. A farmer's body, strong, lean, and sexy. The man drifted to the serious side a bit, but she would help lighten him up. Responsibility weighed him down since his first tour of Afghanistan. He never talked with her about the war or things that happened there.

She would find more ways to put smiles on his face. Just like the ones last night and this morning.

She giggled remembering.

Together with Lucas, the positive possibilities of life could light up the night sky.

She poured coffee into Lucas's mug. He caught her wrist, smiled, and winked. "Thank you."

She nodded, enjoying the sensations of being part of a family again.

"I wonder where he is," she muttered, concerned about her brother's absence. She set the pot on a trivet before sitting down to eat. If anyone minded that Craig was a no-show, it wasn't apparent by their appetites.

Bang! Slam!

The front door opened and closed. Craig rushed in hoisting a side-by-side, double-barreled shotgun. He aimed it at Lucas. "Get up."

"What?" Lucas's fork, covered in potatoes, hung suspended halfway between his plate and mouth.

"Craig, what the heck?" Lia asked. Pushing away from the table, she rose and stood in the space between Craig and Lucas, who remained seated. "We're having breakfast. I saved some bacon for you. This isn't funny. Put the gun down. How do you want your eggs?"

"Lucas, outside."

"You better not hurt my brother," Megan shouted, fear flashing on her face.

Lia turned her back to her brother and faced Lucas. "Finish your breakfast. I'll take care of this."

"No!" Craig cried. "Lucas. Man to man. Outside. If you live, you can finish your meal. Amelia, the two of you have gone too far."

Lia's hands trembled. She reached for Megan's

hand when Lucas rose, dropped his napkin on the chair, and crossed the room. He left the house the same way Craig had entered. Craig followed him out.

"Seriously?" Megan said, standing up. "Make them stop. This isn't funny," she pleaded.

"I know. I know." Lia swallowed hard, her stomach in her throat. Wrapping her arm around Megan's shoulder, she made a fist with her other and released it. Was Craig drunk? Her stomach tightened. It was all too surreal. It had to be a joke.

She and Megan pressed their noses to the window. Lia shuddered. Uncertainty scratched down her back as the scene unfolded outside. "Trust me. Craig won't hurt Lucas. He doesn't have it in him. Let's just pray the gun doesn't accidently go off."

Megan nodded. "I can't believe Craig is this crazy!"

The two men stood ten feet apart on the front lawn, their intensity belying the bucolic setting of velvet grass, pink and red flowers, bluebirds scattering seeds from the feeders, and hummingbirds flitting around the tall posts of the split-rail fence.

"Oh, Craig," Lia sighed, opening the window to hear the exchange between the men.

Her brother always tried to do the right thing, but lately he never stopped to consider what really might be best. Just like a man to be lost and not stop for directions.

Her heart pounded double time. Blood rushed in her ears. Butterflies dove and fluttered in her stomach. She said a silent prayer for Lucas's safety, *and* counted on his rationality in the face of her brother's bizarre behavior. However, Craig's erratic behavior worried her to her bones. He'd taken on so much, carrying the burden of responsibility for her and the farm, all the while trying to carve out a new life for himself in St. Louis. Had he snapped? Had seeing her with Lucas been too much?

"Lucas, I always thought of you as a brother," Craig shouted as he paced back and forth. His fingers flexed around the gun. "So did Amelia. Our father isn't here. So this is my job. What are your intentions toward my sister?" Craig raised the barrel of the shotgun and pointed at Lucas's chest.

"Intentions?" Lucas shrugged. "Funny thing about intentions. Sometimes they backfire, just like yours did." Lucas held out his arms from his sides as though showing he had no defenses, his body language screaming, *I'm unarmed*. He took a step forward. Craig took two steps back.

"I set out to help you, Craig. I know you had good intentions for Amelia, but you can't play God. She gets to decide about her life. She gets to live with the consequences of her actions. Your father was a wise man"—Lucas shook his finger, berating Craig— "he wouldn't be standing here holding a loaded shotgun on me."

"You slept with my sister!"

"I did. I love her."

"Please, don't tell him it wasn't the first time," Lia whispered. She covered her cheeks with her hands and willed Lucas to hear her plea. "Please don't tell him."

Megan looked up at her with wide eyes. "Not the first time?" The accusation hung thick in the air around them.

229

Linda Joyce

"I'll explain later," Lia told her in a rush. She pointed outside hoping to keep Megan's attention focused there.

"So Lucas did more than just spend the night with you in KC."

"Megan, now isn't the time."

"This is too much drama," Megan said. "I'm going to be sick." She ran to the bathroom.

Torn, Lia wanted to follow her to be sure she was okay, but her feet remain glued to the spot before the window. There had to be a way to stop this craziness before someone got hurt.

"Why would you sneak around behind my back?" Craig lowered the barrel of the shotgun from Lucas's chest to his groin. "Why didn't you let me know how you felt about her?"

Lucas didn't flinch. "So the great and mighty Craig Britton could laugh at me? Tell me how a poor, farm-less farm boy wasn't good enough for his sister? How living in the country isn't the life for his sister?" Lucas shouted and stepped closer to Craig. "How many times have you told me that? How many? Christ, if I had a dollar for every time, I could buy your half of the damn farm and give it to Amelia for a wedding gift."

Craig's face wrinkled. Brows furrowed. Nose pinched, as though he smelled something foul. Then he raised the barrel of the gun and pointed it once again at Lucas's chest.

"I love her. And if she'll have me, I'm going to marry her."

Lia squeezed her eyes shut. Her nostrils flared. Her jaw locked. "Enough!"

She stormed outside, slamming the front door. "Craig Britton!" she screamed. Anger pumped through her veins like a rocket blasting off for a trip to the moon. She stomped her way to her brother. "Give me that!" Jerking the barrel of the shotgun, she yanked hard and pulled it from him. "Idiot! What do you think you're doing?"

Craig folded and sank to the ground, sitting crossed-legged. He covered his face with his hands.

Lucas crossed the yard to her as she opened the break-open shotgun. Once the chambers were exposed, she snorted. "The darn thing wasn't loaded. Dammit, Craig. What's up with you?"

Lucas reached out a hand to Craig, an offer to help pull him up. Craig slapped Lucas's hand away and rose on his own.

"Suit yourself," Lucas said, his voice deadly calm. "But don't ever point a gun at me again unless you intend to pull the trigger. I *have* killed men for that."

"Honey," Lia pleaded. "Please check on Megan. She's not feeling well. Let me deal with my brother. I'll let you have a swing at him later. I might even hold him for you."

Lucas nodded. When he reached the front door, he turned back as though he had something to say, but instead, shook his head and disappeared inside.

"Let's talk over there." Lia pointed to the two wooden Adirondack chairs their parents used to sit in and watch sunsets.

Craig sank into the wooden seat.

Lia pulled the diamond pendant so it hung in front of her t-shirt. "Lucas gave me this." She leaned over for her brother to examine it. "He didn't ask me to marry him. He said he didn't want to rush things. When I was ready, when I know it's right, we'll take the stone and have it set in a ring, an engagement ring. Then he'll officially propose."

"Nice," Craig said, letting go of the chain.

"Now for you. A shotgun? Really? You need to tell me what's going on. If I were Zoë, I'd take the butt of the gun and..."

"I get the picture." Craig scrubbed his face with his hands. "You were always the perfect child, always the talented one. From the day you were born, I was told to protect you, watch out for you. You're the baby sister."

"But I haven't been a baby for a long time," Lia said softly. "And I don't want to increase your *ick* factor, but I'm also not a virginal little miss. Lucas wasn't my first."

"I want to cover my ears and sing, *la la la la la*. I don't want to know the details. Not about anything before, and certainly not about what I saw."

"I want you to be happy for Lucas and me. I love him, Craig." She reached and patted his hand.

"But—"

"Blame it on Helen. She was the one who declared the prophecy. I resisted the notion, but I've always cared for Lucas."

"Yeah. I know." Craig's voice carried deep resignation.

"You did?"

"I saw the carvings on the trees down by the creek. Your hideaway. I figured it out. But when I saw the two of you this morning, something took hold, after I waited all night for you to open your present and to share some news about the farm."

Unease crawled up her back like a scorpion walked along her spine. The harvest wasn't in yet. What did Craig have cooking?

He pulled his keys from his jeans' pocket. "I've got to get back to St. Louis. I guess I'll leave you and Lucas to work out the details, figure out a plan. I'll get used to the idea of the two of you together"—her heart softened, and the breath she held escaped. He would come around and all would be okay—"I've got a buyer for the farm."

His words hit her like a bulldozer. Her heart plunged to her feet. She blinked. "You what?"

"Either buy me out in cash, or we sell." Craig stood. "I've given you all the time I'm going to. I'm tired of this, tired of trying to help you do the right thing, and you fighting me all the way." He bent and squeezed her shoulder. "The farm is part of my inheritance, too. I want to invest in something else. This appears to be a bust." He strode to his BMW and drove away.

Lia sank back into the chair. Her brother's words hurt as much as if he'd shot her with both barrels of the shotgun. Her whole world had been wiped away. The paintings. The studio. Now the farm.

And soon Lucas would be leaving for the harvesting season.

What would she do?

Chapter 21

Lucas set his plate of half-eaten food in the microwave to heat, thankful for Craig's departure. What was he thinking? Craig would never shoot him. Amelia proved it. The shotgun had no shells. Damn fool needed his head examined. Maybe the year had been more than Craig could handle. He'd never make it in the military.

"I can't eat," Megan said, joining him in the kitchen, her face still pale, but showing a bit more color. She peeked through the window. "Craig's car is gone."

"Do you see Amelia?" Lucas asked. He pulled his plate out of the microwave and bobbled it. Grabbing a towel to protect his hand, he set the plate down on the table to finish eating the food Amelia had served him only a bit ago.

Megan opened the front door. "Lucas, she's sitting in one of the chairs." She turned to him. "She's crying," she whispered. "Lia hardly ever cries. I wonder—"

Lucas was out of his seat, gently pushing his sister aside, and out the front door.

"Amelia?" Fear had a stranglehold on his gut. He couldn't imagine Craig had hurt her and left, but the man who'd pointed a shotgun at him wasn't the man he'd been friends with all his life. Hunkering down in front of her, he took her hands in his. "Are you hurt, sweetheart?"

She wiped away her tears. "I'm fine." She shook her head as though to stop the tears and clear away the gray cloud Craig had left behind.

"I think he's cracking under the pressure. We both know this isn't like Craig. And I know he isn't doing drugs...nor was he drunk, which makes me worry more." Amelia rose with his help. "Let's go finish breakfast." Amelia's smile was forced. Her eyes still brimmed with tears.

"I was about to start without you," he teased.

They made it to the front porch before Amelia spoke again. "You're leaving tomorrow, aren't you?"

Lucas nodded. He wished he could say otherwise. He would miss her art show opening. Miss the harvesting of her crop. He'd miss her sweet kisses. Miss every inch of her body, her smiles, her sense of humor, and her warmth at night.

Amelia's mouth drew a straight line as though she contemplated something. What? She didn't say. He was reluctant to ask. Prying wasn't his thing.

At the table, Megan sipped orange juice. "Can we pretend what just happened was an episode from *Doctor Who* and now we're back on Earth?" she pleaded. "Amelia, shall I heat up your plate?"

"I've got it. You just enjoy the view and your OJ."

They finished breakfast in silence. Anger skittered in Lucas's gut like a ricocheting bullet. Craig had crossed the line, seriously crossed the line, but maybe he needed serious help. Pointing a gun at him was one thing, but bringing Amelia to tears—

completely unacceptable.

"I hate to eat and run, but I've got to hit the road," Lucas said, rising from the table. He kissed the top of Amelia's head and squeezed her shoulder.

"I'll clean up." Megan popped out of her chair and grabbed the platters of leftover food.

"I'll walk you out," Amelia said, following him.

They stood in silence beside his truck. He opened his arms, and she flung herself at him. "What is it? What did Craig do or say?"

"I'm not sure what I'm going to do." She released him and slumped against the passenger door of the pickup.

Lucas searched her face, her eyes, searched for the deeper meaning to her words. "Now's not a time for riddles. Tell me."

"I don't know where I'm going to go. I don't know what I'm going to do. Craig has a buyer for the farm. I must buy him out now, or the farm is sold."

"That's what he said before he left?" Anger bubbled up and wrapped around Lucas's neck like a noose. It grew tighter until he fought back the choking sensation. The urge to punch something hard, like Craig, took over. He kicked the truck's tire instead. "Dammit! He told you like that?"

"Meaning?"

"He's gone off his rocker completely. He should have told you in a better way."

"You knew?" Amelia stood and crossed her arms over her chest.

"Well..."

"You knew!" She flung the accusation at him so hard it punched his gut.

"Why didn't you tell me?"

"It wasn't my place. I'm navigating new waters here. Our friendship, mine and Craig's, mine and yours, goes way back. Lots of history..."

"But you made love to me! You gave me this!" She tugged on the diamond hanging on the chain. "Am I not your first loyalty?" She stepped away from him.

"Be reasonable, Amelia. It's not that simple. I love you. But the last thing I want is a rift between you and Craig with me in the middle." He took a step closer to her, but she put up her hands for him to stop.

"I don't see a future for us." Amelia unhooked the necklace. She reached for his hand, placing the pendant there. "I can't accept this." She turned away and walked slowly into the house without looking back.

"Amelia," Lucas called after her. She entered the house without a hint of having heard him.

"Dammit. Dammit, Craig," Lucas muttered. Why was it that lately all of his plans took a turn and put him in a ditch? His thoughts flashed to last night. A perfect memory, but he wanted more, an entire memory book with pages of life with Amelia. However, now wasn't the time for talking. Now was the time for doing.

He climbed into his truck. Before driving away, he spied Amelia and his sister watching him through the kitchen window. He blew a kiss.

"Going to see a man and beg about a farm," he said, knowing the words would fade before ever reaching their ears.

He headed down the road and hoped his bartering

skills weren't as rusty as his relationship-fixing skills.

He had to find a way to keep Amelia near. On the farm. A farm. Any farm nearby.

****

Lia cringed and beat her fist on the kitchen counter as Lucas drove away. He hadn't fought for her, for them. Would he bother to contact her before leaving tomorrow? Had she just ended everything? Weariness set in. A nap might not solve anything, but afterward, she'd figure out what to do next. The morning's emotional tornado wore her nerves thin.

"Lia," Megan called from the art studio.

"Yes?" Lia wanted to send the college student on her way back to school.

"Come sit with me for a few minutes."

Lia entered the studio with Jack on her heels. He passed her and climbed onto his bed, circled around, and lay down. Contentment comes easy when you're a dog, Lia mused. The studio wrapped her in a blanket of safety. When immersed in a painting, she often preferred sleeping on the daybed against the wall, taking catnaps between bursts of creative flow.

Megan sat on the rolling stool. "Do you think of Lucas as a big brother?"

"Ah, what?"

"You heard me."

Lia stalled, wondering what field Megan had plucked her question from.

Megan pressed on. "He cares deeply for you, but until—uh, whenever it was when the two of you first did the deed—he wouldn't allow himself to believe you might love him back. So, I'm guessing you *don't* think of him as a big brother. It would be really cool to have you for a sister-in-law. I mean, like last Sunday when you helped me understand Lucas's concerns for me. So, I don't mean to interfere, but you just had a birthday and…"

"Spill it."

"Well," Megan paused. "You're not getting any younger."

"Younger? You think because I'm nearly thirty, I'm old?" Lia snorted and laughed. Nothing about her life gifted her with a sense of youthfulness. Life was hard work. Fun had taken a holiday without her. Did she seem ancient to a college sophomore? Maybe she did need a girls' weekend away with Zoë.

"What's so funny? Most people your age get touchy about the subject. It's not usually a laughing matter."

"Do you realize my brother and yours have been treating me like a child for years? And you come along, bright-eyed and full of life, and you see me practically as middle-aged. Yep, it's funny."

"Does this mean we can talk, woman to woman?"

Lia chuckled. "Absolutely. Talk away." She picked up a paintbrush and twirled it between her fingers. Later she would paint.

"Lucas said he wants me to have the house. We own it together. My parents did a quit claim deed when they left for Arizona. However, I'm hoping you can understand. I. Never."—Megan pointed, punctuating the air on each word—"Want. To. Live. In. The. Country. Again. Particularly in that house. It's great to come home to it while I'm in college. However, I've made up my mind. I can legally sign contracts now. I want to give my share of the house to you and Lucas as a wedding present."

"Whoa. What?"

"Wedding. Present. Does hitting middle age make you suddenly hard of hearing?"

"There's not going to be a wedding. Besides, I can't let you do that."

"You think because I'm in college I can't make this kind of a decision? You're not taking me seriously." Megan scowled.

All too familiar with the sentiment, Lia dropped the paintbrush into a jar with the others. "Megan, it's complicated. It looks like I'm going to lose the farm. I have one small shot at bringing in the harvest, but I don't think it's going to make the mortgage payment and buy Craig out of his share. Craig has a buyer for the farm."

"All the more reason for you and Lucas to get married and move into our house," Megan insisted, rolling the stool closer to Lia.

"All the plans I had...the way I had things worked out. I've failed, Megan. I can't marry Lucas to stay in the country."

Megan jumped up and kicked the stool away. It shot across the room, hitting the kitchen door. "You're not going to marry Lucas to get a place to live. You're going marry my brother because you. Love. Him. Geez, middle age does crap to the brain." Megan shook her head and frowned as though life ahead of her was a minefield, and she might not get out alive.

"Megan..."

"If you say *life's complicated* one more time, I'll

stop speaking to you."

"I'll think about your suggestion," Lia promised.

"I'll go clean the kitchen. Then I need to check on Lucas before heading back to Manhattan."

"You go," Lia urged. "I'll take care of the clean-up."

"And *think* about what I've said."

"I'll give it serious consideration."

Megan hugged her tight. Her bottom lip quivered and her eyes watered, but she didn't continue to plead her case. Lia walked her to the door. Jack waited patiently while Megan hugged him, too.

As Megan drove away, Lia wondered how she'd let history repeat itself. Megan spoke with conviction. She might be younger, but she had a sense of direction for her life, one that didn't include farming. She had every right to walk the path that suited her best, and in truth, only she could know it.

Eyeing her birthday present from Craig, Lia placed it on the dining room table and tugged on the ribbon, releasing the bow. Tearing at the paper, she uncovered a taped, plain brown box.

Sighing, she shook the box. It barely made a sound. The box opened when she pulled off the tape. Inside, several new brushes for oil painting were nestled in a bed of tissue paper along with a gift receipt for a new easel. "Oh, Craig, a perfect gift. Why did you have to spoil my birthday?" He could be so thoughtful to her one moment and irrational about her the next. If he were a woman, she'd think he suffered from PMS.

Plopping on the couch, she cuddled Jack when he joined her. Silence enveloped her. Sleep pulled her under. She nestled into a comfortable position with Jack at her feet and allowed herself the luxury of a nap. The paintings could wait a few hours. When she woke, she intended to find Lucas and hash things out. She'd been way too hasty.

Thoughts of Lucas wound tighter and tighter in her mind, thoughts twirling like a Ferris wheel spinning at warp speed. Restlessness irritated her like a rash. Any chance of her dozing ended when a truck pulled up in the yard.

Lia jumped from the couch. Jack slipped to the floor and scowled, clearly annoyed at the interruption. Throwing open the front door, she shoved the screen door open. "Lucas!" Her heart raced. Misting tears blurred her vision. The world around her changed as though it were a wet-on-wet watercolor.

"Amelia!" Lucas climbed out of the truck, the door left hanging open. He held open his arms. She did a quick hop and jumped at him, wrapping her arms tightly around his neck, nearly a stranglehold. Lucas lost his balance, and they tumbled to the ground. Lucas twisted to break her fall. His back hit the lush grass, and she thudded against his chest.

"*Ahuh*," he said, air leaving his lungs.

"Are you hurt?" She cupped his face and tried to give him mouth to mouth.

Lucas forced her back as he sat, and she ended up in his lap. He coughed, then began to laugh.

"It's not funny." She swatted his arm. "I was trying to be romantic. Two lovers, separated, and then reunited."

"Sweetheart, that's fine," Lucas chuckled. "But we've only been apart for a couple of hours."

Lia drew back and frowned. She started to rise, but Lucas grabbed her around the waist. He rolled and took her with him. A second later, he captured her mouth. His tongue found hers in a dance. The kiss deepened. Urgent. Needy. Wanting. Every nerve in her body hummed. Love was the sweetest emotion. Fluffy and sugary like cotton candy.

She pulled at his shirt. The intense desire to feel the warmth of his skin pushed all other thoughts from her mind.

"Whoa," Lucas whispered. "It wouldn't do for someone to drive by and see the proper Amelia Britton naked on the front lawn."

"Don't make fun of me. You want me just as bad. I can feel that bulge." She nipped at his lips.

Lucas kissed her tenderly. "We need to put this on pause." He rose and helped her up. "I'm heading out tonight." He pulled her into his arms. "There's an equipment issue in Salina."

"No. You can't go now. Not now." She couldn't believe her own ears. She was whining, and on the verge of begging him to make love to her.

"A lot has happened in a short time. I think some space will help us sort things out."

"I changed my mind," she said hurriedly and hugged him tighter. She reached lower and grabbed his butt, a daring move on her part.

Lucas reached into his jeans pocket. "There's more than a bulge down there." He dangled the diamond pendant before her. "I want you to consider all of the issues. All of the problems. Your wants, needs, and must-haves in life. And I want you to do it while wearing this." He turned her around and hooked the necklace around her neck. "I meant what I said before. We'll find a way to make it work."

"Let me go with you," Lia pleaded.

"I'd take you, sweetheart, but you have to finish getting ready for your show."

She hung her head. "You're going to miss it, aren't you?"

"Let's take one day at a time. *Maybe* is all I can say. I might not make it for opening night, but I'm sure I'll get to see it before it closes."

She squared her shoulders. "Fine. We'll take it as it comes."

"Will you call me if you need me?" Lucas lifted her chin.

"Thank you for the offer"—Lia tugged him closer—"however, I'm a big girl now. Clearly on my way to dotage, in your sister's eyes. I can handle things."

"Mind if I call you?"

"That would make this woman very happy." Lia rose on her toes and kissed Lucas's cheek.

"I've got a plan." Lucas took a step back. She hated breaking the heat of their contact.

"That's one of the things I love about you. You're the man with a plan."

"I'll know more tomorrow. And I'll call you tonight so you can tuck me in." He winked, his innuendo sending a zinger of heat to her core.

"Ever done phone sex?" she asked. "Wait, don't answer that. I don't want to know. But be prepared for a sexy conversation tonight." She gave him an exaggerated wink.

Lucas started the truck's engine. "Woman, come

here," he ordered through the open driver's window.

She smiled coyly and sauntered in his direction. She climbed onto the running board. His arm encircled her. He pulled her against the dusty door. His lips crushed hers. When his lips released her, he hung on to her fearing she would melt to the ground. "Remember, you're my woman. We'll work it all out. Tomorrow, I hope to have some good news. Maybe tonight, we'll try Skype."

He held her hand as she stepped down. Taking a step back, she waved. "Call me when you can." She blew him a kiss. As he backed down the drive, she clutched the diamond in her palm.

He was taking her heart and leaving his in her care. Breathlessly, she wrapped her arms over her chest. Joy floated her sky-high. She was light enough to walk on water.

For once, she couldn't wait for the day to be over and nighttime to roll in. She would show Lucas just how *un-prim* and *un-proper* she could be. Even long distance.

Chapter 22

When the kitchen sparkled, Lia headed for the back deck. Gentleman Jack curled on his bed beside the gas fire pit. Lia dropped into a deck chair, flung her leg over one arm, and watched birds gather at the feeders. Many would be heading south for winter soon. Others had already gone. She wondered about a life of travel. It wasn't like she could paint in the back of a semi towing farm equipment. But life wouldn't be that way all the time, she mentally argued. There was nothing more frustrating than not being able to paint when inspiration consumed her.

She closed her eyes and pictured Lucas. Imagined his lips against hers. Dreamed of being wrapped in his embrace and their bodies tangled up together. All frustration evaporated. Happiness settled into her soul. With Lucas, together they could make anything work. Love *would* conquer all.

Opening her eyes, she listened to the silence. Relaxation deepened in her body. Completely calm, she could tackle anything, including battling her brother. For once, she wished for an adult discussion with him to debate options. He always called when he reached St. Louis. But four hours hadn't yet passed. She'd wait an hour or so before calling him. Things ended so weirdly before he left. More like a bad dream. However, he was her brother, and they had to find a way to smooth things over between them...and between him and Lucas.

Her thoughts were interrupted by her ringing cell phone. "Hey. What's up?" she asked.

"Nothing." Zoë said, but the singsong tone of her voice indicated the opposite.

Lia burst out laughing.

"What?" Zoë demanded.

"You lie. Lie detector test—failed. What are you really doing?" Lia managed to say between giggles.

"Okay. You got me. I'm at the grocery store shopping. I'm gonna cook Karl dinner."

"Oh, my. Cooking? That's not safe."

"I know. I hope I don't poison him. However, to change the subject for a tiny second, there's lots of murmurs about you today in town."

"About?"

"I'm not sure where this came from," Zoë said, hesitantly. "Lips are flapping about someone putting his lips to yours. Did something happen last night after the party I don't know about?"

"Nothing." Lia giggled.

"Out with it. What did you and Lucas do? Did Craig catch you kissing down at the creek?"

"I'll tell you when I see you," Lia said. "I'm not talking about this over the phone."

"Be that way. Pork chops or bison?" Zoë asked.

"You want to talk about meat? I have a beautiful diamond hanging on a chain around my neck."

"Repeat that? I didn't copy on this end."

"A. Diamond. Pendant. On a chain."

The squeal from the phone hurt Lia's ear. She pulled it away and put it on speaker.

"Helen was right!" Zoë shouted.

"Calm down. Lucas and I are taking things slow. There's no engagement. He hasn't asked me to marry him...yet."

"I'm sooo happy for you." Zoë gushed. "But you didn't think to call me the second after he gave you a rock? Hello! Girl, I'm your BFF!"

Lia sighed. "Things got complicated...because of Craig. And that's a whole can of bad news I don't want to talk about right now."

"Oh! That's the other reason I called. Have another piece of news for you. Just heard about Gus. He got hurt at a rodeo last night. Spent the night in the hospital. Bad back. Not sure if he's going to be able to meet his contracts."

Those words drained Lia's laughter. "Gotta go." She hung up and dialed Gus's number.

"Hello?" A woman answered, her voice rising several octaves with just one word.

"This is Lia Britton. How's Gus?"

"Lia Britton?" Toni, Gus's wife, asked. The woman's French accent was strong. "Brittons don't have a girl named Lia." The phone went silent.

Lia called back. "This is Amelia Britton. I would like to speak to Gus, please."

"He rests."

"I'm so sorry to hear he got hurt."

"He said he call people to change times. In few weeks, he can do work."

"Give him my regards. I'll wait for his call."

Lia hung up the phone. Doubt welled in her stomach and inched like a worm up to her throat. Uneasiness settled around her shoulders. What else could go wrong?

She ran to the back deck and scanned the undulating scenery covered in green stalks of corn dotted with sections of tall yellow sunflowers, their faces tilted toward the sun. The wind had picked up since that morning. Clouds often blew in and blew out with the prairie wind. A usual day in Kansas. The harvest would net her bargaining power with Craig. Worry was an insidious monster, and she had to vanquish it from her mind.

"No sense in getting alarmed before trouble actually arrives," she chided herself. Heading back inside, she checked the weather reports just for added comfort. Jack scooted in through the dog door and plopped at her feet.

"Nothing out of the ordinary. Daily temperature highs would drop a degree, and the nights would lower by several. The wind would blow. Nothing exciting in the five-day forecast," she said, petting Jack.

Yet uneasiness pecked at her gut like a chicken pecking for bugs. What if a freak ice storm hit, like the one five years ago? Downed trees. Downed power lines. Cars down in ditches. Downed corn meant no harvest. Not only would her half of the crop be lost, but all of Craig's, too. She'd be down and out for the winter, maybe forever.

And with Lucas gone, how would she survive?

Picking up the phone, she punched speed dial for her brother. "Craig, I don't know exactly what to say, but I want to talk with you about what happened this morning. More importantly, I want to talk about your threat to sell the farm. Please call me."

She needed a distraction until she heard from him. From the wall unit in the living room housing the TV and stereo, she pulled out a drawer with CDs. Her mother's collection. Louis Armstrong, Billie Holiday, Bonnie Raitt, Keb' Mo', Trombone Shorty, Winton Marsalis, Tab Benoit. She plucked out a Christ Botti with Lucia Micarelli CD. Both musicians played passionately, and their music would boost her spirits, maybe take her to a place where she could paint while waiting for Craig to call.

The first violin and trumpet notes sang out. Somehow, these two artists captured the emotions of love and anchored them in her heart. Lia hugged herself and glided around the room as though dancing in Lucas's arms. Immersed in the music, when *Emmanuelle* ended, she cranked up the volume and headed straight for the studio. Now she could paint.

The ever-faithful Jack followed her and curled up on his bed. Later they'd go for a run. She'd take him down to the creek and trace the letters she'd carved in the tree many years ago, just to feel extra close to Lucas.

Reds, blues, blacks, with flecks of gold, she painted with the tempo of the music. When Jack barked, it startled her. "What?"

She glanced outside. Dusk blanketed the sky. When a pause in the music came, she heard the phone ringing. Catching a glimpse of caller ID, she rolled the stool over and grabbed for the phone.

"Craig?"

"I'm returning your call." He sounded all official.

"Thank you for the birthday present. I wish I

could have opened it while you were here."

"You had the chance. You were going to open it after the party, remember?"

"I'm sorry. I don't want things to be strange between us."

"How can I help you, Amelia?" His voice was all business again.

"Give me a chance to buy you out," she said, cutting to the heart of the matter.

"Fine. I'll wait until you harvest the crop. I'm not a complete ass. But if you can't come up with *all* the money, then the farm is sold. The buyer is waiting patiently. I can't afford...you can't afford, to lose this deal."

If the harvest brought in enough money, combined with what she had saved in the bank and the sales from her art, she might be able to swing it, even if it meant she only ate mac and cheese all winter.

"Thank you," she said softly.

"No need to thank me. This is a business deal. Nothing personal. As for the rest of your life, I won't interfere."

"You're my brother." She worried about the direction the conversation headed. "You make it sound like you're cutting me out of your life."

"No. But, I won't lie. I'm not happy about you and Lucas. I acted the fool today. I...let's stick to business for now. In time, I hope we'll work the personal stuff out. I've got to go." The line went silent.

Lia clutched the phone. Lucas was away, and now she'd lost her brother, too.

Chapter 23

Lia woke to Jack's barking. The sound set her teeth on edge. She scrunched her face and pulled the blanket over her head.

When Jack continued to bark, she shouted, "What?"

Then she heard the muffled ring of the phone. She lifted her head from the lumpy couch in the sunroom. The ringing continued. Her body ached as though she'd been kicked to the side of the road. She'd fallen asleep last night, same as the night before, after painting as though on steroids to replace the stolen canvases for the show. Three days. That's all she had before the show opened to special guests and critics.

She reached over her head for the phone. When she pushed the talk button, a dial tone rang in her ears. As she attempted to set the phone back on its cradle, it rang again, startling her. She dropped the phone on the floor. Feeling around, she grabbed it along with a dust bunny of Jack's fur. "Hello?"

"Lia, Gus. You been watchin' the news?"

Lia rubbed her eyes. Squinting, she looked through the windows to the world outside. Tumbling leaves and rustling branches. She glimpsed the power of the wind. Not a gentle breeze, but strong and stiff enough to push a dark front down from the north.

Although her eyes could see, her brain had no motivation. She wanted more sleep. "Gus, is there something you need?

"No! I'm calling because you need help."

Lia sat up. Nothing appeared to be on fire. She sniffed. Racing to the window, she scanned the sky for a plume of smoke. Again nothing. Curling up on the couch and pulling the blanket over her feet, she wondered if her brain was just too foggy to connect the dots. "What help do I need?"

"I feel like I'm letting you down. With the storm coming, there's maybe two to three days before it gets here. Everyone's gotta rush to get their crops in, and I'm flat on my back still. I've called around, tried to pull some strings, but I can't find anyone to combine for you. The rest of my crew headed out of town while I'm laid up."

Lia jumped up. "You mean I'm going to lose the crop?" Dread rolled into a tight knot in her chest. Nausea tried to heave its way up. "No! I can't. No."

"I even called a buddy down in Little Rock. Said if he could get here, he could use my combine. Because of the path of the storm, I think south of here will be okay. He's not in any danger, but he already promised his time to another farmer in Columbia, Missouri." Hopelessness rang in Gus's voice like a solider fighting his last battle.

"Gus, please keep trying. In the meantime, I'm going to call Lucas and check his schedule, just in case."

"Lucas is booked. I already called. He's a day's drive away with all his equipment. He's got contracts he's got to fill."

Lia's heart sank. Her life was like a boat taking on water fast. "Gus, thanks for trying. Please don't give up. Don't you have like a black book or something with names of other harvesters? Keep on it. I'll see what I can do."

Phone in hand, Lia paced. She started to hit speed dial for her brother, but he'd shake his head in disgust. He might not say *I told you so*, but even without the words, the sentiment would still ring in his voice. Besides, he didn't have any helpful contacts, only ones wanting to buy the farm.

"You will fail." Craig's words echoed louder and louder.

Lia sprinted to the kitchen and flipped on the coffee maker. She ran to the shower. She needed a clear head and clean clothes. After that, she'd find a way. Until her last breath had been ripped from her body, she wouldn't give up without a fight.

Back in the kitchen, fortified with hot java and reheated bacon on toast, she let Gentleman Jack out to run and sat at the kitchen counter with the inventory for the boxes. If she posted a sale on her website, cut the prices by half, and then managed to sell everything, which was possible though unlikely, she'd make her bills through the end of December. If she finished her paintings and all of them sold at the show, she'd make ends meet until April and buy out Craig. But that left no money for plowing, seed, and planting in the spring, which would bankrupt her and force her to sell the farm.

Could she call Lucas and beg? Offer to pay him half again his regular fee to rescue her crop? Lia sighed. That wouldn't work. Lucas would never compromise his reputation with his farmers. If he didn't get their crops in, they wouldn't hire him again. Dropping everything to help her would be shortsighted on his part. And even if he were willing, she wouldn't let him make that sacrifice for her. He had Megan to put through college. Besides, she'd told him she could manage things. She had to find a way. Boy, she hated the taste of crow.

Lia headed to the back deck and parked on the top step. From there, she could see miles of gentle rolling hills. Her farm. Her crop. Even her neighbor's land. The wind whipped her hair. She twisted it and shoved the makeshift ponytail inside the back of her shirt. Drumming her fingers on her thighs and tapping her feet, she tried to quell her panic. Fear tasted bitter in her mouth.

Squeezing her eyes tightly, she pictured the view from her apartment in the city. Within a few seconds, she began to pant as though out of breath. Too many buildings, too much concrete, too many people. Her thoughts drifted to her city studio. Bright light, paint-splattered floors, though big and wide, still closed in. But also, no longer usable space, and she still hadn't heard back from the fire marshal.

There had to be an angle she'd missed. Life in the city would be a life of treading water. Head above the surface, able to breath, but never getting anywhere. Not a life for her.

Gentleman Jack joined her on the porch. He plopped down on the deck and put his head in her lap. Lia stroked him, needing the calm he offered. His tailed wagged.

"You hated the city. You were only a young pup

then, but you'd have no place to run like this. Okay, Jack, what do we do? When Craig has an investment problem, he does research. Sometimes that means talking to consultants. So, maybe I need a consultant. Who better than Lucas? I won't ask him for help. I'll ask for suggestions. Come on, don't just lie there. Let's get the phone."

Jack followed her into the house. She grabbed the phone and hit speed dial for Lucas. When Lucas didn't answer, her eyes welled with tears. Fear and frustration like she'd never known were using her gut as a pin cushion. She listened to his message, happy to hear the sound of his voice, which gave her a small boost of hope. At the beep she said, "Lucas, I'm guessing you've been really busy because you haven't called. Anyway, it's Friday morning and I'm swallowing my pride. I want to consult with you. When you get this message, please call me back." She hoped he'd call soon. Sometimes cell phone service was spotty in the flats of west Kansas, more unreliable than the Pony Express had ever been.

When in crisis, painting solved the problem. It remained the best way to occupy her mind until a solution materialized.

Lia focused. She put color on canvas. Brushed it. Knifed it. Sponged it. If she had to live with the failure of her crop, at least she might manage to keep the life she loved if she could sell more paintings. Each new one looked more refined and color-intense than the last. The replacement artwork looked better than the stolen originals. Confidence urged her forward.

In all her life, she had never wanted to claim

her namesake more than now. Her father's grandmother, born and raised in Atchison, Kansas, had admired the city's famous daughter, Amelia Earhart, whose drive and spunk were legendary. The very reason Lia's mother named her only daughter after the famous aviator.

Raised on stories of Earhart, Lia grew up imagining the famous female pilot flying planes that flew overhead at crop-dusting time. Like her namesake, Lia now set her teeth with steely determination and risked all to have what she wanted. Only, unlike Amelia Earhart, her course in life didn't put her directly in death's path. So what were her options? Maybe she didn't have to sell all the property. Could she negotiate with Craig's buyer to keep the house, barns, and enough land to have access to the creek? Losing the tree and the hideaway would leave a hole in her heart. She wanted nothing more than to paint on the farm until she took her last breath, hopefully many years from now. But if she couldn't have the farm, maybe a small piece of it?

When the phone rang, Lia picked it up before the second ring. "Lucas?"

"You have caller ID. I'm not Lucas."

"Oh, hey, Zoë."

"You don't have to sound so depressed. I'm calling with good news."

Lia brightened. "You've got a combiner for me?"

"What? A combiner? No. Why would you think that?"

"That's the only good news I want to hear."

"Oh no. The storm. Your crop. I forgot…Gus can't work. What are you going to do?"

"I'm not sure. I may just watch the darn storm roll in and destroy all my hopes."

"I may have some good news."

"You've got a loaded gun and will help me shoot myself?"

"No. I have the prospect of a lease. A shop. I want to capitalize on all those tourists rather than lick stamps for them. I've had this idea about opening a shop. I've talked to several artists in the area. Potters, weavers, and woodworkers. Now, I'm talking to my featured painter. I'd like to sell your work."

The wheels in Lia's head turned. Zoë's idea had merit. She could create enough paintings to show her work at two galleries. A hometown gallery could really work out.

"Are you in?" Zoë asked.

"Yes. My gut says yes."

"Good. Now, I'm guessing you've called Lucas for help."

Lia blew out a breath. "I've made so much out of being able to handle things. I'm embarrassed to ask. But Craig told me I would fail, and I'll crawl over glass to succeed. I'm not giving up until I'm blasted out of here. So, I left a message for Lucas hoping he'd have an idea or two, but…"

"What happens if he doesn't get the message? How long ago did you call? Maybe you need to call him again. That would drive the urgency home to him."

A beep sounded in Lia's ear. She looked at caller ID. Lucas's name and number appeared.

"Got to go. It's Lucas."

She ended one call and pushed talk for the next.

"Amelia?"

"I'm so glad you called."

"I don't have good news. I talked to Gus early this morning. Why didn't you call me sooner and tell me Gus was out of commission? I could have worked something out. Now, there's no way I can get back there in time. I've called everyone I know."

She dropped to her knees. Lucas's words struck like an arrow to her heart. Her eyes watered, and she scrunched them tight to keep tears from falling. Her brain screamed, No! Her last hope of saving her crop had died just like the corn would after the storm hit.

"Amelia? I can help you make it through the winter. If you lose the crop, I'll plow and plant for free in the spring. I'm sorry. I'm sorry I can't do more. I'm sorry I'm not there."

"It's okay, Lucas," she whispered, not trusting her voice not to break. She didn't want his pity.

"I'll call you tomorrow night. I usually take Sunday off, but with the storm…"

"I understand..."

How arrogant of me to think I could handle this all on my own.

"It's good to hear your voice. Call when you can. Bye." She hung up before the tears flowed.

Exhausted, Lia dropped to the couch in the sunroom.

In two days, her show would open.

In three days, her crop would be ruined.

In four days, her life would be over.

Chapter 24

Lia stood up from her stool. Her back muscles protested loudly. She stretched as dawn blazed through the windows of her studio. Her shoulders popped when she shrugged. A diet of coffee and chocolate chip cookies for her last two meals didn't offer much energy. Her stomach rumbled. During the night, the drop in the outside temperature dropped a chill into the room. She turned on the gas fireplace and longed to curl up with Gentleman Jack on the couch and sleep. Forever.

"Thirteen. A baker's dozen." She gazed at the paintings hanging on the wall and leaning up against the counter. They weren't the large twenty-four by thirty-six inches, but fourteen by fourteen square. However, the last one, about half-done, painted mostly from memory, was her favorite. With help from a photograph—one that captured Lucas's smile, the one that made her heart pound with love—she'd painted him. She missed him more than expected, more than she wanted to admit. A deep sadness had settled over her last night when he hadn't called. Working on the painting made her feel closer to him.

"Jack, what do you think?"

The Brittany spaniel raised his head, barked, then made a dive for the dog door, and raced outside.

"Some critic you are."

Lia padded to the kitchen for coffee. Outside, Jack ran in circles and barked, racing back and forth between the front lawn and the barn. After he ran figure eights between the birdfeeders, he ran back and scratched on a glass window in her art studio.

Lia stopped pouring coffee. Over Gentleman Jack's barking, the rumble of a large engine grabbed her attention. She ran for the back door.

While the source of the noise wasn't obvious, the direction of the noise was. She opened the garage door, cranked the four-wheeler, and took off down the pasture path, headed in the opposite direction from the creek.

As she crested a small rise, a behemoth John-Deere rolled across her field a half mile away. The cab of the machine looked like a one-eyed bulging bug, nuclear-sized. Someone had a combine going full tilt, harvesting rows of corn with a single pass. She stopped. Blinked. Looked again. Stared.

Never in her life had she considered herself in need of a knight in shining armor, but the driver of the green beast had rescued this damsel in distress. Someone was saving her corn!

Jack caught up with her. He wiggled as though in a fit of ecstasy. Together they waited for the second pass of the combine. Lia waved as the machine drew nearer. About thirty yards away, the operator killed the engine. The door to the cab opened. A man climbed down.

Jack ran beside Lia as she raced like the wind with the four-wheeler.

"Lucas!" The second she stopped the machine, she launched herself at him, joy giving her body flight.

He swept her up into his arms, lifting her feet from the ground. Her heart sang with a new gladness she never expected.

"What are you doing here?" She managed to get out while peppering him with kisses. Her heart raced as though she'd sprinted thirty yards. Lucas made the world look hopeful.

"And I thought you'd be glad to see me." The smile in his voice warmed her. She planted another quick kiss on his lips.

"Never more than right this minute for a hundred reasons," she said.

Lucas hugged her tighter. Before releasing her, he spun her around before setting her on her feet. He kissed her soundly. Gently. Thoroughly. If she didn't know better, she'd swear the kiss curled the ends of her hair.

"Name one reason, Lia."

"Because I love you."

Lucas smiled the very same smile she'd captured in the painting. Her insides melted. Her knees needed braces to keep her upright.

"I love you, too, Lia Britton."

She drew back. "You called me, Lia." Her heart bounced with joy. Any lingering doubts about whether or not Lucas still thought of her as Craig's little sister were completely erased.

She nuzzled her face against his chest and hugged him tight, not wanting to let him go.

"I've got some good news, Lia."

She drew back to gaze at him. "I can't wait."

"I managed to talk to Craig's buyer. Same

company that bought my parents' farm. I convinced the guy with reason. I suggested that, if the corporation ever wanted local workers, a deal might be in their best interest."

"Deal?" she wasn't sure she wanted to hear what might come next.

"They're willing to take only half the farm, Craig's half. They want a first right of refusal if you ever decide to sell."

"So I don't have to buy Craig out?"

"Nope. They will. We just have to get the corn harvested." Lucas grasped her hands. "If we're going to fight the weather, I've got to get back to work. Might not save the whole crop, but some is better than none."

"But how did you get here?"

"Got a ride with a crop duster who owns several planes. Gus lent me his machine. The path of the storm is a north to south diagonal. Western Kansas won't get it. My crew is still working out there. I've got the rest of today and tomorrow before I head back. Gus's nephew is coming to help with another machine. Karl rounded up trailers to move the crop." Lucas kissed her nose before jogging back to the combine.

"You made all this happen for me? I love you, Lucas Dwyer."

"Make me some coffee, woman," he barked before climbing into the combine's cab. "I love you back, Lia Britton."

Lia backed away with Jack following at her heels.

"I love you!" she called, but he'd already started

the engine and put the machine in gear.

Crop or no crop, Craig was wrong. With Lucas, she'd never fail. He was her heart's desire.

The End
###

Thank you for reading my book. If you enjoyed it, please consider leaving a review at your favorite retailer. Thanks! And now, take a sneak peak of what comes next in the Sunflower series!

Linda Joyce

Excerpt from book two of the Sunflower series. Craig Britton opens the doors to his world.

"Thirty," Craig huffed out, then set the dumb bells back on the rack. He grabbed a towel and mopped his face before heading across the gym toward the men's lounge to shower. Working out five mornings a week before arriving at the office by seven a.m. provided a physical energizing boost and kicked in his brain cells in a way coffee never had— his daily to-do list ran through his mind like a stock ticker on CNN.

His first call of the morning would be to Lucas Dwyer, his future brother-in-law. What man refused a bachelor party? He had to convince Lucas to see reason. The men of Harvest wanted to celebrate with Amelia's future husband. He'd promised his sister the event would be tasteful, but what she didn't know wouldn't hurt her. Yes, he planned an old-fashioned stag party with a bikini-clad woman popping from a cake—something to shock the always-responsible Lucas. Everything was set. He just needed a groom.

Craig dodged treadmill row and continued to the far end of the gym. The only way he'd ever have a bachelor party, he mused, was vicariously through his best friend. Marriage just wasn't in the cards. He enjoyed bachelorhood too much. Rising early on Saturday mornings to play basketball with the guys, and Sunday morning sleeping late after a night of bedroom gymnastics with a date. If he ever needed a taste of family domesticity, he'd pay a visit to Lia and Lucas—and their future children.

His second call, at exactly seven fifty-five a.m. would be to Mr. Harris Haywood, entrepreneurial mogul. Landing the man as a client could increase Craig's visibility and credibility with the moneyed members of St. Louis's top society. It could skyrocket his career. He smiled at the idea, containing a surge of anticipation and continued his even stride rather than running to the lockers.

"Oh, Mr. Britton," a female voice lilted. "Would you sign my magazine?" A chorus of flittering giggles followed the question.

Craig slowed and glanced in the direction of the voices. Three women neatly dressed in navy blue and white matching workout gear moved as though tethered together and headed his way. The middle woman, a blonde in her forties in complete makeup, held up a Sharpie and waved a copy of the *St. Louis About Town* magazine at him. His photo graced the front cover as the Business Man of the Month. Inside, an article detailed his career climb to success.

The cloud of ladies drifted closer to him. Meeting near the juice bar, Craig grinned and made eye contact with each woman, hoping not to disappoint his newest fans. He recognized the woman who'd called out. The god of irony had smiled on him.

"Good morning, Mrs. Haywood. I'd be happy to sign." He recognized her from charity and society events, or mostly photos he'd seen of them.

Through the magazine interview, he hoped to

land new banking clients—being on the receiving end of female attention was an added perk—and the wife of one of St. Louis's wealthiest citizens was singling him out, waving his picture at him and asking for an autograph. What a lucky day!

He'd been schmoozing Mr. Haywood for nearly a year. Rumor was, Mrs. Haywood had the money, and Mr. Haywood had married up. Way up. Maybe the way into Haywood's financial decision-making process rested with the Missus rather than the Mister.

"Shall I personalize this?" he asked, taking the pen from the woman and flashing a smile, his most charming, he hoped.

"Just your signature, please. I plan to auction you off."

"Auction?" What? He managed to maintain a smile while scrawling his signature boldly on the magazine cover, but little pricks of wariness raced to his neck. His jaw tightened.

"The autographed magazine, at a ladies tea, will go to the highest bidder. I was wondering…have you ever considered a photo shoot…without a shirt. I could sell a lot of postcards of you."

"Me?" Could he be more lame in his responses? The woman would think him a total dud rather than a sophisticated dude. He stifled a laugh. A mental image of a room full of designer-dressed society women trading postcards of half-naked men flashed in his mind. "Ah…I'd never considered that." He handed back the pen and magazine not knowing how else to respond. She asked a question, but he sensed it wasn't a request. Beefcake photos could make him the laughing stock of the financial world.

"Charming. You're brilliant with money and still have some humility."

Her word game and scrutiny set his nerves firing caution signals again. The woman might help him, but she could surely ruin him. "It's nice to meet you, Mrs. Haywood." He held out his hand searching for a polite exit. "I'm not really that photogenic."

Her gaze dropped to his hand, then lifted and locked on his eyes, holding his full attention. "This is Beatrice and Saraphina." She pointed to the women accompanying her. He nodded in reply and silently prayed he hadn't offended Mrs. Haywood.

"Bye, now," the women said in unison, before turning, waving, and leaving him alone with Mrs. Haywood. Had she planned this meeting? The hair on the back of his neck began to rise. If so, why?

"Mr. Britton. I'm having a party on Friday. I want to introduce you to my niece. I think, after reading this article about you"—her gaze traveled up and down him—"the two of you have a lot in common."

Something about her voice, her words, made him want to cover his balls. Maybe Harris Haywood wore the pants, but his wife told him which pair to put on. "Oh?" He didn't move in the same social circles as the Haywoods, but surely a niece of a wealthy family didn't need help finding a date...or a mate. But come to think of it, in all his research about the family, he couldn't picture a niece.

"I'm sure you'd find her...very compatible. Pick her up in a limo and bring her to the party next week. I'll send you her address."

Was the woman really pimping out her niece

to him?

Trying not to appear dumbfounded or plain asinine, Craig flashed what he hoped was an easy-going smile. "Thank you for the invitation. I'm sure I'll enjoy meeting her, Mrs. Haywood. What time shall I pick her up?" His brain screamed, "No! Don't do it. It's a trap of the feminine kind." But after a year's worth of work to create a hint of an inroad to the Haywood organization, he couldn't stand by and allow it to blow up in his face like an egg cooked in a microwave. "This is business," he repeated silently to quash the uneasiness thumping in his chest.

"Eight p.m. But don't arrive before nine thirty." She placed her hand on his arm and gave his bicep a squeeze. "If I were twenty years younger Mr. Britton…I think my husband will be calling you about some business. Today." The woman stepped beside him, patted his ass, then turned and left without a backward glance.

Craig swallowed hard. With Mrs. Haywood, he was out of his league. His rising career could burn and fizzle out of sight in less than a nanosecond.

What if her niece didn't like him?

About Linda—Award-winning author Linda Joyce writes about assertive females and the men who can't resist them. Linda's a big fan of jazz and blues. She attributes her love of those musical genres to her southern roots, which run deep in Louisiana. If you walk-through several New Orleans cemeteries you'll find many of her ancestors buried there. She penned her first manuscript while living in Japan, the country where her mother was born and raised. Linda, her husband, and their four-legged boys enjoyed a dozen years in Kansas, the inspiration for the Sunflower series. Now she and her family live in Atlanta, Georgia.

Please connect with Linda Joyce, she always wants to hear from readers!

Website: http://www.linda-joyce.com
Facebook: https://www.facebook.com/LindaJoyceAuthor
Twitter: @LJWriter https://twitter.com/LJWriter
Goodreads: http://www.goodreads.com/author/show/6950241.Linda_Joyce
Pinterest: http://pinterest.com/LindaJoyceWorld/boards/
Instagram: http://instagram.com/lindajoycewrites
Google+: https://plus.google.com/+LindaJoyce/posts